Lost
Memories
of the
Cottage
by the
Loch

BOOKS BY KENNEDY KERR

LOCH CAMERON

The Cottage by the Loch

A Secret at the Cottage by the Loch

The Diary from the Cottage by the Loch

A Gift from the Cottage by the Loch

An Invitation to the Cottage by the Loch

Keepsakes from the Cottage by the Loch

MAGPIE COVE

The House at Magpie Cove

Secrets of Magpie Cove

Daughters of Magpie Cove

Dreams of Magpie Cove

A Spell of Murder

Kennedy Kerr

Lost Memories of the Cottage by the Loch

bookouture

Published by Bookouture in 2025

An imprint of Storyfire Ltd.
Carmelite House
50 Victoria Embankment
London EC4Y 0DZ

www.bookouture.com

The authorised representative in the EEA is Hachette Ireland
8 Castlecourt Centre
Dublin 15 D15 XTP3
Ireland
(email: info@hbgi.ie)

ISBN: 978-1-83618-545-1
eBook ISBN: 978-1-83618-544-4

*In memory of my "antique" grandmother, Mary, and my much-loved aunt, Dot.
They loved tirelessly and now they can rest.*

PROLOGUE

Longing is a strange emotion. It makes me wonder if there is one of those clever German words that explains it better than the English can.

Germany is a land famous for many things – some good, like fairy tales, thick pine forests and sausage – some bad, which we all know, and regret. But, unlike our language, which has limited options for words that express emotion, the Germans have a wealth of detailed language that would suggest, perhaps, that they are better at expressing their feelings than us. Those emotional Germans. Of course, I am a Scot, and we are also an emotional people, though we are for the most part beleaguered with the use of English, with our own notable additions.

Beleaguered is a good word, though. Oh, I ramble, nowadays. Bear with me.

I know this, about these emotional German words, because, in my life in the publishing industry, I once worked with a German author whose works we had translated. And I remember words like *Waldeinsamkeit* – *Wald* (forest) and *Einsamkeit* (loneliness). You can literally translate it as "being alone in the woods," but in the peaceful sense. Or

Torschlusspanik: the feeling of panic or anxiety that comes from the fear of time running out.

It's interesting to note that a lot of those German words capture feelings on the melancholic spectrum, though: *Weltschmerz*, for instance, translates as something like "world-sadness" – the feeling of sadness that comes from being aware of the contrast between the way things are and the way you wish they were.

It's often used to describe the feelings of disillusionment that come with age and experience, as you realise that life doesn't always meet your expectations. I relate to *weltschmerz*. I expect that many here at Apple Orchard Care Home do, too. We know that we are old and infirm – or, at least, those of us still with a reasonably full jar of marbles do. And we wish that we were young again. As Lily Tomlin once said, *ah, to know what I know now, and still have those legs.*

Sehnsucht is the word, though. It means "to yearn or long for," and is often described as a complex mix of sadness and craving, a strong desire to be with somebody or something you love but can't.

Longing for a far-off place, missing home or a particular person, craving to be somewhere or with someone that it's impossible for you to be with.

It is that emotion I feel: *sehnsucht*. Mere *longing* has none of the depth of what I feel. What I have felt for so long is woven into the fibres of me.

As I sit here, in the care home lounge – oh, they try and make us think that it's some kind of swishy hotel we've ended up in, in our last days, but none of us are fooled – I look out of the windows at the gardens beyond, and think about the past. I imagine we all do; at the end of life, there is little ahead. All of what we know is behind us.

We think about our stories; sometimes, we tell them to each other. We say *do you remember such-and-such a time, or such-*

and-such a place, especially if it is not there anymore. If there are places we used to go – to dance, to eat, museums, libraries, shops – that no longer exist, or even houses or flats we once lived in that are no longer there, by talking about them, we can at least temporarily rebuild them in our minds. And if someone else remembers that place, then it can be rebuilt doubly strongly in the realm of memory.

I have found that, as one grows older, the realm of memory grows more and more real. It's the outer world that starts to fade.

But, there are also some stories that we do not tell anyone. Stories that pain us; stories that we wish were not part of our history, and yet they are. Stories that we do not want to rebuild in memory. Rather, we would prefer to demolish them completely. But we can't.

Yet, my *sehnsucht* – my longing for a person it was impossible for me to have in my life – is a story that feels like it now wants to be told. I have made a lifelong habit of not telling it, of holding it close. Even though it is covered in sharp edges, and, though it is woven into the deepest parts of me, it has always hurt to keep it there, like a beast with teeth that wishes to escape.

I have protected my story thus far, but, as the Germans taught us with fairy tales, stories are made to be told. Sometimes they are a cautionary tale, and sometimes they contain information that people need to know and remember.

My story is a little of both of those, as it turns out. And, though I believed for many years that it was finished and in the past, now I can feel it squirming inside me, as if it is chewing itself loose with those sharp teeth. As if it wants to be released. And that thought fills me with fear.

1

——————

'But… I thought… we talked about the future…' Lottie Fox stumbled over her words as she stared, disbelievingly, at Tristan.

'It was a nice thought,' he said, coolly. 'But you must know that we wouldn't be good long-term. You're way too emotional. I need to be with someone chill.'

'And… Chloe… is chill?' Lottie could hardly get the words out.

'Yeah. She doesn't have such high expectations.' He shrugged. 'You know, you have very high expectations from a relationship. You should just relax. Go with the flow.'

Lottie felt this was desperately unfair. She had been "going with the flow", against her own best instincts, for the whole of her year's relationship with Tristan. She could count any number of times that she'd stopped herself reacting to something he'd done, because she wanted to keep the peace. Because she loved him, and she didn't want to scare him off. Because she thought that she'd never find anyone better than him.

One of the things that Lottie had been "going with the flow" with was the idea that she and Tristan were having an open relationship. When they'd started dating, she knew that it was allowed that they would both date other people at the same time. That was how dating worked: you saw a number of people, and then, over time, you might find yourself in a relationship.

That was what had happened with her and Tristan. They'd met on a dating app and met for a walk with his dog. When he'd got out of his car, she'd looked up at him and thought, *uh-oh*. He was gorgeous: unlike some men on the internet who lied about their height, Tristan was definitely six foot three, with a large build and beautiful hazel brown eyes with long lashes. He had a beard and a shaved head, and his profile reminded Lottie of a Roman legionary or maybe a Musketeer: noble, strong, heroic in some way. He could have stood there in a suit of armour and she wouldn't have been surprised.

They'd gone on a few dates and had a lovely time, and things had progressed. She'd known that he was still dating in the background, and that was okay. She wasn't, but she had the freedom to if she wanted to. And, that felt very liberating. Tristan liked to talk about how modern and utopian it was to be able to see more than one person. She should have known he'd break her heart, but she was caught up in him and blind to any red flags.

One night, she was staying over at his house, and as they were going to sleep, he kissed her softly on the shoulder and wrapped his body around her. *Night night, beautiful,* he'd murmured, and her heart had bloomed in love. She'd lain there, awake, her heart hammering, as his breath had deepened.

She hadn't told him that she'd fallen in love with him. Not until months later, when she'd accidentally said it when they were out on a walk in the forest.

It was a brisk, sunny autumn day, and they'd been walking the dog through the trees. Tristan had said something to make her laugh: he did make her laugh in the way that he could be so relentlessly grumpy about some things. *Did you see how that*

BMW was taking up two spaces in the car park just now? I might leave him a note on his windscreen.

Rather than irritate her, it was sort of adorable; she felt like those moments were times when he was being honestly himself, not trying to be charming or interesting. She loved his grumpy old man-ness, which was usually prompted by other people's poor parking or driving. That in itself was sweet: he never seemed to get annoyed about other things, and Lottie thought that if a person only had car-related grumbles about the world, then they really weren't a negative person at all.

I love you, baby, she'd said, without thinking, because her heart was full, and it was the first time in a long time she'd felt so happy.

As soon as she'd said it, she'd clammed up, blushing furiously and wishing she could take it back.

He'd pretended not to hear her.

What? he'd asked, frowning at her. And she'd had the opportunity, right in that moment, to take it back. To swallow the words and pretend she'd never said them. But, something in her wouldn't let it happen.

I love you, she'd repeated, looking him in the eye.

He hadn't said it back.

He'd said, *you know how I feel about you, but I don't believe in saying it back just because someone's said it to me, you know? It feels so transactional.*

And she'd stomped on her own feelings, and assured him that it didn't matter. That he could say it back to her if he wanted to, but there was no pressure. That she would never want to make him feel uncomfortable.

But the unsaid part of that was that she would make her feelings smaller, just to ensure his comfort was uninterrupted.

He had told her he loved her, months later, at the end of a phone call. Right in the final few seconds, he'd said it so quickly that she might have missed it if she'd hung up a second sooner.

After that, he'd said it back to her when she said it first. And that gave her the illusion of safety: if he loved her, then everything would be okay in the end. She just had to be patient.

But he was still seeing other people, and she was too afraid to ask him to stop, because it was hurting her. Once, when she couldn't help being upset at the fact he was telling her about his date with another girl, he'd grown cold and not spoken to her for a week.

If you can't be chill, I can't be with you he'd messaged, at the end of it. And, she'd apologised. She'd run back into his arms, because she'd missed him so terribly. Because he was the only one who *smelt* right, *felt* right, *was* right to her.

And, now, he was telling her it was over.

'But… I don't understand,' she'd stammered, unable to take it in. Just the week before, they'd been on holiday, exploring the Isle of Skye in a campervan. They had had so many beautiful moments together, even though there had been something distant about him. She'd felt there was something he wasn't saying, and now she knew what it was. 'Don't you love me?'

'I love you, babe,' he'd replied. 'But I can't give you what you want.'

'But… all I want is you,' she'd said, feeling wretched. Not understanding what was happening.

'No. I know you want a future, and to settle down and have a family and all that. I don't want that.'

'I've never said that was what I wanted.' Wildly, she thought back through all of their interactions for a time that she might have expressed that she wanted a commitment from Tristan. She hadn't said anything like that, precisely because she knew how he would react.

Of course, he was right: she had wanted a future with him. Of course she had. She loved him.

'I know it's what you want. I can tell.' He'd shaken his head.

'But… Chloe, she *doesn't* want that?' she'd asked, knowing

that it was redundant, knowing that she couldn't argue him back now, and that he'd chosen someone else over her, and so she shouldn't beg to have him back. A part of her brain knew that, if someone wanted to leave, you should let them. If they didn't want to love you, let them. In theory, she knew that she should be with someone who wanted desperately to be with her. Who loved her.

'No. She's chill. I dunno, Lottie. I liked you a lot more when you didn't love me so much,' he sighed, and her heart felt like it split in two.

She'd tried so hard to be the perfect girlfriend: to have no needs, to be relaxed and easy breezy. And it still hadn't worked.

'I'm so sorry, babe. It's been fun.' He'd kissed her on the forehead, then let himself out of her flat, leaving her wondering what on earth had just happened.

2

———

'So, whoever would like to be involved, wave at me, and I'd love to hear your story.'

Lottie stood nervously in the lounge of the Apple Orchard Care Home, having raised her voice to overcome the sound of the heavy rain on the windows. She'd just finished her presentation to the residents of the care home, and she really hoped that some of them would be interested in helping her out.

There was a muted smatter of applause, and then some of the elderly residents turned and started talking to each other as if she wasn't there. No one moved.

This was what Lottie had dreaded: that no one would want to help her with her project, and she'd have to try again somewhere else. It wouldn't be the end of the world, of course, and her tutor on the MA in Sociology that she had begun six months ago had warned her that it might be difficult to find committed, consistent participants at first. There were two other care homes in the area that she'd contacted, but she hadn't liked the sound of them so much, and the staff hadn't been as helpful on the phone.

Instinctively, Lottie's hand went to her neck and found the

locket she always wore. Today, she was wearing a comfy cream coloured T-shirt and jeans, and the necklace was tucked under the shirt's neckline. However, even when the locket wasn't on display, she found the weight of it around her neck reassuring.

The locket was made of rose gold, and it had been her mother's. When her mum had died, she'd left it to Lottie, and Lottie had put a picture of her mum inside it.

On the other side of the locket, there had always been a small curl of hair, caught under the glass compartment. Lottie's mum had never mentioned whose it was, and Lottie had assumed it might have been hers. Whoever the curl of hair had belonged to, she knew that the locket had belonged to her mother a long time, and she cherished wearing it now.

Kimberley, the care assistant who had welcomed her in brightly that morning, put a kind hand on her elbow.

'Don't be discouraged. We'll find some participants for you,' she said, giving Lottie a warm smile. 'They can be a bit reluctant, but we've got some great characters here. Maybe just go and chat to some of them and see what happens.'

'Okay.' Lottie felt strangely nervous, like her first day at secondary school, not knowing anyone. But that was silly, she reminded herself. These were just people, and she was an adult, not an eleven-year-old girl. And, she had to find participants for the practical project part of the assessment for her MA.

Lottie had begun her MA in the previous autumn. If she was honest, she'd started it because she needed a focus in her life, and she didn't know what else to do. It seemed like a cliché but she'd needed to invest in herself; she'd needed to heal.

Lottie still couldn't think about Tristan without wanting to cry. Since he'd dumped her completely out of the blue, she'd felt as though she'd been walking around with her heart cut out.

It had been six months, and it still hurt.

She missed everything about Tristan. She'd had to move because her old flat was riddled with memories of him: the lamp he'd repaired, the shelves he'd put up for her, the sheets he'd slept in with her, the garden outside where they'd barbecued and danced under the moon, shared their dreams together. She couldn't even look at her Tupperware for the memories it held of taking leftovers to his flat and cooking together in his little kitchen.

It had been so sudden. She hadn't seen it coming.

It got too serious, he said. *You wanted too much.*

The thought of those words haunted Lottie. She still didn't know what *too serious* was, but he'd told her he loved her, numerous times. Breaking up with someone with no real reason, with nothing to say apart from some kind of teenage excuse, wasn't love. It wasn't what Lottie thought of as love, anyway. Love required consideration of the other person. It required the careful holding of their heart.

'Lottie, this is Gretchen Ross.' Kimberley appeared at her side and indicated a bright-eyed woman with her hair in a loose grey bun, sitting at one of the tables. She held a book in her lap – Lottie recognised it as a popular and rather raunchy bestseller that was in all the shops at that time – and was squinting at it through her glasses. 'Gretchen, I wonder whether you might be interested in helping Lottie with her project? I expect you were listening, just now?'

'I was.' Gretchen smiled up at Lottie, her eyes twinkling. 'And, what a nice idea it is, too. Though I'm not sure how many of us have life stories worth recording.'

'Gretchen. Don't be modest. It's not your colour.' Kimberley tutted, then turned to Lottie. 'Gretchen Ross has had a life most of us would envy. She's dated celebrities, had a high-flying career, travelled the world... I'm sure she'd love to tell you about it.'

'Kimberley. You're exaggerating, I must say,' Gretchen said, haughtily, but with a smile playing around her lips. 'However, I'd be happy to talk to you, young lady. Do sit.'

'Thanks.' Lottie sat down in the chair to Gretchen's right. 'Do you think there would be others who'd be interested in talking to me? I wanted a selection of voices, ideally.'

She wouldn't think about Tristan today. Today was about her MA, something she was doing for herself.

'Oh, I expect so. I'll introduce you around, if you like. The girls I play bridge with would talk your ear off, given a cup of tea and a biscuit or two. Some of the others are quite interesting, once you get past the fact they're all ancient.' Gretchen rolled her eyes theatrically. 'Of course, sadly, I too am an antique.'

'Well, that's sort of why I'm here.' Lottie liked Gretchen immediately. 'I'm studying sociology and intergenerational studies in particular. Looking at the value of sharing life stories, not losing the wisdom of our elders. I actually look forward to getting to be your age. All that wisdom, and peace,' she sighed. 'I feel like you're beyond heartbreak and all the savage parts of being my age.'

'Oh, dear. Heartbreak isn't good.' Gretchen reached for Lottie's hand and gave it a squeeze. 'I'm all ears, dear, if you want to spill the beans. I've been there too.' A shadowy look passed over Gretchen's face.

'You have?' Lottie asked. 'What happened?'

'Ehhh. You don't get to be my age and not have your heart broken. I'll tell you another time, perhaps.' Gretchen shook her head, as if she had made her mind up about something. 'But, please don't wish your life away and want to be my age. Believe me, it's a pain in the derriere,' she sighed. 'And that's just the arthritis. I won't bore you with the angina. And I miss my figure,' she added. 'Time was, I had a lovely figure, just like you. Oh, I had some fabulous outfits!'

'I don't think I have a lovely figure, but I'd love to see pictures, if you have them,' Lottie ventured.

'Oh, you do. Curvaceous.' Gretchen nodded. 'You're welcome to come up to my room and look at my albums. I've got them going back to the seventies or before, even. Of course, everyone has pictures on their phone now, but I still like getting them printed and arranging them in a book. I'm old school in some ways, though I do use social media. Look, I've got all the apps.' She picked up a modern smartphone from the table and touched the screen, which lit up. 'I believe in keeping up with what young people are talking about and doing. Keep your brain young, then the rest of you will follow. Sort of,' she added with a giggle.

'That's cool. You're probably better at social media than me,' Lottie said. 'And I'd love to see your albums, at a time that's convenient.'

'Oh, there's no time like the present!' Gretchen said, breezily. 'I'm happy to chat now.'

'You are? I'm happy to come back another time, really,' Lottie said, but Gretchen was already standing up carefully, leaning on the table for support.

'No, no. It's morning time, which is the best for me. I go rather downhill in the evenings. I've had some coffee and the book was boring anyway,' she chuckled. 'If I can take your arm, dear, then we can go.'

'All right, then.' Lottie smiled, and held out her arm for Gretchen, who took it.

'I've got cake, too,' Gretchen said, as they walked slowly to the lifts in the corridor outside the lounge. 'You never know when you'll get an interesting visitor.' She said something else, then, under her breath, that Lottie didn't quite hear.

'What was that?' Lottie asked, but Gretchen shook her head.

'Nothing, dear. Just that some visitors, you wish they'd never arrived,' Gretchen said, brightly. 'I've certainly had some gentlemen friends that outstayed their welcome. Let's put it that way. All an age ago, of course. Now: cake!'

'Oooh, cake,' Lottie chuckled. 'That sounds perfect.'

3

———

'*Well-behaved women seldom make history.* Have you heard that, saying, dear?' Gretchen pottered slowly into her flat, still holding Lottie's arm for support.

'Oh, yes. It's on T-shirts and mugs and all sorts,' Lottie said.

'Hmm. The commodification of everything. Well, for many years, I had that slogan above my desk. It was a cross-stitched picture that I made one summer on my daily train commute into the office. That was when I'd just started in publishing, as a secretary in one of the typing pools.'

Gretchen settled herself in an easy chair and pointed to a little kitchen at one side of the flat.

'Dear. Will you go and make some tea? My legs aren't quite up to it. The cake's in the tin. It's a fruit cake, quite good.'

'Of course.' Lottie busied herself with the kettle and found a jar of loose-leaf tea and a white teapot with a floral design.

'Tell me about you, Lottie,' Gretchen called out as Lottie made the tea. 'It seems that if I'm going to tell you everything about my life, I should know something about you.'

'Okay – what would you like to know?' Lottie asked, opening the little fridge to look for milk.

'Tell me about your family. Your parents, where you're from. And if you're married, do you have children? I didn't see a wedding ring, but of course that doesn't mean anything these days.'

'I'm not married. No children,' Lottie said, keeping her voice light, but the painful emptiness in her chest echoed.

'That's a shame. A lovely girl like you.'

'Ha. Not sure about that,' Lottie said, pouring milk into a china jug and setting it on a tray that she could see was obviously intended to be the tea tray.

'Aren't you? Why not, for goodness' sake?' Gretchen asked. 'Surely your mother must tell you what a pretty girl you are. And intelligent, too, studying for your Master's degree.'

'My mum died a few years back,' Lottie said, shortly. It wasn't anything she wanted to talk about, still, even though she was over those first two years where the grief had been unbearable. She reached for the locket, keeping it under the T-shirt but tracing its outline with her fingertips, through the cotton.

If she was being totally honest, maybe part of the reason why the experience with Tristan had bowled her over so totally and completely was because she was still feeling the loss of her mum. Her support structure was gone.

Lottie and her mum Emma had always been close. Her dad hadn't been there for most of her childhood. And, that was okay, Lottie always told herself, because Lottie and her mum were everything for each other, as well as Lottie's grandparents, Sharon and Graham. Lottie's life had been happy: summers at her grandparents' house or on windy Scottish beaches, winters at her and Emma's little house in the Edinburgh suburbs, keeping warm by the log fire, toasting marshmallows, reading books.

'Oh, dear. I'm so sorry to hear that. And your father?'

'I don't see him anymore,' Lottie said, shortly. The situation with her father wasn't something she ever liked to discuss. 'I got his hair, but I don't know what else. Otherwise, I look like my mum.' Her hair was one of the few things Lottie liked about her appearance: it was long, a dark blonde, and had always been thick. She tended to wear it plaited, or twisted up in a bun. Tristan had liked to run his fingers through it, and, with him, she'd worn it loose.

Since he'd ended it, she hadn't worn it down once.

'It's lovely hair, dear. What was your mother's name? If you don't mind me asking.'

'Emma Fox. She died three years ago,' Lottie said. She didn't want to go back into her memory and dredge up the final weeks of her mother's life: a death that had hit suddenly and out of the blue.

'Emma?' Gretchen asked, looking around. Lottie thought she sounded a little startled.

'Yes. It was very sudden,' she said. 'A problem with her heart. It's called Sudden Arrhythmic Death Syndrome. It's rare – affects about 500 people a year in the UK – but it happens. When someone's heart just suddenly goes without any warning.'

'She didn't have any heart conditions before then, that you knew of?' Gretchen asked.

'Not that we knew of. She was only forty-eight, but she may have had and just not known it.'

'Oh. I'm so sorry, dear,' Gretchen said, slowly. 'That's an awful thing for a young girl. To lose her mother, and at such a young age too. How old are you?'

'Twenty-eight. I was twenty-five when she passed,' Lottie said, shortly.

'Oh, my goodness. It's no age at all.' Gretchen let out a long sigh.

'I'd rather talk about you, though, if that's all right?' Lottie set the tea tray on Gretchen's coffee table and put her phone next to it. 'That's what we're here for.' Lottie had brought the tray over with two delicate bone china cups on matching saucers – the design was floral, to match the teapot – with a matching milk jug and the fruit cake, plus a couple of small plates. She felt very protective of talking about what had happened with her mum. It had been so sudden: such a shock, so out of the blue. Her mum had been standing on a train platform and suddenly collapsed. Someone at the station had called an ambulance, but by the time they'd got to Emma, it had been too late.

'Of course. I didn't mean to pry. I just...' Gretchen trailed off, frowning.

'What?' Lottie got the impression that Gretchen was about to say something more, but then she shook her head and smiled.

'Oh, nothing, dear. An antique woman and her antique thoughts, that's all,' she said. 'Come on. Let's start your recording, or you'll never get anything for your project. You must nudge me if I stray off course, though. I am prone to wander.'

'I'm sure that whatever you tell me will be fascinating. Let me set up the voice recorder though, before you go any further.' Lottie tapped the voice record app on her phone and made sure it was facing Gretchen. 'Okay. fire away. You were telling me about the typing pool.'

'Oh, yes. They still had those then. It's hard to believe it now, with the internet and laptops, apps and drones delivering your dinner, but there was a time when, if you wanted anything communicated to someone else, you had to summon a woman – it was always a woman, then – to your oak-panelled office and dictate your message. The other option was that you could give us your sacred words on a little tape, and we'd listen to that and tap away at our typewriters, frowning, listening to your voice drone on about contracts and royalties and advances.' Gretchen chuckled.

Quietly, as Gretchen spoke, Lottie cut a couple of slices of the cake that she'd brought over from the kitchenette and handed a slice on a plate to Gretchen, who took it with a delighted smile.

'Yes, I did my share of frowning and typing. And I did more than my share of listening to men, and noting down what they had to say. Fortunately, that didn't last forever.' Gretchen took a delicate bite of the fruit cake. 'Yummy. Thank you, dear.'

'It's your cake. I just sliced it.' Lottie grinned. 'It is lovely, though.'

'It is.'

'So, you started in the typing pool. But at some point, you became hugely successful.' Lottie remembered what Kimberley had said when she'd introduced her to Gretchen: *She's dated celebrities, had a high-flying career, travelled the world.*

'I suppose you might say that, yes. But I never intended to work in a publishing house. It was just something that came up: fate, you might call it. I've always been a strong believer in fate. In Scotland, there's a saying: *what's for you won't go past you.* I believe that.' Gretchen met Lottie's eyes for a long moment, and nodded, as if she was confirming something to herself. 'It's funny how things work out,' she said. 'Life has a habit of surprising you.'

Lottie had the sudden, strong impression that Gretchen might have been talking about something else: there was a kind of subtext to her words. But, Lottie had no idea what she meant.

'Not always in a good way.' Lottie raised an eyebrow. 'But, I know what you mean.'

'Hmmm,' Gretchen said. Unexpectedly, she wrapped her arms around herself and gave a shiver. 'I don't think you do know. But you might, one day, and I hope for your sake that it's the good kind of surprise. Because there are plenty of bad ones out there. I assure you.'

4

GRETCHEN

Eenty teenty tirry mirry, ram, tam, toosh,
Crawl under the bed, and catch a wee fat moose.
Cut it in slices, fry it in the pan,
Be sure and keep gravy, for the wee fat man.

It was odd, talking to Lottie. I started telling her my stories and, then, tonight, as I got into bed, I started humming that song: *Eenty teenty tirry mirry, ram, tam, toosh.* I probably haven't thought about it in seventy years or more, but it suddenly appeared in my mind. Like the process of recounting my past opened a door somewhere.

I wonder whether I will tell her my whole story. I've never really told anyone the whole truth, but perhaps it's time now. I feel that I need to tell it, once and for all: all the secrets, all the parts that I have kept to myself, out of fear or mistrust or shame.

There is something about Lottie: something that she needs, too. She wouldn't be doing this research project – talking to old codgers in a retirement home – if she didn't need human connection, and perhaps some sense of perspective on her own life. There has certainly been heartbreak there, and some loneliness. I know both of those feelings.

I have been lonely most of my life. Even now, I live among all of these people, but I feel it. The daily social grind does nothing for me; there are no soulmates here, no friends of the heart. Perhaps I have always kept myself slightly apart from other people, when it really matters. Because of the secrets I carry.

Eenty teenty tirry mirry, ram, tam, toosh. I had no idea what it meant then, or now. Just one of those silly counting rhymes you learn in the playground. But, it took me back to a memory.

I was playing among the headstones. It was a grey day up on the hill at Loch Cameron Chapel, that I recall. My mother was there to lay flowers on my grandmother's grave, and she'd taken me along. I never knew my grandmother, so I didn't find the graveyard a sad place, although Mother cried whenever they went there. I never liked to see Mother cry, but she would never accept my little efforts to make her better: if I put my hand in hers, she'd release it. If I tried to kiss her cheek, she'd brush me away. She didn't like to be witnessed when she was sad. So, while Mother talked to her mother's grave – I remember thinking that it was a strange practice, but also that adults were full of strange behaviour – I counted the headstones, chanting my nonsensical little rhyme. I remember skipping between the mossed-over stone slabs. Some were quite old. Their names had been scrubbed off by the wind and the rain. Some were newer and could be read. I liked to read the gravestones. Mother said once she thought it was ghoulish of me, but what else was I supposed to do while she was otherwise engaged?

I always liked to read, wherever I was. So, I read the stones.

Ernie Smith, 1802–1845, Gone But Not Forgotten. Goldie Kopper, Beloved Wife. They became names that I remembered, always walked back to, running my fingers over their names over many years. I like to think that remembering people's names, even when you didn't know them, is a kind of love. I hope that, one day, someone will see my name on a gravestone and remember it.

I remember stopping at a little stone wall which came to my waist – I was six or so at the time, so it wouldn't have been that high. Beyond the wall was a cluster of stones that looked less cared for, slightly offset from the main area, under a yew tree at the edge of the graveyard. I tried to scale the wall but couldn't quite get over it: my legs were too short, and I fell backwards onto the wet grass. I remember hearing my pinafore rip, and then Mother's voice:

Gretchen Ross. I cannae take my eyes off you for one second, can I?

Mother picked me up. My leg had a graze, and my white pinafore was ripped at the hem. I knew that Mother would be far more concerned about mending the tear than my injury. I hadn't cried – it hadn't hurt that much, and I was an adventurous girl, always getting in scrapes – but Mother had a grim look in her eyes and I remember wondering whether crying might have softened it a little.

I said sorry as meekly as I could. Then, my curiosity got the better of me: *why are those graves over there, beyond that wall?* The grass was long in that part of the graveyard and there were no flowers resting against any of the stones.

Don't go over there, Mother replied, in the way that adults have of not answering questions. *It's not for you.*

But why is the wall there, Mother? I asked, doggedly.

Mother looked away and took me by the hand. *Come on, Gretchen. Time to go. Those women are something you never want tae be.* Mother marched through the graveyard to the gate at its edge.

Women? I probably frowned. *All of them?*

They're women that had babies out of wedlock, Mother explained. *Some of them that died young.*

What's wedlock? I distinctly remember imagining the iron padlock that Father kept on the outhouse, where he kept his tools. *Wedlock* sounded like something hard and heavy; something designed to keep you inside.

Marriage. Like me and Father, Mother said. *Babies are supposed to come inside marriage. Not out of it. God frowns on women that commit the sins of the flesh outside holy union.*

We had walked away from the chapel by that time, but I looked back at it, on the top of the hill. Grey clouds were forming around it, and I recall wondering at that point if God was frowning down on me. I gripped Mother's hand tighter, thinking *I'll be good, don't frown on me,* without knowing what *sins of the flesh* meant.

The women had babies and weren't married, and then they died? I asked, imagining a vengeful God sitting at the top of the hill above his chapel with lightning at his fingertips, ready to strike down sinful women. *Why did they die?*

Some of them died in childbirth. Some of them... regretted their sin, Mother said.

What does that mean? I was now wide-eyed. I had regretted things before: stealing a piece of cake, whispering at school when I was supposed to be reading silently, being bored in church. I wondered if these things were sins, and whether God would punish me for them if they were.

It means, just be a good girl, and you won't end up alone on the wrong side of the wall, Mother said briskly, as we turned onto the lane at the bottom of the hill, which led onto the high street. *And when you get older, remember to stay pure, because God is always watching.*

I remember her saying that so well: remember to stay pure. But I was only six, so I had no idea of what Mother meant by being *pure.* I remember imagining white bedsheets fluttering in the breeze, on a sunny day when Mother had done the laundry, scrubbing at the cotton on her washboard, her forearms lathered with soap and with the fresh smell of bleach in the air.

Pure meant *clean.* I knew that. I surmised that Mother must have meant that I should remember to bathe and wash my face, and stop my clothes getting muddy and ripped like I'd done that day, falling off the wall.

I'll be good, Mother, I said, as we walked along. I never forgot that day, and, when I got older, I started to understand what those graves on the wrong side of the wall really meant.

Good girl, Mother said, resting her hand briefly on my head of messy curls. *Don't let me down.*

I did let her down, of course. Terribly and heartbreakingly.

Over the years I thought back to that day many times, and wonder if it taught me anything. I don't know that it did, apart from a sense of shame that was never mine to own, but which I carried around with me like every woman did, at that time, and perhaps does still: the shame at the potential for dissent that your body holds. The awful worry that your body will accidentally betray you; betray your family, your village and the whole of society.

But, like that childhood song, the shame played in my mind: memorised forever, ready to re-emerge when triggered. I tried hard to be a good girl. But, it turns out that being *good* means hardly living at all. And I wanted to live.

Finally, now, perhaps something in me wants my truth to be heard. Perhaps that's why I thought of that day, after talking to Lottie. But, how can I ever tell the truth, after all these years? And, if I do, will she be willing to hear it?

5

'I can look back at my career and conclude that much of it was because of my father. Father believed in education. Mother didn't, particularly, but she wouldn't argue with him. In those days, and in little villages like Loch Cameron – that's where I grew up, it's a few villages away – people didn't put a lot of importance on educating girls, but Father insisted. For that, I'm forever grateful to him.' Gretchen was in full flow again, the next day: Lottie had enjoyed their talk so much the day before that she had returned to talk to her again.

'Oh! I live there too, now. I just moved into a house share in the village,' Lottie said, pleased they had Loch Cameron in common. It gave her more of an insight into Gretchen.

'Indeed! It's a lovely place,' Gretchen nodded.

Gretchen talked volubly, gesturing often with her gnarled hands, only stopping now and again to sip from her bone china tea cup. Lottie made sure that she topped it up every time it got low. However, at times, she seemed to lead herself towards something and then shy away from it: Lottie got the impression that Gretchen had something to say and yet was reluctant to say it.

'He insisted that I go to a good school some villages away, and made sure that I stayed to the end – not that I needed a great deal of encouragement, because I loved school.

'But, sometimes, girls wouldn't stay to the end of school and get their qualifications. They'd leave because they'd get pregnant and there would be a scandal. Or, more often, their mothers would want them to help at home and they'd miss the final years, including the exams, because who needed school qualifications when you were destined for a life of cleaning, cooking and making babies?' Gretchen stopped talking for a moment and stared at Lottie. She looked as though she was about to say something.

'Gretchen?' Lottie asked, gently. 'What is it?'

'I... nothing, dear,' Gretchen said, after a pause. 'Just got distracted. Where was I?'

'Cooking and making babies.' Lottie repeated Gretchen's words.

'Hmm. Well, I stayed to the end of school and got the qualifications that were available. I still had to learn cooking and sewing and all the things that people thought girls needed to know, in those days. But I also learned history, biology and English literature.' Gretchen's eyes lit up. 'In fact, we were blessed with a rigid but passionate bluestocking, Miss Enright, who read us the poetry of Robert Burns every week in a quavering but committed tone, and her love of literature helped bank up the fires of my own developing passion.

'I still think fondly of Miss Enright, perched on the edge of her desk with book in hand, reading to us teenage girls with her bun askew and her woollen socks pulled up to her knees. She must have been dead for many years now – I'm hardly a spring chicken myself – but I like to think that she still exists, somewhere, delighting in the poetry of the great Rabbie Burns.' Gretchen smiled mistily, lost in her memories for a moment.

'So, Miss Enright inspired you to love books?' Lottie asked.

'Possibly, but I was destined to be a reader: I've lived a life of books, and I wouldn't have it another way. We always had books in the house. That was Father's influence, again. He was a great reader, though he'd never had much of an education himself,' Gretchen replied, thoughtfully.

'And, because they were there, and because there was little else to do except mending and cooking and cleaning – which I studiously avoided – I grew up reading, reading, reading. When I'd read everything we had in the house, which was a strange concoction of religious tracts, history of the British Empire – much of that would be frowned upon these days, of course – and poetry, I sought out the library and became a regular there. Aged ten, I got my own little blue cardboard library card, with LOCH CAMERON LIBRARY stamped upon it, and I went there as often as I could, always taking out the maximum number of books and returning them faithfully.

'The library isn't there anymore. It closed a couple of years back: budget cuts came for it, and the argument at the local council was that no one was using it. It was sad, but it was probably true: some libraries have kept up with the times and now provide ebooks and games to rent, places to hang out for the young ones. My daughter Stella actually worked there for many years. She was a real part of the community.'

'Wow. That's amazing, Gretchen.' Lottie smiled.

'Indeed. The Loch Cameron Library was a game old bird: she had beautiful Arts and Crafts woodwork inside – rows and rows of polished oak shelves, a fireplace, the date carved over the door as you went in – but she didn't keep up with the times, so they closed her. It's a lesson for us all. Keep up, or you're destined for mothballing.' Gretchen chuckled. 'Anyway, I digress. I do that. You'll have to nudge me if I stray too far off course.'

'That's sad. Does your daughter work at another library now?' Lottie finished her slice of cake and cut another.

Gretchen had said that her daughter *was* a real part of the community. What did that mean?

'No,' Gretchen said, shortly. There was a silence.

'No?' Lottie echoed, surprised at the sudden change in Gretchen's demeanour. She had been charming and effervescent, but at the mention of her daughter, she had become instantly stony.

'No,' Gretchen repeated. Her smile had disappeared. 'Some things are better left for another day. I don't want to talk about Stella. Not yet.'

'I didn't mean to upset you. It's just that you mentioned she'd worked at the library, so...' Lottie trailed off.

'You haven't upset me. But you don't have an automatic right to know everything about my life,' Gretchen snapped.

'Of course,' Lottie said, slightly taken aback. Gretchen had been so open so far; she didn't seem to want to hide anything. 'I know that.'

'Thank you.' Gretchen sighed, and stared out of the window for a moment. 'Where was I? Oh, yes. Education and babies.' There was another silence as she seemed to think about something; Gretchen looked as though she was going to say something more for a moment. 'I just...' she began, then stopped.

'What, Gretchen?' Lottie asked, gently. Of course, everyone had things they didn't want to talk about. Lottie did. Why shouldn't Gretchen? Her course tutor had prepared Lottie's MA group for this. Capturing people's stories was a deeply personal experience, and was entirely subjective. Memory was subject to bias, change and obfuscation, and some memories never wanted to be told at all. At some point in this process, Gretchen might find that there were parts of her story that were difficult to tell. All Lottie could do was be supportive and patient.

'Nothing, dear. Just my vintage brain. I was telling you

about education and qualifications.' Gretchen blinked, and her easy demeanour returned. Lottie wondered what it was that was on her mind: what she hadn't wanted to say.

'Girls were going to university by then, but I wasn't allowed that much freedom. Mother said that universities were hotbeds of sin, and a girl didn't need higher education. She believed that a degree would have unbalanced me: that if I was too brainy, I would lose out on a baby and a husband. I think she saw it in almost biological terms: some kind of heavy, maladapted brain, taking all the blood from a delicate little uterus, making it shrivel and die.

'Ultimately, in a way, that is what happened, but not in a biological sense, as far as I'm aware. I chose not to marry and produce a baby in my uterus. How much of that decision was anything to do with blood supply to my brain, I'll never know.' Gretchen was back to what seemed like her usual self, but her tone was sardonic. Lottie was starting to learn that her new friend was a complex woman; sharp, bright and intelligent – someone who, perhaps, didn't suffer fools gladly.

'So, after school, I had a few choices. Not many, but any choice is a good thing, and there are plenty of women in the world today who still don't have any,' Gretchen continued, taking a sip from her teacup.

'My choices were secretarial school, nursing, factory work or to stay at home and help Mother until such time as a local man would swoop by and rescue me.

'I chose secretarial school, after bargaining with my mother that I would leave my home village of Loch Cameron and move away to Edinburgh, on my own.

'That was a difficult enough arrangement, I can tell you. My mother was hardly the meek type, and, in those days, it was still thought that girls should stay close to home, live with their families and get married as soon as possible. Only then could you move out, move in to a little house with your new husband and start churning out babies.'

'Ouch.' Lottie made a face. 'Not that those are bad things, but when that's the only choice...' she trailed off.

'Exactly. I didn't want to do that. Mother resisted me going. She said I was too young at sixteen, trying to persuade me into nursing, which was hilarious, considering that I almost fainted at the sight of my own scraped knee. I told her in no uncertain terms that I had no desire to replace anyone's bedpan or change bloody bandages, and after a while she agreed, having been my mother for all those years and knowing that I was hardly the practical type in that way, she had no choice.' Gretchen sighed.

'Finally, she agreed – or, Father persuaded her, I never knew which. I had to live away, in a boarding house, and the bargain with Mother was that I could go as long as she chose the boarding house.

'It was a little like a nunnery. The place was run by a very strict widow, Mrs Carstairs. We weren't allowed gentleman callers, drinking or smoking indoors and she used to measure the length of our skirts with a tape measure before we left in the morning.

'Of course, all of us girls left Mrs Carstairs' house with our skirts worn obediently to the knee. This was 1953 and pencil skirts were in vogue, as well as the rather lovely full-skirted dresses one sees have made a return nowadays as "vintage" wear. As a living antique myself, I fondly remember my own "vintage" wardrobe.'

Lottie smiled, enjoying listening to Gretchen.

'Mrs Carstairs was a despot with that tape measure, but she was also concerned with the tightness of the skirt as well as the length. Length-wise, we didn't present her with too many problems, as the miniskirt would come later, in the 1960s. But, I certainly preferred my pencil skirts fitted to the point of it being slightly difficult to walk, and if Mrs Carstairs saw one of my skirts, in particular – a lovely black one which gave me a very significant wiggle – she'd send me back upstairs to change.

'So it was, and so it shall ever be: one can never get teenage girls to wear sensible clothes, and society should give up trying.' She shot Lottie a cheeky grin. 'I think there's something majestic in teenage girls. All that verve and youth and rebellion. The wild poetry in their hearts.'

'I guess so. I didn't love being a teenager.'

'Nobody does, dear. But then, you look back and realise you were resplendent.'

Lottie laughed. 'I think I was awkward and spotty and I had terrible dress sense.'

'Tsk. One mustn't speak negatively about oneself. You were resplendent,' Gretchen insisted. 'Anyway, after my stint at secretarial school, under Mrs Carstairs' watchful eye, Mother demanded that I return home for a while. I think she was concerned for my virtue, though she needn't have worried: despite the wiggle skirt, I was still only eighteen, and hadn't found a tremendous number of opportunities for wickedness between Mrs Carstairs, the bus to secretarial college and the college itself, which was only for girls.

'On returning to Loch Cameron, my parents' cottage, where I had grown up quite happily, seemed very small. The village seemed small, too: it is, of course. But what reveals itself as quaint and desirably homely when you're older is anathema to the young, who want excitement and adventure, wide horizons and – in my case – cities.

'But, for a while, I was stuck there, and so I had to make the best of it. My beloved library needed an assistant, and I applied, and was successful. I do wonder, in retrospect, whether there were any other applicants for the job.

'Still, for a couple of years, I worked there quite happily:

reshelving books, taking returns, repairing books sometimes when they started to fall apart. I loved being among books, and when I wasn't doing librarian tasks, I was free to read. I must have read every book in that library at least twice: romances, history, geography, politics: I even pored over the local maps and books about Scottish wildlife. I was so bookish that I even dated the owner of the local bookshop, here in the village. Later on, of course. I was older then,' She frowned for a moment. 'Not that it turned out that well,'

'Oh dear. I'm sorry,' Lottie said.

'No, no. Just life, that's all,' Gretchen waved her hand dismissively.

'And your daughter followed in your footsteps, later on,' Lottie prompted, and then regretted mentioning it. Gretchen had said she didn't want to talk about her daughter; not yet, anyway. But Gretchen just smiled and nodded.

'Indeed, she did. And, then, one day, I looked at the newspaper and saw that Dunne's Books in Edinburgh were advertising for secretaries, and I knew. I knew it as deeply and as truly as I knew that I wasn't meant for a village life, and so I applied. A month later, I had started in the typing pool. Many years later, I was Editorial Director at Hatch Publishing.'

'Editorial Director! Wow. That sounds like a story, how you got there.' Lottie sat forward, keen to hear more. She felt as though she could listen to Gretchen talk all day.

'It is, dear. And I'm happy to tell it to you. But I want you to remember one thing for me. Okay? Are you ready?' Gretchen pointed her index finger at Lottie, determinedly.

'Yes,' she grinned. 'Ready as I'll ever be.'

'Okay. This is it. Never let them tell you that you can't do exactly what you want to do. All you've got to do is want it enough, and work hard. That's the secret, darling. You don't listen to anyone else, and you do whatever fills you with absolute joy. Then, the world is your oyster,' Gretchen said, a look of fierce determination on her face.

'That's what you did?' Lottie asked.

'That's what I did.' Gretchen nodded, but her birdlike, wrinkled hands fidgeted in her lap, and Lottie got the sense that Gretchen had something on her mind.

6

———————

GRETCHEN

After Lottie left, I sat for a while, staring at my photo albums on the shelf.

I got the blue album down and leafed through it. It's been a while since I looked at it, though I know exactly what's in it and in what order: the pictures of him, of me, of the children. Specific days, poses, memories. Silly faces, serious looks, incriminating details in the background.

Do I regret it? No. I made the choices that I made. I stand by that.

Does it still hurt to remember? Yes.

The thing about the past is that it's not like a photo album. Not really. The past is not a series of disconnected moments, posed for and created. Isolated and captured, fixed fast on a page.

Looking at a photo album provides us with the illusion that the past is static, but that's wrong.

The past is a living being. A continuum of influence. The past never stops being in the present.

I put the album down on the bed and get up slowly, button up my mustard handknitted cardigan. I make my way carefully to the small kitchenette you get here as part of your little retirement flat. I've gotten used to it by now: so much of how I live now is a miniature version of before, when I was young and free and was permitted a full-sized kitchen and sharp knives of my own.

Now, I'm too old and infirm to be truly free anymore: I exist in this baby-fied hinterland, jollied along by the young, who think they know better than me. I consent to be here, albeit grumpily, but I dislike not making my own meals anymore. I dislike the group activities – bingo! Boring films with no sex or swearing! Knitting! Until I came here, I didn't know that knitting was a group activity. No one wants to talk about books: at least, not the books that I like.

Plus, the constant pressure to be amenable is tiring.

I have never been particularly amenable, and age doesn't improve a person's patience or general good humour. At heart, I have always been a lonely soul, and I have no really close friends here. In fact, I've made closer friends in these late years with the young women who have come to live at my old cottage, now that I don't live there. I have more in common with the young, in some ways. And there has been something in the experience of helping those girls that has helped me, too; I may have regrets about my life, and those regrets may have kept me more alone than I should have been. But some of those relationships have brought real friendship and love into my life.

At least I'm still allowed to make tea.

My hands shake as I fill the kettle with water and set it on the gas hob, turning the knob with difficulty and pressing the ignition at the same time.

Time was, none of these little things even entered my mind as a difficulty. Now, setting the kettle on to boil takes a concentrated effort. I hate being this old and infirm.

I shuffle to the small fridge, lean down and open the fridge door. Take out a pint of milk and set it on the counter. Even that effort tires me out. My angina must be getting worse, or something: I never used to be this easily exhausted, but just an hour or so talking to Lottie and a gentle sojourn to the kitchenette makes me feel as though I've run a marathon.

How quickly age comes for us all, even those of us that have resisted it so fiercely.

I realise that my mind has wandered again; I re-clasp the sense of unease that talking to Lottie provoked in me. The train of thought I had started was about the past, and now the remembered rush of dread about recounting some of that past, floods through me.

What could talking about the past dredge up now? There is a fear there: a fear of something rotting and long-submerged coming to the surface and poisoning me, threatening to drown me, making me remember things I don't want to remember.

I know what lies there, and I am the one who has buried it, deep on the ocean floor of memory.

I reach for the kettle and pull my hand away at the steam which I have forgotten is there. I almost drop the damned thing: I fumble, and manage to set it back on the hob without scalding myself.

Idiot, I think. *How many years have you made tea for yourself, perfectly safely?* Now, the thought of uncovering some of those purposefully-submerged memories – like kittens, drowned in sacks, which people did once, in less kind times – just that *thought* almost wreaked violence on my aged skin.

The past is always with us, and, in my experience, trauma never becomes less keen. Memories can hurt, and I am afraid of the pain.

I rub the wrinkled skin of my wrist with my fingers. The miasma of wetness from the steam of the kettle lies on my skin, and I wipe it away. It seems symbolic: a warning. Be more careful, or these perils will hurt you.

I stand there, hanging on to the top of the counter, and feel the rush of panic subside into a wave of sorrow that lashes me from within. My own reservoir of grief is deep, like the loch, and, over the years, I have drowned many kittens in sacks there, as horrible as that may sound. But, at the time, we think we do it for the greater good.

Yet, over time, the secrets we drown start to poison the water.

The past is not something we can file away and forget. It stays with us, and, if we disturb its waters, it can pull us under.

7

———

'Need a hand with the drying up?' Fred appeared at her elbow and made her jump.

'Oh. Sure, okay. Thanks.' Lottie handed him a wet plate, and he took it, tea towel in hand.

'So, how are you settling in?' he asked.

'Okay, I think. There are some birds in that tree outside my window that chatter a lot, first thing in the morning,' she said, shyly. *What a stupid thing to say,* she criticised herself. *The first thing you could say to a new person, and you choose that. Well done.*

'Magpies. Like this?' He imitated the *chack-chack-chack* sound that had been waking her up most mornings. Lottie laughed at the accuracy of his impression.

'Yes. Exactly. They're loud.' She shot a glance at Fred, then looked back at the dishes in the sink. He was a nice-looking man, medium height, wearing glasses, khaki shorts and a bland, sports-style T shirt. They'd met when she'd moved in, though Fred had just been on the way out somewhere and had just given her a hurried hello in the hallway as she'd been carrying in her bags. Her other housemate, Celine, always seemed to be out too, and remained a mystery.

'Yeah. I hear them too, but my room's at the front of the house. So, I get the kids playing on the playground on the weekend. Not that I begrudge them their fun,' he said with a smile.

'Right,' Lottie chuckled. Loch Cameron was a small village, and their rented house was up on a new development called Gyle Head which featured forest to the right, and a view over the loch if you walked away from the houses a little. There was a nice community feel there, and the housing development had been built around a central play area for the children.

Lottie didn't mind it at all; for the past few years she'd been living in some fairly soulless blocks of flats in Edinburgh, where there were frequent sirens at night and where she didn't know her neighbours. Some children playing and some magpies chattering was a welcome change.

'So, how are you finding Loch Cameron? So sorry I wasn't around to help when you moved in. I had to help my girlfriend with her car.' He took a mug and dried it, then put it away in the cupboard.

Ah. So, he has a girlfriend, Lottie thought. A man who would voluntarily help out with the washing up wasn't going to stay single for long.

'It's been good so far. I've hardly been here, to be honest.' Lottie stacked a saucepan on the drier. 'I'm doing my MA, and I'm up at a care home a couple of villages away, interviewing residents. It's the best part of the day getting there, chatting and recording, coming back and writing up the stories. Some of them are really interesting.' She thought about Gretchen Ross, and smiled.

'Wow. That does sound interesting, good for you. How come you decided to do an MA? Pursuing an academic career?'

'No. Well, not really, I mean, I'm open to whatever happens. I just... needed a change.' Lottie was keeping her answer intentionally vague, because she didn't want to explain that she had decided to move away from Edinburgh because she'd had her heart broken. It would sound stupid. 'The course I wanted to do was here, so I came up for the year.'

'Fair enough.' Fred nodded. 'You couldn't find a similar course a bit closer to home? They have universities there, I reckon.' His eyes twinkled.

'I know, I know,' she replied, chuckling. 'But it's a good course, the one I'm doing. And, I don't know. I always remembered a picture of Loch Cameron my grandparents had on their mantelpiece. It was some kind of Christmas card from an old friend of theirs or something. Just this really pretty scene of the loch surrounded by snow-covered trees, and the castle in the background with all the lights on. Like a fairy tale.' She paused for a moment. 'And, if I'm being honest, the idea of getting as far away from home as I could was appealing.'

'Why's that?' Fred asked, drying another cup.

'I'd rather not go into it, if you don't mind,' she said, carefully, feeling the hurt of the breakup burn in her heart. *Oh, no. Not now*, she thought, imagining her hurt as a ball of smouldering molten iron, and pulling a heavy door closed on it. It was like her heart was a forge; sometimes she imagined pouring water on the molten iron, and it steaming and fizzing violently. Yet, the flame never seemed to go out.

She desperately wanted to let go of Tristan, but she just didn't seem to be able to.

And, there was the added bruise of the loss of her mum. Lottie had got over the worst of it: that was true. But, she still missed her mother every day. She missed having someone to confide in, someone who knew her better than anyone else. She missed her mother as a link to her own childhood. She missed her hugs, the way she laughed, the jokes they shared.

Lottie's dad had left them midway through Lottie's childhood. She rarely took those memories out of the dusty drawer and examined them: they made her uncomfortable.

For some years, when she was younger, there had been long absences, when her mum had told her that Daddy was away with work. Lottie still didn't know if that was true or not; her dad had been in sales, and that could involve long trips away.

She'd tried screaming and crying, once, when he'd left. For a work trip, supposedly. She'd been young, perhaps six, and she'd hung on to his trouser leg and refused to let go. *Daddy. Daddy. Please don't go.*

And her mother had pulled her off her father's leg and said, *Stop it. Don't make a fuss, or Daddy might not come back at all.*

And, so, she hadn't made a fuss after that, when her father had left on his long trips. They never knew when he might be back: the trips weren't regular timings, a week in every month or something at least that could be got used to, scheduled, allowed for. In the end, he was just *away*, and Lottie would see him for an afternoon about once a month, if she was lucky.

And that had always left her feeling anxious because there was no predictability, no certainty, no consistent attention. She would be ignored for most of the time, apart from the occasional bright days when she would be the apple of her father's eye, and then discarded again until the next time.

She got used to it. That was how it was, and there was no point complaining, because complaining got you nowhere.

Worse, it might mean that if her dad did want to see her, then she wouldn't want to spoil that chance by being cross, or worse – needy. In the end, when she'd been about twelve, her mum had told her that Daddy wasn't coming back at all. He had another family, and he was going to live with them. Permanently.

Lottie had asked Emma, some years after that, whether that was where her dad had been before; for all the weeks when he was supposedly away with work. Her mum had given her a wry smile. *I think so, sweetheart*, she'd said. *I was just trying to protect you.*

There wasn't much that Lottie could reply to that. She had hugged her mother; Emma Fox was the best mum anyone could ask for. It wasn't her fault that Lottie's dad had deserted them. But, it left Lottie with the sense that, perhaps, she wasn't good enough.

She had never felt like the one who would be *chosen*. Her dad hadn't chosen her and Emma. And, as she'd grown up, she had never really felt *chosen* or special by any boyfriend. Lottie would get crushes on boys when she was younger, and put them on a pedestal in her mind. She'd fantasise about them, do everything she could to chase them, and then be disappointed when they left her.

Lottie believed in happy ever after. She was a romantic. But she hadn't managed to find anyone yet who wasn't going to treat her like an option, and she didn't know how to change that.

Lottie's grandparents were still alive, though they were elderly. Since Emma had died, Lottie had got into the habit of visiting them about once a week; they'd have dinner and talk. Sometimes, she'd help her grandmother in the garden, or do the crossword with her grandfather. Being in Loch Cameron, she was missing out on that. But she'd felt like she had to get away.

'So, what do you do?' she asked, changing the subject.

'I work at the bookshop in town. Been local all my life, I'm afraid. Nothing glamorous.'

'I envy the fact that you've lived here all your life. Loch Cameron's so lovely.'

'It's nice, aye. Can't complain. But then, on the other hand, you do get kinda used to it. Then you go elsewhere now and then, and remember that not everywhere has a picture-postcard loch with a fairy tale castle looming over it.'

'Exactly.' Lottie chuckled. 'And the high street's quite

quaint too. Cobbled walkways. The shops are really cute. I've walked past that bookshop, actually. What's it called, again?'

'Pageturner's. Not very original, I guess. It was a family business for years and then got put up for lease. My mum retired and decided that she'd take it on. She's one of those people that can't sit down and do nothing. Anyway, she thought she'd just keep the name, because that's what people know it as.'

Lottie had walked past the shop but not been in it: however, she remembered what it looked like, because she'd stopped to look in the window. The shop sign was written in a slightly flaking gold italic script above old fashioned lead-lined windows, and there was a wooden trolley of books on sale outside, covered in a plastic cover, and a black wooden sign with gold lettering that said:

NEW & SECONDHAND BOOKS
WE BUY BOOKS

She would have gone in that day, but the shop was closed and a hand-lettered sign in the window said

OUT FOR LUNCH,
BACK SOON, DEAR READERS

'I walked past but it was closed for lunch. That was you, then. How funny!' she said, lightly. 'I liked your sign.'

'Small world, huh. Yeah. I close up for lunch some days and go for a walk around the loch, or run some errands. You know. It's hardly a sprawling metropolis, Loch Cameron. People don't seem to mind.'

'I'll have to pop in next time. I love a bookshop,' Lottie said, earnestly. 'And from what I could see inside, it looked really interesting.'

'Ah, thanks. Definitely pop in next time you've got time and

I'll give you the guided tour! It's got a lot of really nice original features – beams, a lovely old fireplace in the back, and there's even a spiral staircase up to a mezzanine! Wear practical shoes, is all I'd say.'

'Ha. Okay, that sounds great. I will.' Lottie put the last plate on the drier, just as Fred reached for it. Their fingertips touched briefly, and Lottie looked up as their eyes met unexpectedly. Just briefly, there was a moment that passed between them. A moment of connection.

Lottie blinked, and withdrew her hand.

'Anyway. Work to do,' she said, to break the sudden odd feeling that had replaced her easy chat with Fred.

'Right, Celine and I were going to pop into the village later for something to eat, if you fancy it?' he asked, hanging up the tea towel. He didn't appear to have noticed the strange energy between them. Or, Lottie thought, he had, and was politely ignoring it. Silly moments like that happened all the time, probably. It was just one of those things.

'Oh, right. Maybe. I do have a lot of transcribing to do, though,' she said, knowing that she wouldn't go.

'Well, the invitation's there. We'll give you a knock when we're heading off.' Fred gave her a kind smile, and she felt bad for knowing that she wouldn't go.

'Okay. Thanks,' she said, instead. 'Anyway, I should get on.'

'Those stories won't write themselves!' he said, flicking on the kettle. 'I'd love to hear some of them sometime.'

'Oh. Sure. That would be lovely,' she said, wondering why he was being so nice to her.

Fred is just a nice person, she thought pointedly. *Some people are nice. Some people – some men – just want to be your friend. He has a girlfriend. He's your housemate. That's all.*

'Well, come out tonight and you can tell us then,' Fred said, playfully. 'I promise Celine's quite nice when you get to know her.'

'All right,' Lottie acquiesced. *What's the point in hiding at home for one more night?* she asked herself. She could stay in and break her heart over Tristan every other night of the week, after all. 'I'll come.'

'Excellent!' Fred clapped, looking unashamedly nerdy, which was somehow adorable. 'We were thinking around seven? Don't dress up, just FYI. It's very much a fleece and walking boots sort of evening. We're planning to get some food from a food truck that's started coming to the village, and sitting by the loch with a few beers or something.'

'Right. I'll leave my high heels at home.' Lottie nodded. Not that she had any. She'd lived in either pyjama or jogging bottoms for the past six months, and a selection of grey T-shirts and pilled sweatshirts with faded slogans. 'I guess I could get to know some of the Loch Cameron locals.'

'Well, we might meet some of them. I just feel like I need to manage your expectations slightly,' Fred chuckled. 'If you haven't gathered already, it's mostly elderly gossips and families, but there are some younger people too, here and there. Not hugely glamorous.'

'Haha. Okay. No glitterati, then?' Lottie replied.

'Not unless you count the middle-aged ladies who run the crochet club. They're no strangers to a nice A line skirt and a cardigan. Of course, we have quite a young and attractive laird, and his partner, who is also very good looking. They're quite glamorous, I guess. And us, of course.' He put his hands on his hips and posed.

'Oh. Beautiful. I'd better put on my cleanest jogging bottoms, then.'

'You better had. Celine's French. She has standards.'

'Noted.' Lottie chuckled. She wondered whether Gretchen, her new friend at the care home, would opt to go out with her new housemates. Not that this was a big night out: they were just going down to the high street to get some food. Still, it was more socialising than Lottie had done for a while.

She thought back to what Kimberley, her contact at the care home, had said about Gretchen: *Gretchen Ross has had a life most of us would envy. She's dated celebrities, had a high-flying career, travelled the world.*

It sounded as though Gretchen wasn't a woman who had ever said no to a social occasion, and Lottie felt inspired by the thought. If Gretchen would say yes – she would probably love to be able to walk down to the high street and get some fast food, instead of being cooped up all day long – then she, Lottie, would go, and enjoy herself.

As she changed into some slightly newer jogging bottoms and a nicer sweatshirt, Lottie wondered what Gretchen might have to say when she spoke to her next. There had been a couple of moments when it had seemed as though Gretchen had been about to say something, and held herself back.

Time will tell, Lottie thought. But, she found that she was curious about what Gretchen had to say. What secrets could she be hiding?

8

___

When they arrived on the high street, Lottie was surprised to find a hubbub of people gathering around a food truck parked opposite the Loch Cameron Inn. As they approached, Celine sniffed the air and pointed to it excitedly.

'Oh. It's the Shrimp Shack!' she said, a grin lighting up her usually serious expression. 'Lottie. We 'ad the best fish finger sandwiches from these guys last time. Zey just started coming to the village like a couple of months ago,' she explained, skipping over to the queue and gesturing to Lottie and Fred to follow.

Lottie looked at the menu which was written on a blackboard on the side of the food van – a very cool-looking repurposed silver trailer which had its front cut out, and in which two young guys with beards and wearing beanies were cheerily serving customers.

Crab Mac n' Cheese
Po Boy Sandwiches
Fish Finger Sandwich
Tempura Prawn & Bacon Sandwich
Cajun Squid Wrap

Sweet Potato Fries

Lottie's tummy started to rumble.

'Wow. That all looks delicious,' she said to Fred, who grinned.

'Yup. I'm having the crab mac n' cheese.'

'That sounds amazing. I think I'll have the same.'

'We should get some fries as well. Celine, what are you having?' Fred called out to their housemate who had edged her way into the queue ahead of them.

'Cajun squid wrap,' Celine called back, rubbing her hands together excitedly. She caught Lottie's surprised expression. 'What is it, Lottie?'

'No, it's just... I'm loving the enthusiasm.' Lottie smiled.

'Bah. I'm French. Food is life,' Celine said with a shrug.

'I'm actually friends with one of the guys that runs the truck,' Fred interjected. 'We went to school together.'

'Oh? Which one?' Lottie looked up at the serving hatch, where the two men were working.

'Callum. Redhead. Or, ginger beard. I guess you can't tell with their hats on.'

'Right.' Lottie watched Callum for a moment, noticing his strong biceps under a black T-shirt and a red and white striped apron. She cleared her throat and looked away. 'He's actually a bit too tall to be in that truck, isn't he? Looks like he has to hunch just to get in there.'

'Yeah. He's a big lad. Played rugby at school.' Fred nodded. 'Not like me, I was always reading comic books. Then when sports didn't work out, Callum got really into food, and the laird gave him a loan to get the food truck up and going. It's been doing great, he said. Last time we spoke.'

Lottie regarded Callum out of the corner of her eye. *Rugby player, huh.* She wasn't given to thinking about men in a sexual way; that had never been who she was.

Yet, her relationship with Tristan had opened her eyes when it came to sex. That was part of why she missed him so damned much: their physical connection, their chemistry, had been out of this world. She'd only have to see him and want to jump on him. In bed, Tristan had made her feel so good. His body was strong, lithe, beautiful. His thighs were like tree trunks. She'd used to sit on his lap sometimes just for the pleasure of feeling them beneath her.

Do not – and I repeat, NOT – think about Tristan's thighs, she berated herself.

'That's great. So, the laird – is that Hal Cameron?' Lottie asked, drawing her gaze away from Callum.

'Yup.' Fred nodded.

'He supports local businesses a lot, then? Or was that just a lucky favour?'

'Nah, he's pretty supportive of local businesses, because we don't allow chains up here at all. You might have noticed. No big supermarkets, no fast food franchises, no cookie cutter shops. It's all independent businesses up here. That's how we survive. Otherwise, the big companies would put us out of business, and there'd be nothing here.'

'I had noticed that, actually. It's strange to be somewhere you can't order thai food to be delivered in under thirty minutes, or hundreds of miles away from a drive-thru coffee.'

'Well, I don't know about hundreds of miles away. But definitely a long way.' Fred chuckled. 'However, you can get coffee from the little shack up on Gyle Head, by the playground. Or the Inn does a pretty good cappuccino, to be honest.'

'I've had one from the shack. It *was* good.'

'Their home-made granola bars are pretty special, too,' Fred said, jamming his hands in his pockets and shaking his head in wonder at the loch. 'You know, I've lived here all my life and I'll still never get over that view.'

'You're right. It's stunning,' Lottie breathed. An orange sun was setting on the horizon, and the whole sky was turning a deep pink. It had been a warm day – warm for Scotland, at least – and the sky was completely cloudless for once. The loch's surface was so glassily clear that it reflected the setting sun like a mirror, and the orange and the pink glimmered on its surface like a jewelled blanket.

Next to the loch, the tall turrets of Loch Cameron Castle cast a long shadow over the ornamental gardens below, and the rich green of the woodland surrounding the loch was lit with the warm sun, bringing out the depth of colour of the fir trees and the deep pinks of the bougainvillea and rhododendron bushes that had burst into bloom over the summer.

'Hey, Fred,' Callum greeted them when they stepped up to the front of the line. 'How's it going?'

'Yeah, good, thanks. Callum, this is my new housemate, Lottie.' Fred laid a hand on Lottie's arm. For a moment, she felt that same strange flicker of electricity; a similar moment of connection as when she and Fred had touched hands in the kitchen. She crossed her arms over her chest.

'Hey, Lottie. How are you?' Callum gave her a friendly smile. 'Are you new to Loch Cameron? Haven't seen you around.'

'Yeah, I just moved up here,' she said, a little shyly. Callum was handsome, with an open expression and clear blue eyes that had little laugh lines at the edges.

'Makes sense. I would've remembered you.' He winked, and something about how he did it made Lottie smile. 'Now, then. What can I get you?'

They gave their orders and went to stand alongside Celine while their food was made to order. The smell of the meat on the grill and the savoury smells of cheese, hot bread and char-grilling made Lottie's mouth water.

Celine and Fred got into a good-natured argument about which was better: the food from the van, or the pub grub at the

Inn behind them. Fred was valiantly defending the Inn, which, he said, had cosy old-world charm, and its food was hearty and tasty and came in large portions. Celine was firmly on the side of the food truck.

'And, the truck has two hot guys, am I right, Lottie?' she asked, nudging Lottie, who had been only half-listening to their banter, and half-watching Callum move around the truck with surprising grace. He might have had to hunch to fit in the space at all, but there was something in the way that he held himself that kept her attention.

'What?' Lottie had only half-heard Celine.

'I said, the guys that run the food truck are hot, no?' Celine repeated, chuckling. 'Don't think I can't see you watching.'

'I wasn't! I was... just making sure I listened for our number being called,' Lottie said, weakly.

'That Thomas can call my number any day of the week.' Celine put both hands onto her cheeks and shook her head in wonder. 'I love the Scottish guys. So wholesome and big. Do you have a boyfriend?' she asked.

'Umm... No, I don't,' Lottie said, not wanting to say more.

'Why not?' Celine zipped up her jacket. 'Agh. I love Scotland, but it gets so chilly.' She looked up and gave Lottie a nudge. 'Oh. Don't look now. Speak of the devil.'

Lottie frowned and looked up to see Callum walking over to where they were standing, carrying a paper bag.

'Thought I'd bring it over and get a breather from the van for a minute,' he said, handing the bag to Lottie. 'It gets hot in there.' He took off his beanie and ran a hand through his thick auburn hair.

'Thanks,' Lottie said, shyly.

'No problem. We should hang out, you guys. Tom and I were thinking of doing the quiz at the Inn next week, if you all wanted to make up a team, maybe?'

'That sounds good. Fred can bring this girlfriend we keep hearing about,' Celine interjected. 'I'm not sure that she's real.'

'She's real.' Fred sounded embarrassed. 'For goodness' sake! We haven't been seeing each other that long, that's all.'

'Yeah, right. We'll see.' Celine winked at Lottie. 'Maybe she's just a figment of your imagination, Freddie.'

'Well, she's not, so give it a rest,' Fred sighed. 'Her name's Helen, and she's a pharmacist.'

'Fantasy pharmacist,' Celine scoffed. 'I'll believe it when I see it. Callum, we would love to come to the quiz with you and Tom.'

'Great,' Callum laughed. 'I'm good at sports and Tom's pretty good at history, but we could do with some other expertise on the team. Fred, you're into books, right? So that covers a lot.'

'Yeah. Celine's great at politics. And she's a translator.'

'Awesome. How about you, Lottie?' Callum's voice softened as he turned to her.

'Oh. I mean, I'm studying sociology. If any questions come up about cultural policy, I'm in. Or the arts. Music, maybe.'

'Perfect.' He held her gaze for a long moment, and Lottie felt herself blush under his gaze. 'It's a date.'

'Oh... okay,' Lottie said, aware that she was acting like a preteen girl, but she was completely unable to stop herself.

'Well, I better get back to it. See you at the quiz.'

'Oh, sweet lord,' Celine hissed as Callum gave them a little wave and headed back into the van. 'Come on, Fred. We have dinner, go and get some wine from the supermarket. Screw cap. We'll see you on the bench.' She guided Lottie to a free bench at the edge of the loch and waved Fred off impatiently.

'I think we have a date, Lottie, eh?' Celine made a little squeal noise and put her arm around Lottie's shoulders. 'Ah, I'm so glad you've moved in to the house. It's been dull, just with Fred. He tries his best, but I can only talk about books for so long, you know? Now there's another girl in the place, we can have fun, no?' She opened the food bag and handed Lottie a tub of crab mac n' cheese and a wooden fork.

'I mean... sure. I guess I could do with a little fun.' Lottie took the tub and opened it, breathing in the delicious savoury aroma.

'That's the spirit, *cherie*.' Celine grinned. 'Life isn't just all work, work, work, eh? I feel like you need to cut loose a little. You have a sadness in you. Whatever it is, you let it free, eh? Life is too short.'

Lottie looked out at the loch; the sun had almost completely set, but the sky was still a deep violet: the last pink light of the evening reluctant to leave.

'You're right, Celine,' she said, and took a bite of the mac n' cheese. It was delicious: rich, creamy and filling. She took another spoon, and another. She let out a long sigh which felt as though it had been trapped inside her for months. Years, perhaps.

'Of course I am right,' Celine chuckled. 'Yes, I think you and I will be friends, Lottie.' She patted Lottie's hand. 'I am glad that you are here. And I think that Loch Cameron is a good place to come and heal whatever it is that has hurt you. I myself have loved living here. But that is another story for another time.' She gave Lottie a wry smile. 'Oh. Here Fred comes with the wine. Do you think he really has a girlfriend? I don't know how anyone could find him sexy,' she said, as Fred approached.

'I'm sure he does, if he says he does,' Lottie said, lowering her voice as Fred approached. 'And I'm sure there would be girls – or boys – who would think he was nice.'

'Pah. Nice,' Celine scoffed. 'You can keep it.'

As Fred approached, carrying a bottle of wine and some cocktails in cans, Lottie thought that *nice* was a very underrated quality. And she wondered what it would be like to have a boyfriend who might not break your heart.

9

GRETCHEN

I am not the first woman to be frightened of a man, and I won't be the last.

This is something I know.

Even if I didn't already know some of what can happen between a man and a woman – the bad things, the secret things, the whispered things that aren't discussed in the open – a walk through the chapel graveyard would educate me. The women dead before their time: childbirth, worn down in a life of misery, an accident in the home.

Not that those things are written on the headstones, but I learned as a child that a graveyard speaks in its own code: Old Maid; Taken Too Soon; Fought Bravely.

But, knowing something and being able to act on it – and not being paralysed by fear – is quite another thing.

I have always known that there is a dark thread of violence that can run through relations between people. Not just men and women, of course. Sometimes, parents and children, too. But, my own childhood was relatively peaceful and loving. There certainly wasn't a sense of dread in the house, that anything lurked under the surface, waiting to strike.

At first, I didn't feel that with him, either. Everything was lovely. He was charming. Affectionate. He couldn't do enough for me.

I trusted him.

I shouldn't have.

We were having dinner at his house and he found a spot of dried food on his fork. He held it up to the light and looked at it for a moment. It was a Sunday evening. I'd made a casserole.

I wasn't really listening to him when he said *this fork is dirty*. He repeated it, and I looked over, distractedly.

Oh. Must've missed a spot with the cloth, I said.

Get me another, he said. I looked up and frowned, then, because it was a strange thing to say.

Get it yourself, I said. *You're a grown-up*. I was a little cross at his tone. He was being rude, and it wasn't like him.

He got up, and I went back to eating my dinner.

Then, he had my hair in his fist, pulling my head back so fast that it snapped my neck.

Get me another fork. A clean one, he repeated, staring down into my eyes. I couldn't reply: partly the shock, partly he had my neck at such a severe angle that it was hard to speak. He pushed me, then, his fist at the back of my neck. *Go on.*

He let go, and I stared at him in disbelief.

What was that for? I asked, coughing. In reply, he launched into a diatribe of abuse.

I was too messy about the house, he said. I lived in "a flea pit" and that I should spend less time at work and more time being a good housewife to someone.

He stood, towering over me, it felt like, shouting all these terrible things. He was the only man who would ever want a woman like me who was such a sluttish housekeeper, and I should be grateful that he was here.

He ended this sudden, long series of harsh criticisms of me by slamming his hand down on the table. It made a huge bang, startling me, and then he picked up my dinner plate – and threw it across the room. It shattered on the wall, and I watched the remaining food on it slither down the wall.

Clean it up, he said, and walked out.

I cleaned up the mess.

It was so sudden, so out of the blue. I was in love with him. But how could I love someone who would do that? And, if what I suspected was true – the thing I hadn't yet told him – then that left me in an even worse situation than I originally thought.

I have never told anyone about that day. I don't know if I can ever tell anyone: not even Lottie, this sweet girl who listens to me ramble on so patiently. For all these years, I have felt a terrible sense of shame.

I know now that it wasn't my fault. But, for a long time, I thought that there was something in me that drew him to me. Something in me that made him do these terrible things.

Now that I am older, I know that is not true. But I still hold back from telling it, even though I am weary from holding it inside me.

10

___

'Hey, you.' Fred looked up from the counter as she pushed open the door of the bookshop. 'I didn't expect to see you. Welcome to Pageturner's!'

'Ah, well. I was passing and realised I hadn't been in yet. Hey. This is really cute!' Lottie exclaimed, looking around. The bookshop was small, but Lottie felt instantly cosy on entering it. Dark wood bookshelves lined the walls and a couple of matching tables were piled with colourful hardbacks. There was a pleasant smell of beeswax in the air, and the wood of the shelves and tables gleamed.

At the front of the shop, Fred stood behind a wide, dark wooden shop counter which held a laptop, some messy piles of paperwork, a number of half-drunk mugs of tea and piles of books with Post-it notes on them. Looking around, Lottie noticed a dinky spiral staircase.

A couple of tourists were browsing in the corner – Lottie assumed they were tourists because they were wearing hiking boots, expensive-looking sportswear and brightly coloured rain macs. Loch Cameron residents seemed fond of jumpers, cord trousers and wool skirts; despite the existence of a nice boutique clothes shop, the village seemed a little stuck in the past in some ways.

'Thank you. We try.' Today, Fred was wearing a simple dark green jumper and jeans, and she thought for a moment how nice the colour looked on him, bringing out the green flecks in his hazel brown eyes. 'Did you want a book, or just came in to case the joint?'

'Casing the joint. A hundred per cent,' Lottie chuckled. 'It's really nice in here, though. I wouldn't mind having somewhere like this to work.'

'Aww. Well, you might not think that when the mice come out and play,' Fred tutted, and grinned. 'I'm glad you popped in, actually. I was clearing out one of the cabinets in the back, and I found something interesting. A notebook belonging to the guy who used to own this shop, Alexander O'Connell. It mentions a Gretchen, and I know that you're interviewing Gretchen Ross up at the care home. I thought they might be connected, or she might want to see it or something.' He picked up a plain, spiral-bound notebook from his desk and held it out to her. 'I mean. There are only so many Gretchens, right? Mind you, having looked at it, I'm not sure you should show it to her.'

'Why not? Yes, I remember her mentioning something about it now. In passing, though. She was very dismissive about it. Gretchen had a bit of a thing with the guy that owned this place.' Lottie took the book and opened it.

Gretchen,

~~*I don't know how you could do it*~~
~~*I trusted you*~~
I wanted a family with you. It could have been so lovely between us. It was good between us. You've broken my heart.
I can't see you anymore.

Alex

'Oh my goodness. What happened between them?' Lottie looked up, meeting Fred's eyes.

'I don't know. Something certainly kicked off, but it's not clear what.' Fred looked over her shoulder as she turned the pages of the notebook. Lottie was deeply aware of his presence, again; the pleasant aura of masculinity that he exuded in a gentle, grounded way. She tried to ignore it.

On the next page there was another note, full of more crossings-out.

Dear Gretchen

~~*I miss you so much. I feel as though my heart has been cut out.*~~
I am heartbroken. You could have had everything with me. I wanted a life with you.
I am heartbroken. I can't think or work. I've closed the shop.
Please, please reconsider.

Alex

Then, one page, with a single sentence, written in angry capitals:

YOU BITCH. I'M GOING TO TELL EVERYONE ABOUT WHAT YOU DID.

'Wow. This is intense.' Lottie recoiled from reading that.

'I know. Horrible, isn't it?' Fred agreed. 'So, what do you know about this man, again? I mean, I know he owned the shop, and then mum bought it from his nephew, I think. Some Irish guy.'

'Gretchen and this Alex were an item for a while,' Lottie said, flicking through the rest of the notebook. 'I don't know anything about it, though.'

'I mean, it looks like Alex was pretty upset in these notes, like he was rehearsing or making notes for something he wanted to say to her.' Fred pointed to the handwriting.

'Right. Well, I guess I could ask her what happened between them.'

Lottie leafed through the notebook. There were more notes and diary entries; some of them looked like stocktaking lists or book orders, but here and there, there were other, more personal entries. All of them seemed hurt and angry, with frequent capitalisations and crossings-out.

'Hmm. D'you mind if I take this?' She looked up and met Fred's eyes.

'Not at all. I'll let you know if I find anything else, but you're welcome to it,' he said. 'Seems like there's a bit of a mystery there. I kinda want to know what happened.'

'Me too. I'll let you know what I find out,' Lottie said, putting the notebook in her bag. Gretchen's story had just got even more interesting, and she couldn't wait to see her friend again to find out more.

11

———

The next day, Lottie got to the care home at midmorning, burning with curiosity about the notebook that Fred had given her. But, as she sat down next to Gretchen and started their now familiar routine – tea, biscuits on a plate, a polite hello and a catch up – she wondered whether sharing the book with Gretchen was a good idea.

Gretchen, however, seemed to know that Lottie was hiding something and fixed her with a gimlet stare.

'What is it, dear?' she enquired, curiously. 'You look like a cat on hot bricks.'

'Umm...' Lottie prevaricated. She didn't want to upset her new friend, and the notebook held some potentially distressing entries.

'What, dear? Spit it out,' Gretchen insisted.

'Oh, it's just that I was at Pageturner's yesterday, and Fred – he's my housemate, do you remember? He works there. Well, anyway, he found some notes written in a book by the man that used to own the shop... Alexander. I remembered that you said you dated the guy that worked there, once... but you said it didn't go well. I guess I wondered… if you really wanted to see them.'

'Alex?' Gretchen's tone was guarded. 'Goodness. Well, yes, I suppose so. It's been a long time. He's passed, now, I believe,' she sighed.

Lottie took the notebook out of her handbag and handed it to Gretchen.

'It's not that… pleasant, what he wrote. But I still thought you'd want to see it. I don't know. Maybe I shouldn't be giving it to you.'

'Of course you can give it to me. As I said before, it's all a long time ago now.' Gretchen put her glasses on with her left hand and held the book up to her eyes. 'That said, it's quite strange to see his handwriting, after all this time.'

She read some pages, laying the book on her lap and turning the page with her free hand. She didn't say anything, but, after a while, she took a deep breath and looked up.

'You're right. You shouldn't have given this to me.' Gretchen handed it back to Lottie, who took it, surprised.

'I'm sorry. I—'

'You should be sorry. Lottie, I've given you everything of my story that I wanted to give you. That… Alex… that isn't anything I wanted to think about again. And now, I have to.'

'I'm sorry, Gretchen. It was thoughtless of me.' Lottie was taken aback by Gretchen's change in tone. She was normally so cheery. The little girl in Lottie was instantly scared: she never wanted to make anyone angry.

'Things happened between us that I don't want to remember. I loved him so deeply, and he hurt me. My advice? Don't go for the ones that give you butterflies in the beginning. You think it's love, but it's a lack of balance. Alex kept me off-balance for our entire relationship.'

Gretchen wiped away a tear from her cheek, then picked up

the teacup that Lottie had placed on her bedside table and took a sip.

'I'm sorry, Gretchen. Forget I said anything,' Lottie said, her anxiety making her tummy clench in its familiar way.

'I don't want to talk about it,' Gretchen said, staunchly. She pressed her lips together firmly, as if she was stopping the words leaving her mouth.

'I'm sorry. I just thought—' Lottie apologised again, mortified that she had upset her friend.

'No, you didn't think,' Gretchen interrupted her, sounding tired. 'Just because you come here and listen to my stories, don't assume that I'm going to tell you all of them. I don't want to tell you everything.'

'I don't assume. I didn't... Fred gave me these and I guess I thought you'd want to see them. These notes are all about you.' Lottie flicked through the pages. 'But, you're right. I'm sorry. I don't have any right to ask you about just anything.'

There was an uncomfortable silence.

'Oh, Lottie. Forgive me.' Gretchen took in a deep breath and let it out again. 'It was just a bit of a shock, reading those words. He was so angry. I suppose I'd forgotten, a little. Or, I wanted to.'

'I'm here if you want to talk, Gretchen. But you're right. You don't have to.' Lottie took her friend's hand, her heart still pounding with anxiety that she might have upset her friend.

'One day, I might tell you about Alex,' Gretchen said, rubbing her forehead with her fingertips. 'But not now, sweetheart. Okay?'

'Gretchen. I'm sorry.'

'Don't be sorry. But I'm not feeling that well, dear.' Gretchen looked pale, and Lottie noticed how paper thin her skin was. 'Can you leave me be for today? I need to sleep.'

'Of course.' Lottie stood up and let go of Gretchen's hand,

which fell back onto the coverlet of the bed like a limp bird. 'I'll come back soon.'

'Good.' Gretchen closed her eyes, coughing a little. Her breath was more difficult than it usually was, Lottie thought. She felt concerned; she didn't want to leave Gretchen when she was clearly feeling so low.

'Do you want me to stay?' Lottie asked.

'Leave me to sleep, dear. I won't relax if you're here.' Gretchen shook her head.

'All right, then. I'll see you soon, though,' Lottie said, gathering up her things. 'Are you sure you're okay?' She couldn't shake the feeling that something was wrong. That she should stay and watch over Gretchen.

'I'm fine, dear,' Gretchen said, opening her eyes and giving Lottie a tired smile. 'Don't worry yourself. Be gone with you.'

Lottie nodded, putting her bag on her shoulder. She *was* worried, but she obeyed Gretchen's wishes and left, pulling the door closed softly behind her.

12

'In my first role as editor, I was the only woman in a team of ten editors and a number of more senior colleagues: commissioning editors, publishers, editorial directors. All the editors were supposed to be paid the same, but, of course, I was paid less than the rest of them, because I was a woman.' Gretchen was in full flow with her story again, as if the last time that Lottie had talked to her hadn't happened.

Lottie was cautious about interviewing her again, because of the way they'd left it the last time: she'd felt that she had offended Gretchen, or touched a nerve. There was definitely something distressing that Gretchen didn't want to talk about, connected to this Alexander from the bookshop. Lottie had decided to leave it for now, but she was keen to probe Gretchen for more of her story. She felt certain that Gretchen had something she wanted to get off her chest, and was fascinated to know what it was.

Someone who had lived so vividly – as Kimberley had suggested to her – would also have many other amazing and perhaps salacious stories, Lottie was sure. An affair with a famous author? Some kind of press scandal? Political intrigue? Gretchen could have so many stories to tell.

Gretchen, lying in queenly fashion in her bed, had shown Lottie how to use the remote control that made the top and the end of the bed raise and lower, in order to achieve maximum comfort.

'The rationale then was this: a man was responsible for supporting a family, ergo, his salary should reflect his responsibilities. I, as a young single woman, was not deemed to have as many responsibilities, so I was paid less than my male counterparts, even though many of them didn't have families anyway.'

'That's terrible,' Lottie breathed, checking that her voice recorder was on. 'Shall I make tea?'

'Yes, please, dear. And open the window, would you? It's stuffy in here. Smells of old woman. I usually would spray a bit of Elizabeth Arden around before visitors came, but I didn't get round to it today.'

'Of course.' Lottie went to the window which looked over the lovely gardens of the care home, and opened it so that the air flowed in. It was a beautiful July day and she'd revelled in the scenery of the drive, coming over: there was a point where the road narrowed and you turned off the unremarkable A road, and entered a countryside full of wide moorland and tussocky heather. In one field, shaggy brown longhorn cows grazed peacefully, and she'd rolled down the windows of her car to breathe in the fragrant air.

'Thank you. Ah, that's better. Yes. They thought there was an unshakeable logic to their way of ordering the world, but I knew from looking at my cheque at the end of the month that their logic was seriously impeding my opportunities to eat and pay rent. Still, when I became an editor, I was thrilled. For the first time, I would have the opportunity to shape books. I would be able to work with authors. I would work in the beating heart of publishing, and be among greatness,' Gretchen continued, and snorted. 'Hmph. That was what I believed, anyway.'

'That didn't happen?' Lottie was boiling the kettle and setting everything out on the tea tray. She gave Gretchen a curious look.

'Not exactly, dear. On my first day as editor, I turned up to the editorial office early. We were supposed to start at eight thirty, and I'd got there at eight to make a good impression and make sure that I had plenty of time and wasn't rushed. Until then, I'd only ever worked in the typing pool at Dunne's, and then, in the office outside editorial, as an assistant.

'Being an assistant at Dunne's was a very small step up from the typing pool, but it meant that my job didn't *just* consist of typing anymore. As an assistant, I posted out edited manuscripts to authors, filed contracts and answered the phone. But, I still typed a lot: letters, new versions of manuscripts, which, once they'd been corrected, I had to decipher and recreate.

'I was so excited to leave my desk on the other side of the door and walk into editorial because I belonged there, and not because an editor had clicked his fingers at me because he wanted something.'

'I can imagine.' Lottie returned with the tea tray and set it down carefully. She was feeling buoyed up by listening to Gretchen's inspiring story. Just the very act of being in Gretchen's presence made her feel empowered. Lottie felt as though she could do anything when she was with Gretchen.

'I'd taken a lot of care over my outfit that day. Clothes were always very important to me, and still are. You might look at me now in my old lady body, and doubt that I ever looked svelte and glamorous, but believe me when I say that I looked damn good then. I was always slim – it was genes, rather than a particular effort on my part. I never dieted, but at work I did often forget to eat, so that may have contributed to the fact that I stayed a size ten until I was around forty years old.'

'Lucky you,' Lottie said, glumly. 'I've always struggled with my weight.'

Gretchen leaned forwards and peered critically at Lottie.

'In what way, dear? You look fine to me.'

'I've just always been bigger. I eat well – I mean, I do enjoy food – and I walk a lot. I just can't seem to get rid of it.'

'You are a normal size for a woman.' Gretchen waved a gnarled hand at her. 'You're lovely. Women are supposed to have curves.'

'Oh, that's very kind. But I don't think I'm lovely.' Lottie felt very uncomfortable.

'Don't you? Why not?' Gretchen frowned at her. 'Although, dear, and ignore me if I'm being too antique in my opinions here – I know that you young girls have different fashions nowadays, and it's wonderful to be comfortable and practical. I have a few tracksuits myself – but those loose clothes really aren't doing anything for your lovely figure.'

'Oh. Well, I don't really pay attention to my clothes,' Lottie admitted. She was wearing some loose grey jogging bottoms that had lost all shape a long time ago, and a bobbly jersey T-shirt in a faded pink. She had put her hair into its usual plait and then pinned it around her head like a Dutch girl – she liked to do that sometimes, though the weight of her hair pulled on her scalp after a while – and she hardly ever bothered with makeup. She hadn't thought that her clothes would be an issue, coming to talk to the elderly, but clearly she'd been wrong.

Gretchen looked like she was going to say more, paused, and then continued her story.

'On my first day in editorial, I wore a black skirt suit with a white scoop necked blouse underneath it and black heels. In those days it was much more common for women to wear stockings, and so I wore those too. I distinctly remember the fact that one of my suspender belt clips wasn't working very well, and it kept coming untethered. I should say that I am glad that women in your generation don't have to deal with the underwear we used to have. All clips and boning, corsets and girdles and this and that. Nowadays if you want to hold things in place, you have these amazing scientific fabrics. *Spanx*. A couple of the girls here have them, though you could break a hip trying to get them on at our age.' She winked at Lottie, who giggled. 'I didn't mean to make you feel self-conscious about your appearance, dear. Please feel free to wear whatever you're comfortable in to see me. I just meant that it seems a shame to cover up a beautiful figure like yours with clothes that – if you'll excuse me – look like they should only be used to paint the drawing-room in,' she added.

'Well, I have had these a long time,' Lottie admitted, looking at the joggers. 'They're just comfy, though.'

'Comfort is important. I expect you have some lovely dresses in your wardrobe. Something that nips in you in at the waist and shows off that lovely bust and bottom,' Gretchen said, kindly.

Actually, when Lottie thought about it, she didn't have anything like what Gretchen described. She hadn't bought a dress in... well, she couldn't remember when. She'd never had a lot of confidence in her body, and, since being a teenager, had tried to cover it up as a general rule. She lived in jogging bottoms, loose T-shirts, sweatshirts and cardigans. She'd always thought that was just her style.

'Hmm,' she said, noncommittally. 'Go on with your story, anyway.'

'Yes. Right. When I arrived at the office, I was the first one there. I remember that I hovered uncertainly in the corner, wondering which would be my desk. At just before eight-thirty, the assistants started to arrive at the office outside, so I went to talk to them, since they were my friends and, just the day before, that had been my desk in the right-hand corner.

'Twenty minutes later, some of the editors started to file into their office. I followed them in and stood in the doorway expectantly. *Get us some coffees, Ross,* one of them said. Charles O'Flanagan. I had never liked him, because he spoke to all of us assistants exactly like that. He'd clearly forgotten that I'd now joined the editorial office. Or, he hadn't forgotten, but he wanted to put me in my place, whatever he thought that place was.

'*It's Miss Ross, and you can get your own damn coffee, Charlie,* I said. *Which one's my desk?* I remember he blinked at me, like I'd just reeled off a lick of Russian or something. *I'm an editor now,* I said. He just shrugged. He said, and I'll never forget this, *they just hired you because of women's lib. It's all for show. Not like you'll be able to do the job.*'

'He didn't!' Lottie was outraged on Gretchen's behalf, but Gretchen nodded sagely.

'Oh, he did. That was Charlie all over, the misogynist little twit. *We'll see, won't we?* I said, brightly, though it was a horrible thing for him to say, but then, he *was* horrible.' Gretchen paused for a moment, swallowing. Lottie had the same sense that she had had before – that Gretchen wasn't saying everything; that she was keeping something back.

'What is it, Gretchen?' Lottie asked. 'Did something happen with this Charlie?'

'Hmm. You know, some of these things… they're not easy to talk about.' Gretchen sighed and shook her head. 'I'll get to it, Lottie. In good time.'

'Well, you can tell me. I know what some men are like,' Lottie said, grimly.

'I have no doubt, dear. Sad that you have come to that conclusion, at such a tender age.' Gretchen raised an eyebrow. 'You can imagine what it was like, applying to be the only woman in an office like that,' she added.

'I can. Horrid.' Lottie nodded.

'It was, but I wanted the job so much, so I had to try. I'd

interviewed for it without much hope; sitting outside the personnel office, I'd been the only woman in a row of carbon copies of the same young man. When they'd offered it to me – despite the fact that I knew I was qualified and I knew I could do the job well – I'd known that I would be the only woman in that office, and I'd wondered whether I was fulfilling some kind of quota.

'I never knew if that was what it was; why I got that first editorial job. And, over time, I stopped worrying about it. At the end of the day, dear, I got my foot in the door and that was all that mattered. After then, all I had to do was prove myself, and work three times as hard as everyone else. And, the joke was on them, in the end. Because I was by far the most successful in my career out of any of them.'

'Even Charlie?' Lottie prompted her, wanting to probe her further. Had this Charlie been a boyfriend, she wondered?

'Oh, especially Charlie. He was as lazy as he was rude. Even in the patriarchy, you have to make at least a bit of effort to fail upwards, if you have a penis. You have to be seen to get some results, even if they're absolute rubbish. Charlie spent all his time at the betting shop and the pub.' Gretchen rolled her eyes theatrically. 'Sorry for saying *penis*, dear. But you know what I mean. It's a perfectly fine thing in itself, but unfortunately, it often comes with a nasty dose of entitlement. I don't know when that begins. When they learn to pee standing up, perhaps.'

'Probably.' Lottie snorted. 'I get the sense that you and Charlie had some sort of relationship, though. From the way you talk about him.'

Gretchen's expression darkened. 'I definitely didn't have a romance with Charles O'Flanagan,' she said, shortly.

'Well, it just seems like you had some kind of link to him. To mention him at all,' Lottie said.

'I don't want to waste my time talking about him,' Gretchen

said. 'This was a time in my life when I was surrounded by toxic men. I...' She bit her lip. 'It was not a happy time,' she said, shortly, and Lottie could feel the pain underlying those words. She wondered what had happened between Gretchen and this Charlie. She wanted to ask more, but she didn't want to upset her friend again. Yet, there was definitely something Gretchen wasn't saying.

13

GRETCHEN

I am enjoying telling my story to Lottie. I am enjoying seeing myself reflected in her eyes: Gretchen Ross, the grand old dame, the raconteur. I am enjoying telling her the stories I know will warm her heart. They're real; I wouldn't lie to her. The things I'm telling her did happen.

I can tell that Lottie wants to know more. She is searching for the truth. There are questions in her about her own life, too. She is a girl who is searching for herself as well as my story.

But, there are some stories I won't tell her, because I want Lottie to believe that good triumphs over evil and that bad men get their comeuppance. Sadly, that isn't always true.

I have regrets. One doesn't live a life as long as mine and not have them.

But, of them all, there is one that outweighs the others. One big regret that sits on my conscience like a vulture, picking the meat off my bones. Over the years, it has taken so much from me that I am hardly more than skin and gristle; and, still, it sits on my chest, slowly weighing me down, down, down. The thing that changed my life forever; the thing I can never forget.

.   .   .

'A man could die of thirst here.' Charlie O'Flanagan leans back in his chair, his feet on his desk. My desk is opposite his now, and if I look up, I'll see the worn soles of his cheap brogues mashing the top of a manuscript he's supposed to be working on.

I ignore him. I know he thinks I should get up and put a pot of coffee on. But, I don't respond.

I am proofreading a manuscript. A novel by one of our more mid-list authors. They won't trust me with a book by a high-profile author yet – mid-list means that the author is doing okay, sells consistently, but never gets into the top tens of anything, isn't a bestseller. Isn't a huge name, like some of the people we publish. I am using the proofing marks we used then, that the typesetter will understand when I write them in the margins in their special, archaic code.

'Ugh. Does anyone else want a coffee?' Charlie pipes up again. 'Ross. You're closest. Put a pot on, there's a good girl.'

I have to look up now, because he's addressed me personally.

'I'm busy. Put it on yourself,' I say, annoyed that he's made me lose my place and my concentration, and even more annoyed at being called a *good girl.*

'Come on, Ross. Don't play games. We don't know how to use the machine,' Charlie wheedles. A snicker goes around the office, and one of the other editors, Graham, laughs.

'I wouldn't mind one, if there's a cup going,' Bob, the managing editor, says from his corner desk. I look over at him, and he shoots me a warm smile.

Bob is not a bad man. He listens when I give him updates on the manuscripts I'm working on and he doesn't make overly offensive remarks about my outfits or my hair, but he's still a middle-aged white man in the 1960s who probably doesn't see anything wrong with me being the designated coffee maker in the office, because I possess a vagina. So, I get up, with a sigh, and go over to the coffee machine.

I know that not all men are like them. Or, perhaps they are, but working with men is very different to being their girlfriend or wife or sister.

I have a boyfriend at this time, Alex. He is appalled at the things I tell him about the men I work with. He says that he would never treat a woman in this way, and he has suggested more than once already that I leave. But I refuse to.

Behind me, I can hear them talking among themselves, snickering at some in-joke that they find amusing. I am never included in their jokes, and I know I am often either the butt of them, or I have to listen to jokes in which the woman is always the victim.

What do blondes and beer bottles have in common? They're both empty from the neck up.

Why haven't any women ever gone to space? It doesn't need cleaning yet.

It's those, and so many more. Sometimes, I know that they share dirty jokes in an effort to make me feel uncomfortable. It's a boy's club in this office, and Charlie and some of the others want me to know that I'm only there under sufferance. The rest of them, like Bob, are oblivious, and just laugh along. *What's the difference between an oral and rectal thermometer? The taste.*

I have learned to be tough. To ignore the jokes and not take offence; sometimes I smile at a dirty joke, not because I find it funny – the humour level is about the same as the playground – but because I know I need to try and fit in.

I am standing at the percolator, removing the used filter, when I feel hands on my hips. I spin around, finding Charlie behind me.

'Just thought I'd come and see how it's done,' he says, smoothly, now placing a hand on the small of my back, as if he is a close friend giving me support at an emotional time, or a date, ushering me through a busy restaurant. Neither of these things are the case, though, and his sudden, unwanted touch fills me with a horrible sense of threat and unease.

I can touch you whenever I want, and I can intimidate you whenever I want, is what Charlie's hands on my body are saying.

I shrink back, dropping the used coffee filter full of wet coffee grounds on the floor between us. Wet coffee grounds spatter my stockings.

'Butterfingers,' Charlie snickers, raising an eyebrow. 'Not sure you should be making us coffee after all, Ross. We should get one of the secretaries to do it, eh.' He glances down at my stockings. 'Go and clean yourself up. You look like a tramp. And you're going to stink all day now.' He makes sure that he has said all of this in a loud voice so that everyone in the office can hear him.

I blush deeply, completely mortified. I feel sick. I want to run away.

'You're dirty, Ross. You stink.' He leans in closer to me, lowering his voice so that only I can hear his last comment. 'Dirty girl. I should clean you up.'

I am being punished for talking back, for threatening Charlie's perceived dominance in the office – perhaps, I am being punished simply for existing. For daring to be a woman in this space. And, in that moment, I am diminished. I am not the Gretchen Ross that is later victorious over men like Charlie; I am not the Gretchen Ross who is in charge. I am not the marvellous and caustic Grand Dame recounting her adventures to a young student, in which I gloss over moments like this when I was made to feel weak and powerless, and when I didn't yet know how to fight back.

In this moment, I am a young woman who is being harassed in her workplace, which is at that time a place with no safety for her.

I run to the ladies' bathroom and strip off my stockings in one of the stalls, dropping them into the waste bin. Then, I sit on the lid of the toilet and sob my heart out.

I do not tell Alex about what happens that day. I do not tell anyone, out of fear and intimidation. I do not tell Alex because I do not want him to think that I am dirty or that what Charlie did *was* somehow my fault. Because it is always the woman's fault.

Alex is a good man. I know that good men exist. But I don't want to ruin what we have. And there is something in me that fears I might.

14

'Next question. How many years did Manchester United win the FA Cup Final? With bonus points for every correct year that they won.' Eric Ballantyne, the landlord of the Loch Cameron Inn read the next quiz question.

Lottie sat next to Celine at the table, with Fred and his girlfriend Helen next to her and opposite Tom and Callum. The quiz was in full swing, and they were one of ten teams competing. Lottie had been surprised at how seriously everyone was taking it, and felt slightly that she should have done some preparation for it, like reading some trivia books or watching some quiz shows on TV.

'Twelve. They've won twelve times.' Callum leaned forward, lowering his voice so that people at the other tables wouldn't be able to hear. 'And I think, 2016, 1990? What else?'

'1977. Against Liverpool,' Tom added.

'Right. Any other years?' Callum looked around at the rest of the table.

'No idea, mate,' Fred admitted with a shrug.

'No, sorry.' Lottie shook her head. 'Football isn't really my thing. Though I do feel like they were quite successful in the nineties. Were there other years they won that, in particular?'

'Yeah, I think you're right, definitely.' Callum gave her a big smile. 'I just can't remember which years for sure.'

'1996, I think,' Helen contributed. She hadn't said much so far, but Lottie thought that she seemed nice, if not a little reserved. Fred had seemed happy to see her when she'd met them outside the Inn, but they'd only kissed lightly on the cheek, and they hadn't spoken much to each other at the table.

'Yeah. That sounds right, but I just can't remember, for some reason. I'll put 1996, I'm sure you're right,' Callum said, writing it down.

'He's distracted,' Tom said, amused, looking at Lottie and then back at Callum.

'Well, who can blame me?' Callum replied, giving Lottie an appreciative glance. 'May I say, Lottie, you're looking very pretty this evening?'

'Yes, she is! Callum, you are such a flirt. I expect this from a French man but not you.' Celine clapped appreciatively.

'Just say it like I see it.' Callum grinned.

'Oh. Errrm... thanks.' Lottie blushed violently, feeling suddenly awkward. She was wearing a dress as opposed to her usual joggers and sweatshirts or baggy T-shirts, but only because Celine had taken one look at what she'd had on and made her go upstairs and change.

She'd brought one wraparound dress with her when she'd moved to Loch Cameron and worn that, despite the fact that she felt exposed in it. She didn't like her body: it was too big, too rounded. She was painfully aware that the top of the dress, which was green, was a V neck and it exposed more of her cleavage than she liked, and even though the dress showed off her waist, she was very aware of her tummy underneath it. The V neck also showed off her locket.

She did like the colour of the dress, however, and she thought it was probably quite a good contrast for her hair.

'We missed the next question.' Fred cleared his throat. He raised his hand. 'Sorry, could you repeat the question?' he asked, pointedly.

'The question is: Which author penned the original vampire classic *Carmilla* in 1872?' Eric read from his questions.

'Oh! I know that!' Fred sat forward excitedly. 'Sheridan Le Fanu!'

He and Lottie said it at the same time, caught each other's eye, then laughed.

'Oh, you're a vampire book fan?' he asked, as he reached for the quiz answers sheet to write it down.

'Yeah. Love them. *Dracula* is probably my favourite,' she confessed.

'Oh, it's the classic. For a reason. I love an epistolary novel,' he said.

'Me too.' Lottie grinned, knowing she was being nerdy about books but not caring.

'You know, we have a vintage copy of *Dracula* in the shop. And a Folio edition. They're both gorgeous. You should pop in and I'll show you,' Fred said, lowering his voice so that everyone could hear the next question. It was something about capital cities.

'I'd love that,' Lottie replied.

There were a few more rounds of questions, and then an interval.

'Ah, it's the break. Come on, let's get some drinks in. Lottie, give me a hand?' Celine stood up and stared meaningfully at her. She followed her housemate to the bar, where they stood, waiting to be served.

'Callum likes you,' Celine began, with no preamble.

'What?'

'Come on. It's obvious.' Celine gave the woman behind the

bar their order with a smile. 'Dotty, this is my new housemate, Lottie. Dotty and Lottie, ehhh. You should be friends.'

'Very nice tae meet ye, dear.' The older lady behind the bar gave Lottie a big smile. 'Been in the village long?'

'Not long, no. I'm studying up at the Highlands University,' Lottie explained.

'Ah, how lovely. Well, you'll be winnin' the quiz, then! I'll get yer drinks.' She busied herself pulling pints and pouring glasses of wine.

'He just told you how great you look in that dress. Which you do,' Celine continued the conversation.

'He was just being nice,' Lottie said.

'Pffft. Men aren't nice for no reason.' Celine rolled her eyes and then looked over Lottie's shoulder. 'Oh. Wait. He's coming over.' She elbowed Lottie in the ribs and moved along the bar. 'You can take the drinks. I've got to go to the ladies.'

'Celine!' Lottie hissed, but her housemate was gone.

'Need a hand?' Callum smiled down at her, and she felt her legs go a little rubbery.

'Sure. Thanks.' There was a short silence while they watched Dotty load the drinks onto a round tray. 'Enjoying the quiz?' she asked, shyly. She was all too aware of Callum's powerful physique next to her; he was tall, wide and muscular in that rugby player kind of way. Lottie had the sense that he could definitely throw her over his shoulder without any trouble at all.

'Yeah. It's fun. Are you?' he asked.

'Yes, though I only think I've got a couple of the questions. I'm not that competitive.' She picked up a beer mat and turned it around in her hands for something to do.

'Ha. Me either. Well, I'm competitive all right, but if it's not sports or food, I'm kinda dumb. I wasn't the smart kid in school like Fred. Always messing around at the back of the class. Or trying to make the girls laugh.' He gave her a wry smile.

'I'm sure that's not true.' She smiled back, earnestly.

'No, you're right. I was never that funny,' he replied.

'Ha. That's not what I meant, and you know it,' she chuckled.

'Made you laugh, though, didn't I? Just a little bit.' His eyes twinkled at her. 'Also, I wanted to repeat, how pretty you look tonight. I noticed your hair when we met, which is beautiful. May I say that the dress is... very flattering.' He gave her a wide and confident smile. 'And this is really nice. Old fashioned but pretty.' He reached for the locket around her neck and stroked it gently.

Was it possible that Callum was flirting with her? It crossed her mind that it was possible that Callum and Tom had some kind of bet going on, like those sporty boys often did. They'd choose a target – a shy girl, someone not very confident, like her – and see who could be first to get her into bed. The thought of it made her want to go and hide in the bathroom.

She turned away, picking up the drinks tray; him touching her locket had been such an intimate gesture that she didn't quite know how to respond.

'Well, I should really get these back to the table,' she said, coldly.

'I'll take it,' he offered, reaching for the tray. Lottie gripped it harder.

'No, I'm fine,' she insisted.

'I'm sorry. Shouldn't I have said anything, about your dress? I didn't want you to feel uncomfortable,' he said.

'Don't worry,' she replied, trying to make her tone light. 'I don't normally wear anything like this, that's all. I guess I feel a little self-conscious.'

'Well, you do look gorgeous. That's just the truth. Let me take the drinks.'

'I've got it,' she insisted.

'Lottie. Please let me be a gentleman here.' He gave her a

winning smile and a little bow. 'You're going to show me up otherwise.'

'Fine.' She let him take the tray.

'Lottie?' He looked down at her, his eyes soft with surprisingly long lashes. 'I... I'd really like to take you on a date one night, if you'd like that. That's what I've been trying to work up to, coming over to talk to you.' Callum looked uncharacteristically shy.

'Oh.' Lottie was at a loss for words. 'Umm... Sure. If you want.'

'I do want. Can I have your number?' He maintained eye contact and Lottie could feel herself getting hot.

'Umm. Okay.'

'Write it on one of those beer mats. I'd get my phone out but I've got my hands full,' he said. Obediently, she found a pen on the bar and wrote her number on the back of a beer mat, and awkwardly put it on the tray. Out of the corner of her eye, she could see Celine at the table, giving her a thumbs up. She ignored it, but she thought suddenly of Gretchen. Would her new friend be proud of her, going out on a limb and giving her number to Callum like this? Lottie wondered about talking to Gretchen about her love life. She thought that Gretchen would likely have good advice about it.

'Great. I'll give you a call,' he said, and sauntered back to the table. Lottie stood at the bar for a moment, wondering what had happened. Cautiously, she followed Callum back to the table and sat back down in her seat. Celine was grinning at her, and she pretended to be looking for something in her handbag to avoid her look.

Yet, when she looked up, she caught Callum's eye, and watched as he picked up the beer mat with her number on, and slid it into his pocket.

15

———————

'How are you enjoying Loch Cameron, dear?' Lottie's grandmother, Sharon, sounded more or less her usual self, though she coughed more than she used to because of a medication she took after a heart operation that made her throat dry.

'It's fine. Nice. Quiet,' Lottie said, walking to her window and looking out onto the playground at Gyle Head. It was a Saturday and so there were children playing out there today, meaning it was a little less quiet than usual. 'Mostly.'

'It's a nice little village. Interesting that you chose to go there.' Her grandmother coughed.

'Interesting how? It was cheap for rent and it's near to the care home,' Lottie said.

'Oh, no reason. Interesting, because it's such a quiet little place. A girl your age might want more distraction.'

'A girl my age likes the quiet. You know I'm not one for big nights out. And... especially after everything that's happened,' Lottie said.

'I know, dear. How's it going at the care home? And the interviews?' Sharon changed the subject deftly; her grandmother knew that she didn't like to talk about losing her mother, or what had happened with Tristan.

'It's good. I've found this one lady who is really keen to chat, and has a lot of interesting stories. Some others too, but she's the best.'

'Oh, that's wonderful, Lottie. I'm so pleased. I'll tell your grandpa. He's so proud of you, of getting your Master's degree. We both are.'

'I know. Thanks.' Lottie was always a little uncomfortable taking praise, but her grandparents had never been anything but loving. 'How is Grandpa?'

'Oh, you know. Same old. Watering my begonias at the moment. Graham! Phone!' she called out. 'He'll want to say hello.'

'So, have you been to Loch Cameron?' Lottie asked, while she was waiting. 'I don't remember ever coming with Mum. Or her mentioning it.'

'Oh. Once, a long time ago,' Sharon said, offhandedly. 'Pretty place. We went around the castle.'

'You came with Grandpa?'

'What? Oh. Yes. Probably. I don't remember that well.' Lottie could tell that Sharon was holding the phone away from her ear, and she could hear her grandmother talking to her grandpa. 'No. She's on the line now, Graham. Have a quick word.'

'Hello, trouble.' Lottie's grandfather's voice appeared on the line, as warm and affectionate as always. 'How's tricks?'

'Good, thanks, Grandpa. How are you?'

'Oh, ye know. Survivin' your grannie's route marches.'

'They're just walks, Grandpa. They're good for you,' Lottie giggled. Her grandfather always referred to the daily walks that Sharon had been making them take for the last few years as *route marches*, as if they were a military operation and not the pleasant amble around the village they really were.

'Aye, I suppose so, hen. She keeps me in line, eh. What're ye up tae, my little pigeon?'

Her grandfather had a variety of pet names for her, and he absolutely refused to stop using them, even though she was well into her twenties.

'Grandpa. I'm not a pigeon.'

'Aye, y'are. Small and curious.'

'Pigeons are voracious eaters. They're pests.'

'Nawww. Intelligent birds, aye. They're just survivin'. What would ye prefer, find somethin' tae eat by bein' smart, or go hungry?' he chortled.

'Eat. But I don't like pigeons,' Lottie insisted.

'Fine, fine. My little crow maiden. How's that?'

'Better. Crows really are intelligent. Though I'm not that little.'

'Aye, y'are,' Graham repeated. 'You'll always be ma little one.'

'Grandpa. I'm twenty-eight,' Lottie said.

'That's what I'm sayin'. No age,' he chuckled. 'Listen tae us. Ye always have a sensible chat wi' yer Grannie, and nonsense wi' me.'

'That's because you're silly by nature,' she replied.

'Guilty as charged,' he said, sighing. 'But you know I'm here for ye, anytime. Night or day. Ye know that, don't ye, sweetheart? If ye need me, just call. I'll be there.'

It was an uncharacteristically serious thing for him to say, and Lottie frowned, wondering what had prompted it.

'I know, Grandpa. Don't worry. I'm okay.'

'All right. I'm just sayin'. Anyone or anythin' upsets ye, ye give yer auld Grandpa a call,' he repeated. 'Yer my little bird, aye. I'm not so aged that I can't be of use if needed.'

'I know,' she repeated, a little bemused. 'I'm all right, though. What's brought that question on?'

'Well, ye know. After that lad,' Graham said, a hard tone

coming into his voice. 'If I ever get a hold o' him, I willnae be responsible fer my actions.'

'Grandpa. You're eighty years old,' Lottie reminded him.

'Doesnae matter. A man has a duty tae his loved ones,' her grandpa said, stoically. 'All's I'm sayin' is, yer a little heart-broken still... and away from home, in Loch Cameron... I just want ye tae be safe an' happy.'

'Why wouldn't I be safe and happy here?' Lottie blinked. This was the second time that her grandparents had acted strangely about the village she was living in.

'No reason. Just... bear it in mind,' he said, obliquely.

'Grandpa. What's up?'

'Ah, Lottie. Ye know, I worry about ye. Bein' away from home. Havin' lost yer mum. Bein...' he broke off and laughed gruffly. 'Ah, listen tae me. I'm emotional in ma old age.'

'What were you going to say? Being what?' she prompted him.

'Oh. Bein'... alone, over there in Loch Cameron,' he said, vaguely.

'It's Loch Cameron. It's hardly a dangerous neighbourhood,' she said, confused. Why was her grandfather being so strange, all of a sudden?

'I know. I know. I just worry about ye, that's all,' he said. Lottie thought that didn't give her any insight at all about why her grandfather was being weird, but perhaps it was his age making him sentimental.

'Anyway. It's good tae hear ye, my little turtle dove. My little blueberry muffin.' Lottie could hear the smile return to her grandpa's voice: he was back to his usual silliness.

'Well, at least it makes a change from birds,' she said, smiling.

'Aye. I'm nothin' if not creative.'

'You are that. I love you, Grandpa,' she said, wishing she could give him a hug.

'I love ye too, Lottie,' he said, his voice tender. 'To the moon an' back. Never forget that.'

'I won't.'

'See that ye don't. Okay. I'm gonna pass ye back to yer grannie, because she's gesturin' at me. Okay, okay, Sharon. Keep yer hair on,' he grumbled. 'Speak soon, darlin'.'

'Speak soon.' Lottie felt her heart tug at his familiar voice. She missed her grandparents.

'Sorry about that, darling.' Sharon returned to the line. 'He's just protective of you. He means well.'

'I know. It's fine, I love Grandpa.'

'Well, we both love you very much. We have to go, though, because we've got Jo and Vicky from next door popping over in a minute to show us their holiday photos. They're lesbians, you know.' Her grannie was always a little more practical and businesslike than Lottie's grandpa, but she still thought that she detected a slight undercurrent of something *off* under Sharon's tone. However, she couldn't work out what it was.

'I know, Grannie. You've told me.' Lottie chuckled, nonetheless.

'Well, I just think it's very nice,' Sharon said, sounding slightly aggrieved.

'What, the fact that they've been on holiday? That they're lesbians? Or that they live next door?'

'Don't be sarky. You know I just mean, they're nice girls. Good neighbours.'

'Okay. I'm just teasing you. I'll call you next week, okay?'

'All right, darling. Take care. Love you.'

'Love you, too.' Lottie ended the call and stared at the children in the playground outside. She had always been loved. She had always felt cared for by her mother and her grandparents, and they had never lied to her, as far as she was aware. Yet, there had been something in that phone call. A sense that her grannie and grandpa weren't being entirely truthful, and it bothered her.

What could they be worried about in Loch Cameron? And, if there was something, why wouldn't they tell her what it was?

16

———

GRETCHEN

It's hard to turn up for work every day after what happened at the coffee machine.

In many ways, what happened with Charlie that day – and the constant harassment and low-level abuse which went on for far longer than a day – was a precursor to what happened with Alex. Even though I have never thought of myself as a naïve person – Gretchen Ross, always ready with a quip and a smart reply! – I was naïve, then. But I was young, and the world was arguably more savage to young women (or indeed most people) than it is now.

I believed that I could walk into a job that I was qualified and intelligent and talented enough to do, in a male dominated field at the time, and just do it without any opposition. I was naïve.

I never thought a man would hurt me, or harass me, or frighten me. I was naïve. They did.

It's difficult enough to gee myself up every day to walk into the office. But after Charlie lays his hand on me in that threatening way – tells me I'm dirty, that I stink, makes me feel like a common prostitute just for being there and daring to talk back to him – it's so much worse.

I shrink into myself. I am not proud of that, because, usually, I do not shrink. I have always been ballsy (the irony of that phrase), I have always been brave. And yet, I can't help it.

I go to work, but I don't interact. I don't look anyone in the eye. I do my job, but that's all. I don't try to talk to anyone. I hide in the bathroom at lunchtime instead of trying to hitch myself onto their group at the pub, which was where they go most days, often for longer than the permitted hour.

I stay late when I have to, but if it is just going to be me and Charlie in the office, then I leave. I don't want to be alone with him for a second. I am terrified of what he might do.

One day, I can't get out of bed and ring in sick. I've never done this before apart from when I really am ill, and it feels awful. But I can't face Charlie. I can't take another day of the underhanded threat that now exists between us.

At this time in the early sixties, I'm living in a little bedsit in the Edinburgh suburbs which has mould by the windows and is completely covered in wood panelling. Mother hates me living alone, and hates the bedsit, but I am now in my mid-twenties and live according to my own rules. The bedsit is all I can afford, but despite its mould and the fact that it takes a long bus ride to get into work and back, I still like the independence it gives me.

However, for the first time since I have moved in, I feel alone and vulnerable here.

Since that day with the coffee machine, Charlie knows he's knocked my confidence. Every time I look up, he catches my eye and raises an eyebrow or gives me a snide grin that tells me he knows exactly how uncomfortable he is making me. He deliberately laughs louder, tells dirtier jokes and is in general more offensively laddish with the other men in the office, all to create a wall of masculine threat that will put me in my place.

And, how badly Charlie wants to put me in my place. I can feel it radiating from him.

People have the idea that if a boy likes you, they'll pull your pigtails in the playground or push your face in the dirt. Some well-meaning person might look at my work situation with Charlie and say, *he likes you. He just doesn't know how to show it.*

They would be very wrong. There is no affection for me in Charlie's mind. And, of course, we should never tell girls that violent or abusive behaviour from a boy means affection.

It doesn't mean that at all. It means that some boys and men will hurt you and tell you that it's love. And, if you listen to those well-meaning people around you – sometimes your own family and friends – you will continue to be hurt, and ignore your own bruises and even infections and worse, because you think that's what love looks like. They will say, *love has its ups and downs. You need to stick with it. He's a good man.*

Sometimes, those men are very good at appearing to be the good man, on the outside. And even your own parents and your best friends cannot see through the lies. They will judge you for making a life-changing, heart-rending decision, not knowing what the threat of him is.

But, that's a story for another time.

The day that I ring in sick, I lie in my bed and stare at the ceiling, wondering what to do. I consider leaving my job. That's how bad it is; I can't see a way that I could change anything. If I report Charlie, what would I report him for? I can't prove he's done anything wrong, and it would either be a case of he says/she says – in which case, I would definitely be the one to be disbelieved, being the newest to the office and being a woman – or, Bob would just give me a concerned stare and say something like, *he's just joking, it's office chitchat, you have to learn to toughen up and take it on the chin. We all talk to each other like that.*

The thing is, of course, that they don't all talk to each other like that at all. No one has ever leaned in close to Bob and called him dirty; no one has ever intimidated Bob, put their hands on his body in a sexually suggestive way and certainly no one has made him so fearful of going to the office that he calls in sick.

That day when I stay at home, I realise that I am on my own at work. There is no one to support me in that office; I have no friends, and I have no allies. If I want to make it work, then I have to hunker down and accept the way things are.

It isn't an inspiring or exciting realisation, but it is realistic, and the next day I go back to work knowing that I choose to be there; knowing that I can walk out if I want to, but I don't want to. Not now.

I have worked too hard to get to this meagre editorial job, and if I leave now, then all of my efforts will have been in vain. Goodness knows if I'd ever find another position, especially if I am *that woman* and leave under a cloud; if I'm a *troublemaker* and report a man I'm working with after such a short time in the job, I know how that will be perceived at other workplaces.

No, I have to fit in. I have to endure the less salubrious elements of this job, and trust that, one day, things will improve.

Morning, Ross. Make us a coffee, Charlie says as soon as I get in. *You feeling better? Women's problems, was it? Disgusting. Women shouldn't be allowed to have jobs if they're going to take a week off once a month.*

I'll make you a coffee, Charlie, I say, meeting his aggressive stare for the first time in a while. His expression flickers slightly; instantly, I know he feels the change in mood between us. *Can't guarantee I won't spit in it, being such a hormonal bitch. But, then, you didn't notice before, so I guess you won't notice it now,* I say. My eyes are cold and I don't smile.

It's a gamble. I know that I need to fit in, but I also can't live another day being Charlie's punching bag, so I'm going to play their game. I have always been imaginative, and I imagine pulling on a suit of armour. If this is war, then I will need to become a warrior.

I hold his gaze, and hold my breath. A titter of laughter runs around the office and it feels like a crack in the icy dam of their boys' club. I will never be one of them, but I have to show strength, otherwise I am done for. If I can crack that wall, then maybe I can become accepted enough so that I don't hate every day I'm here.

I hope you've washed your hands, he retorts. *If you're on the rag, I don't want that in my coffee either.*

Can't guarantee that I have, I say, much more airily than I feel. *But you do know that's not how menstruation works, right? It doesn't come out of our hands? That's called stigmata. You have to be a Catholic saint or something. Menstruation means that blood comes out of my vagina, Charlie. Not my hands.*

There's another, louder, run of laughter through the office. I am relieved. The more that they laugh, the less power Charlie has over me.

I don't want to be so crude in the office, but it's all I can think of in the moment.

Jesus, Ross, he says, and a flush of colour blooms in his cheeks. *Just shut up, will you? You're making me sick.*

Goodness, I say, picking up his dirty mug from his desk and taking it to the coffee machine. *And they say women are the delicate ones. All I said was "vagina". Bit of a foreign concept for you, perhaps.*

Right, that's enough, you two, Bob says, chuckling. *Do some bloody work.* Bob apparently thinks this is all part of the *office chitchat*, in the same way that he was absolutely tone deaf to Charlie harassing me before.

I make coffee for everyone, and when I get to Charlie's desk, I deliberately spill his on the manuscript he's working on.

Whoops. Sorry, I say, insincerely. *Time of the month.*

I know from his eyes that it isn't over between us, but there is some comfort in refusing to be his victim anymore.

When I think back to this time, I wonder how I can ever tell that dear young woman the truth. Because I do not want to be responsible for ruining her trust in the world, if she still has it. I had my naivete ripped away from me. I do not wish to take it away from another woman. Yet, if Lottie hears my story, perhaps it may, in some small way, help prepare her for the horrors that do exist in this world.

But, as well as that, I am afraid to tell Lottie all of this. Because if I tell her the story of Charlie O'Flanagan, then it brings me one step closer to telling her the story of Alex O'Connell. And that is one story I do not wish to tell.

17

―――――――――

'Now, I'd been in the editorial office for six months when Charlie got the sack. Thank goodness, because he was awful to work with.' Gretchen stirred two lumps of sugar into her tea. It was the next day, and Lottie had was desperate to record more of her story. She had woken up that morning thinking of all the questions she wanted to ask Gretchen, but one loomed large in her mind: what was Gretchen's big secret? She knew that her new friend was holding back on something, and Lottie wanted to know what it was. There had been a few times now when Gretchen had seemed as though she was about to say something and then decided against it.

'I won't tell you the awful things he used to say to me. But it's all in the past now.' A dark look crossed Gretchen's face.

'You can tell me, Gretchen,' Lottie prompted her. 'Feel free to tell me anything.' She knew that her curiosity was getting the better of her, and that rule number one in interviewing the elderly was to let them talk and not push too hard where the subject was painful. But she also felt that Gretchen had something that she *wanted* to say. If it was the case that she just needed a little more encouragement, then Lottie didn't want to be the reason that Gretchen didn't say what she needed to – to get it off her chest – for a lack of feeling as though she *could.*

'Hmm. Some things are too dark, dear,' Gretchen demurred. 'I...' she let out a long breath, and then shook her head. 'I wouldn't want to tell you some things. I—'

'What is it, Gretchen? You can tell me,' Lottie said, knowing that whatever the secret was, it wasn't too far from the surface, now. It was like this secret, or whatever Gretchen was keeping back from her, was an iceberg under water, and she and Gretchen were rowing a boat on top of it. Perhaps Gretchen feared that the iceberg would capsize the boat.

'No, dear. It's not something I'm ready to talk about,' Gretchen said, and Lottie felt the iceberg sink under the water again. There had been a moment where they both might have faced it and navigated around it, but that moment had disappeared again.

'Anyway, when Charlie got the sack, I thought, I'm going to have his desk and his job,' Gretchen continued, tapping her fingertips on her lap.

'Why did he get the sack, again?' Lottie asked. Her phone buzzed and she glanced at it briefly; since Callum had taken her number at the pub, she'd been expecting him to call and ask her out. But she'd heard nothing. She kept expecting it to be him when she got a text or a call, but it hadn't been so far.

'General uselessness.' Gretchen shrugged. 'The truth will out, as they say. Our boss at the time, Bob, was about as effective as a chocolate teapot, but even Bob couldn't overlook the fact that Charlie was always late, never met a deadline and his editing was full of errors. But the thing that did it was that he fell out with an author he was working with, and he complained to Bob. Charlie had reworked a whole section of this author's book without consultation, and not only was the author rightly annoyed by it, the reworked section absolutely didn't work at all. He'd made the book much worse.'

'Oh. That doesn't sound good.'

'Indeed. And guess who got the wonderful job of putting it right?' Gretchen rubbed her eyes and blinked hard, wincing as she did so.

'You? Gretchen, are your eyes okay?' Lottie asked.

'Hmm. Yes, they're all right. Don't fuss. I'm just old,' Gretchen tutted. 'So. Charlie left and I had to correct the mess he left behind. I made a good job of it and smoothed things over with the author, and Bob was pleased. Relieved, really. We didn't lose the author because of me.' She nodded, with a gleam of satisfaction in her eye. 'And, I can't say that I was sad to see Charlie go. Not that there weren't more like him, because there were. I had to learn how to work with that kind of man and endure it for a long time.'

'It seems like you came out on top, though,' Lottie said. 'It's inspiring.'

'Hmm. If you knew the truth, darling, you wouldn't find me so inspiring.' Gretchen smiled and patted Lottie's hand. 'But I have to admit that it's nice to inspire you.'

Lottie had talked to a few more residents, including Gretchen's friends Muriel, Mavis and Evangeline, and she was gradually making headway with them and their stories too. But, in truth, Gretchen was by far the most interesting. Mavis only really wanted to talk about her grandson Jonathan, who worked in the local court as a legal assistant and, it seemed, fed her lots of details about legal cases that should have stayed confidential.

Evangeline was nice, and she'd just started telling Lottie about her career as a palm reader – Lottie felt hopeful that might be interesting – and Muriel was sweet but became distracted very easily. When Lottie mentioned it to Gretchen, Gretchen nodded. 'Alzheimers. It's a terrible shame, but it started about a year ago. She can be fine one minute, and the next she's in her own little world. She's pretty much stopped playing cards with us now.'

'I suppose these things can creep up on you,' Lottie replied.

'Hmm. Indeed they can.' Gretchen looked away for a moment. Lottie had the impression that there was something on her mind, but then Gretchen cleared her throat and frowned, looking directly at Lottie's neck. 'What's that?' she asked.

'What? Oh, my locket?' Lottie touched the necklace. 'My mum gave this to me. I haven't taken it off for a long time. Since she died, I think.'

'A locket,' Gretchen said, staring at it. 'What does it have inside?'

'A picture of my mum. And there's a lock of hair on the other side.' Lottie opened it and showed Gretchen.

'Goodness.' Gretchen stared at the picture for a long moment, and then at Lottie. 'I... I haven't seen a locket like that for many a year.' She stared for longer at Lottie's face, as if she was assessing her features in some way.

'Oh. Well, I think they used to be more in fashion than they are now,' Lottie said. Gretchen continued to stare at the locket. 'Would you... like to see it, close up?'

'Oh... I...' Gretchen reached out for it. 'I'd love to.'

Lottie opened the locket and held it up for Gretchen to see more closely. The old woman's fingertips stroked the curl of black hair and an odd expression flitted over her features for a moment before she pulled her hand away.

'Gretchen? Are you okay?' Lottie frowned, closing the locket and tucking it under her shirt again.

'Ah. Yes, dear. I was just meandering in my thoughts there, for a minute. Forgive the antique brain.' Gretchen gave her a sudden, bright smile. Lottie thought that the way she had touched the hair in the locket was a little strange. It gave her an odd feeling that she didn't entirely like.

'Now. Where was I? Oh, yes.' Gretchen nodded. 'So, I

applied for Charlie's job, and, again, there I was in a row of identikit young men in their suits, sitting outside the personnel office. And, I thought, there's no way I'll get this promotion. They've got me in the editorial office now, tokenism has been satisfied, they don't need to promote me any further. So, you can imagine my surprise when I got the job.'

'Definitely,' Lottie said, but she was still a little confused by the moment with the locket.

'I was baffled, but I was, of course, absolutely delighted. They sat me at Charlie's old desk, and you can imagine, that was a wonderful revenge for all the times he expected me to make coffee for him, talked down to me, asked me to check his contracts before they went out.

'I did do all those things, actually, but the joke was on him because I let so many mistakes go through on purpose – of course, he was far too lazy, and drunk, to check what I'd done – that he, for instance, sent a mis-typed contract to a very important author.' Gretchen grinned broadly at Lottie. 'I may have had a quick word with the girls in the typing pool for that one. It paid to be friends with them.'

'You didn't!' Lottie widened her eyes.

'Oh, I did. If he'd checked what he was sending out, he would have seen that she'd *accidentally* typed in the offered advance at fifty thousand pounds instead of five.' Gretchen shrugged. 'Not my fault if he was too slack to check his work. Because of course he did check contracts, like he was supposed to. And he definitely didn't dictate them drunk.'

'Oh, my! What happened?' Lottie asked.

'Well, the powers that be had to step in and make things right with the author in question, but there was a big to-do because they had a powerful agent who was absolutely adamant that his client deserved the amount that had been put in writing. Obviously, he knew it was a mistake, but agents are tricky so-and-so's, and he was very excited about getting twenty per cent of fifty thousand pounds. At the time, that was a ridiculously huge advance. As it was, five thousand was very generous.'

'And Charlie got the sack?'

'Charlie got the sack. For things like that and the problem with the manuscript that got given to me to put right. Couldn't have happened to a nicer fella.'

'Wow.'

'Ha. Indeed. But he deserved it. And, I always felt that, as someone who had the odds very firmly not on their side, I had to use whatever advantages I did have to get ahead. Mind you, of course, I'm saying all this with the full knowledge that I did have one major advantage going for me, which was that I was a white woman. In those days, I was a rarity as a woman outside of the typing pool, but if I'd have been a woman of colour, there's no way that I would have got as far as I did. I am aware of the privilege that I had, and still have.'

'Of course.' Lottie nodded. 'Not everyone of your age would see it that way, though.'

'No, well. I pride myself on staying up to date with my thoughts as much as I can. And I've had a life in books, so it makes sense that I read a few of them now and again.'

Lottie looked around her, at the shelves and shelves of books, and the piles of them on the floor.

'Just the odd one?' she joked.

'Just one or two.' Gretchen nodded. 'Now, I must say that although all the men I worked with were all quite sexist – this was the sixties still, after all – not all of them were bad people. Bob, who was the managing editor at that time, knew I was good at my job and I think he was part of the reason why I got that promotion. He never asked me to make him coffee and he asked my opinion on manuscripts. Because he used to do it, the rest of them started asking me my opinion as well. Of course, they were asking me to *get the female insight*, but it was something.' Gretchen blinked and rubbed her eyes.

'If you're tired, we can do this another day,' Lottie said, concerned that their talks were too demanding for Gretchen, but the older woman shook her head vigorously.

'I'm fine, dear. My eyes are just a little sore. I'll close them for a while. Why don't you tell me a little more of your story, while I have a little break? It'll help me regroup.'

'All right. What do you want to know?'

'Hmm. Your mother was named Emma. Where did you grow up?' Gretchen asked, a little blearily.

'The Edinburgh suburbs. Fairmilehead,' Lottie said. 'My grandparents live in Kirkliston.'

'Near the airport. I know it.' Gretchen frowned. 'Are they still with us? Your grandparents?'

'Yes. Grandpa's eighty. Grannie's seventy-nine. They're still going strong, though.'

'And you get along with them? Good people?' Gretchen asked. Lottie wondered if she had a reason for asking, or whether this was Gretchen's natural inquisitiveness showing through.

'They're wonderful.' Lottie thought about her recent phone call with her grandparents. 'Though I spoke to them yesterday, and they seemed a bit weird about me being in Loch Cameron.'

'Really?' Gretchen opened her eyes wide.

'Yeah. They wouldn't really go into it, but they just kept saying things like, *let us know if there's a problem*. I'm not sure what they think is going to happen.'

'Hmm. Probably just concerned for you, being away from home.' Gretchen looked thoughtful. 'What are their names?'

'Sharon and Graham. Why?'

'Oh... I knew a couple who lived in that area once. Work acquaintances.' Gretchen blinked. There was a pause. 'Now, where was I?'

'Oh. Umm... The female insight, I think,' Lottie prompted her.

'Oh, yes. Hmmm. Well, the editors used to ask me about the female characters a lot. Quite often, of course, if it was a male writer – and it was, overwhelmingly, at the time – they'd always written these terribly two-dimensional, identikit female characters. They definitely didn't pass the Bechdel test in those days. I was always having to point out that women didn't think obsessively about their own breasts, and that they had lives outside of talking to each other about men.'

'Really? That's... I want to say shocking, but, yes. Sadly predictable.'

'Hmm. Indeed. So many terrible inaccuracies, too. I remember reading a James Bond novel – not published by us, I might add – in which Fleming claims that women who can't whistle are lesbians.'

'What?' Lottie thought about her recent conversation with her grandmother about her gay next door neighbours, but even though Sharon was elderly, even she was progressive enough not to entertain such a bizarre idea.

'I know. And you just know that's not even the worst of it. Not by a long chalk.'

'Goodness.'

'I know, dear. I know. You have to remember that this was a world where airlines could have a policy to make their stewardesses undress during a flight.'

'*What?*' Lottie did a double take.

'I'm serious. One of the airlines – an American one, naturally – had a policy at one time, in the seventies or eighties, I think, so a little later than the era I'm talking about – but not that long after – where the stewardesses had to remove one layer of their uniform every hour or so. The uniform had, I suppose, a jacket on top of a skirt and tunic, then there was this kind of bikini thing underneath. Can you imagine?'

'I can't, really.' Lottie was wide-eyed with disbelief. 'Really?'

'Really. You're too young to remember, thank goodness. The outfits that they used to have to wear. The terrible way they got treated. Groped. Talked down to. As if they were just pretty dolls to serve drinks, not the people who were there to save your life if things went wrong. I'd love to see firemen disrespected in the same way.'

'It's no wonder feminism happened,' Lottie said. 'Not a minute too soon.'

'Exactly. As Marge Piercy said, *Freedom is the real abundance*. That's from one of her poems, though I can't remember which, now. Freedom to do your job without being sexually harassed is nice. At that time, it was a bonus. Thankfully, now, it seems to be a given. For most women, anyway.'

'I like that. Freedom is the real abundance,' Lottie repeated.

'It's true, though, isn't it? All this talk of manifesting abundance, these days. On social media and what have you. It's all very laudable, I mean – who wouldn't want a life of abundance?' Gretchen said. 'But, really, the best thing that money gives you is time. Time and freedom to do what you like. And it was freedom that the women were fighting for then, whether that was reproductive freedom, social freedoms, cultural freedoms. Freedom to pursue a career, to get paid the same as a man, to enjoy the same freedoms as a man. Some might say we still don't, in some cases.'

'Amen.' Lottie rolled her eyes.

'Hmm. Anyway, I didn't burn my bra because I didn't like not wearing one. But I read all the books by the famous feminists, and I thought, yes, this is a thing. This patriarchal culture we live in. Because I had to work inside it every day, live inside it every day, like we all did. And I thought hard about how I could change it and make it better for other women, and I decided that the thing I could do could be inside the work world. So, I worked hard to rise up in the ranks at Hatch until I could be the one making decisions. And when I was, you better believe there were some changes.' She gave Lottie a wry smile.

'Oh, I do believe it. Like what?'

'We'll get to that.' Gretchen took a biscuit from the packet that Lottie had brought with her, and dipped it in her tea. 'I have yet to tell you about my greatest success.'

18

———————

'Now. Do you know how publishers get to look at manuscripts from writers in the first place?' Gretchen asked, looking at Lottie beadily.

'Not really,' Lottie admitted.

'That's all right. No reason for you to know. Most of the time, publishers have relationships with literary agents and they submit manuscripts for consideration from their clients. But then, some publishers accept submissions from the general public too, or they do so at particular times of the year. Nowadays, that's more common than it was. At Dunne's in those days, we had occasional open slots for submissions, and the task of looking through them fell to me.'

'And was there anything good that got sent in?' Lottie leaned forward, interested.

'Sometimes, yes. That's the thing with submissions. There's a lot that isn't right – either it's terrible writing, or incomplete, or the writer doesn't understand some basic element of a book, like plot or structure. Or, quite often, it's good, but not what you publish. A lot of writers seem to think that if a book is good enough, a publisher will just change their publishing strategy and take it anyway. They don't.'

'It sounds like a lot of hoops to jump through,' Lottie commented, taking a biscuit from the plate.

'Oh, it is. I'd never be a writer. It's a savage industry.' Gretchen shook her head. 'Anyway, sometimes something does come in direct. And, in my second year of being an editor at Dunne's, something did.'

'Oooh. What was it?'

Gretchen named a huge bestseller from the past.

'Oh! There was a film made of it, right? I saw it when I was a teenager. Me and all my friends all watched it together at one of their houses when her parents were away. We felt so scandalous.'

'Ha! Oh yes, there was a film and a TV adaptation, merchandise, all sorts of things. I believe that there's a very active fan base still. Of course, Jenny had a hugely successful career after that. She lives in the Caribbean now.'

'Wow.'

'Definitely wow. She had a wonderful life. She deserves it! She worked very hard to write that book, and all the ones after it. She had three kids, and her husband left her for another woman. She worked, and in the evenings, when the kids were in bed, she sat down and wrote that book. The one that I found in the slush pile.'

'Gretchen. That's such an amazing story.'

'It is. And what's more amazing is what happened because of it. Now, you'll remember that I mentioned I worked with a man called Bob, and all of them were always asking me about the female perspective?'

'Right.'

'Yes. Well, I found this book, and I knew after the first three chapters that it was going to be a publishing sensation. And that was precisely because of where the world was at that time.

Jenny had written this fabulously sexy and exciting page-turner, but what was even more brilliant about it was that it was a book about women. Their friendships, their relationships, their careers. Women weren't the little secondary characters or the love interest that got killed off in various creatively misogynist, woman-hating ways, like in James Bond and the rest. I took it and put it on his desk and said, this is the female perspective, Bob. If we publish this, millions of women will read it. You can take early retirement.'

'That was you, sticking it to the patriarchy,' Lottie whooped. 'I love it!'

'It certainly was.' Gretchen smiled. 'That book – I mean, you'd read it now, and you'd think it was dated. And it is, now, though it's still an excellent book about female friendship. But, at the time, it was controversial. And, by that, I mean that a lot of men didn't like it. Because the women in it had abortions, divorced their husbands, worked, made their own decisions. Were modern women, essentially, and didn't spend their whole time talking to each other about men or just breast boobily down the stairs every five minutes.' She rolled her eyes.

'*Breast boobily?*' Lottie started to laugh. 'What?'

'You know, dear. Where male authors write female characters that are obsessed with their own bodies in a very sexualised way, or where they exclusively describe female characters as overtly sexual. There are several famous examples, but some wit on the internet came up with *she breasted boobily* as a kind of catch-all phrase. To some men, breasts are adjective and adverb as well as noun.'

'Wow. Just, wow.' Lottie chuckled. 'Though I do know what you mean. I think I've read some of those books.'

'We all have.' Gretchen rolled her eyes again. 'Some of us had to read many of them, and publish them, even though they were utter trash. When I look back and remember the absolute gall of hearing my fellow male editors claiming that books by women – romances, often – were "trash", but they thought these books by brainless misogynists – with all the breasting boobily, and women staring soulfully at their own breasts in mirrors – were "edgy intellectuals". It still grinds my gears. Intellectuals, my eye! Breast-obsessed little boys that mummy didn't love enough. Probably never even met a woman. Certainly couldn't write one.'

'Gretchen. You're terrible,' Lottie sniggered. 'Though, I agree. So, what did Bob say? About Jenny's book?'

'I could see that he had his doubts, but he took it home and read it. And, then, he let his wife read it.' Gretchen grinned. 'And Sabrina – that was his wife, lovely woman – absolutely loved it. In fact, she called me up a couple of days later in the office – I was the one that answered the phone, obviously, because I had a vagina.'

'Obviously.'

'And Sabrina said, "Miss Ross, first of all, I can only apologise for the fact that you have to work with my husband all day long and thank you for not putting arsenic in his tea. Second, may I invite you over for dinner. Third, if Bob refuses to recommend that book gets published, then you can tell him that he won't be enjoying any marital relations for a very long time."'

'Oh, my goodness. That is amazing. I *love* Sabrina,' Lottie breathed. 'I want to punch the air!'

'Oh, my. Yes. She was absolutely wonderful. We became very good friends after that, in fact.' Gretchen wiped a tear of emotion from the corner of her eye. 'I miss her. She died some years ago now.'

'I'm sorry.'

'Not at all. Sabrina was a true inspiration. And I always told everyone the story because I wanted to make sure that people knew how instrumental she was in Jenny's career. And in mine,' Gretchen continued.

'So, what happened next?' Lottie was agog. She definitely

hadn't expected anything like this when she'd sat down to interview anyone at the care home.

'Next, we gave the book to all the women in the typing pool. I made the copies myself. I didn't mind. I knew that they'd all love it. And they did. The week after I gave out the copies, every single woman in the typing pool came into the editorial office and told Bob and all the rest of them that if they didn't sign Jenny up, they were going to walk out.'

'And that persuaded them?'

'That persuaded them.' Gretchen smiled mistily. 'I mean, Bob was already on board because of Sabrina, but the rest of them had to be convinced. But when they saw all the girls come in clutching their photostat copies, they knew. So, we published it.'

'And it was a huge success?'

'It was. The press loved Jenny. She was a real rags-to-riches story, and it helped that she was very bubbly, very eloquent and wise and charming when she was interviewed. She became a bit of a darling in the media and started getting invited onto TV chat shows, panel shows, that kind of thing. You know when your author's on *Wogan* and *Parkinson* that you're doing well. Those were chat shows of the time.'

'And what did it do for your career?' Lottie sipped her tea. 'Did you get a promotion because of it or anything?'

'Not immediately. But, yes, after a while, when Jenny was doing so well in the charts, and we brought out more books in the series, I was promoted a couple of times. First to Commissioning Editor and then Senior Editor. And, soon after that, I got headhunted by Hatch Publishing, where I spent the rest of my career.'

'It's such an inspiring story, Gretchen. You don't really hear about what happens to get a book into the shops, I suppose. About all the people who work on it behind the scenes.'

'No, indeed. And, even if it sounds like I'm tooting my own

horn, you wouldn't believe the amount of work an editor puts into a book, alongside the author. People think that all we do is correct the spelling and decide on a nice cover, but it's so much more than that. Editors shape the books they work on. We make suggestions for the plot, advise on rewrites where the author hasn't really hit the right kind of tension at the right time, help writers with character development, commercial viability, all kinds of things.

'And then, when the manuscript is as good as it's going to get, the editor liaises with the designers and marketing and PR to make sure the book gets the best cover, that it's marketed in the best way, all that.'

'It's an awful lot of work, by the sounds of things,' Lottie said.

'It is. I mean, with some writers, the editor writes half the book, too. I'm not even joking – all editors know what those books are, and some of them go on to win awards. The writer's been signed because the powers that be think they're some kind of genius, then it's the editor that has to sort the book out.'

'Oooh. What books are those?' Lottie asked.

'Oh, my dear girl. If I told you, I'd have to kill you.' Gretchen rubbed her eyes again, and Lottie recalled she'd done it before. Clearly, their conversation was taking a toll on the elderly woman. 'Anyway, that's not usually the case, obviously, usually the writers are talented and hardworking professionals.' Gretchen pulled a face. 'I have to say that.'

'Of course.'

'Anyway, that was a long story. But that was how I started at Hatch. It was the seventies by then, and things were starting to change. The poor American stewardesses were protesting about being sexually harassed and having to wear those ridiculous outfits. And, when I joined Hatch, I went in as a senior editor, and there was already another woman in the editorial team.'

'Progress, then,' Lottie said.

'A little, yes.' Gretchen closed her eyes and rubbed her temples. 'But, as they say, God gives with one hand and takes with the other. I sometimes feel that any liberties I won as a woman, I paid for in blood and tears.'

'Oh. Gretchen. That sounds awful.' Lottie frowned. 'What do you mean?'

'Hmm. Ignore me, that was unnecessarily dramatic.' Gretchen paused, then nodded to a cupboard at the back of the room. 'But...I suppose this is as good a time as any to give you something. I remembered it after your last visit,' she said, blinking tiredly. 'If you go to the cupboard over there, by the bookshelf... yes, that's it,' she said as Lottie got up and walked over to where Gretchen had indicated. 'There are a couple of notebooks in there. Red leather. Yes, that's it.' She nodded as Lottie held them up with a questioning expression on her face. 'Bring them over here, would you?'

Lottie handed them to Gretchen.

'Now, then. With me telling you all about my life, it made me remember that I used to keep a diary when I was younger. Not for a long time now... I mean, nowadays, I wouldn't have anything interesting to write in it. But I thought you might like to have them, for your project.' Gretchen tapped the cover of one of the books. 'Only two, I'm afraid. There were more, but I don't know what happened to them. It's very possible they were lost in the move here, or my antique brain just can't remember where I've put them.'

'Wow. That's really kind, Gretchen. Thank you! Are you sure?' Lottie opened one of the leather journals carefully. Inside, page upon page of carefully handwritten pages opened up to her.

'Of course. I'm just sorry that I didn't remember them before now, dear. They're yours, if you want them. Feel free to quote them.'

'Goodness. I can't wait to read them. Thank you. This is incredibly thoughtful of you.'

'You're welcome, dear. I just want you to know... what's in there. I want you to know, because I care about you.' Gretchen coughed. 'And I trust you. And...' she trailed off. 'I might not have much longer, dear. And some secrets... you shouldn't take them with you.' She closed her eyes.

'I care about you too.' Lottie was touched.

'Those diaries might ... give you some clarity on the subject. I know you're curious about my life, and there have been things that... well, we've got close, and I shied away from saying it. I know that. I... I've found it hard to tell you. But they will, I think.'

'All right. Thank you.' Lottie had to admit that she was wildly curious about what was in the leather journals now. For a while now, she'd been curious about whatever big secret Gretchen had been avoiding telling her: her friend seemed to be suggesting to her that what she wanted to know was in these journals.

'That might have to be it for today, dear.' Gretchen closed her eyes. 'Promise me something?' she added, her eyes still closed.

'Anything,' Lottie said.

'Don't judge me. For what's in there,' Gretchen said, sounding tired. 'I did what I thought was best. Sometimes, that's all you can do.'

'I would never judge you, Gretchen,' Lottie said. 'You're my friend.'

'Thank you, dear.' Gretchen let out a long sigh. 'Perhaps the problem is that I've judged myself so harshly, for all these years.'

19

———

'Hey, Fred.' Lottie had just got home from the care home and slung her handbag onto the kitchen table. The thud it made reminded her – as if she could forget – that she'd brought home Gretchen's diaries. She couldn't wait to read them.

'Good evening, housemate,' Fred said. 'Good day?'

'It was good, thanks. Interviewing Gretchen Ross. How was the bookshop?' she asked, politely. *Do not flirt with Fred*, she told herself, sternly. *Just because he is nice, just because he has eyes you want to lose yourself in and hair you want to tangle your fingers in.*

'Quiet. As per,' he replied. 'No one breaking the door down for books, as usual. Sad times. The decline of Western civilisation. You can tell I've been reading the French philosophers again,' he sighed, theatrically, for her benefit.

'Well, if you want to hear something interesting, I've got Gretchen Ross's diaries to read. You can bet they're pretty sensational,' Lottie chuckled.

'Oooh. How come she gave them to you?' he asked, turning his head over his shoulder. Fred had started the washing up;

Lottie thought guiltily that she hadn't done it much since she moved in.

'I guess to sort of help fill in information about her life.'

'Wow! That's very trusting. She must really like you a lot,' Fred said. 'Can you read some of it aloud?'

'What, you want to hear them?' Lottie said. She was definitely interested to find out what was in them, but she had assumed no one else would be that interested. The fact that Fred wanted to listen warmed Lottie's heart.

'I'm curious. I sort of know Gretchen, I mean, she was always around when I grew up in the village. Quite a character,' he added.

'Right... I forget you're a Loch Cameron native.' Lottie sat down. 'Gretchen had quite a life.'

'I bet. I'm intrigued,' Fred chuckled.

'Me too.' Lottie opened the first journal and focused her eyes on Gretchen's copperplate handwriting. 'Right, then. Here we go.' She started to read aloud.

12 May 1986

Interviewing for my new assistant. They were all pretty young women and reasonably qualified for the job, but I couldn't imagine working with any of them. None of them had much chutzpah, though it pains me to write that.

I would like to employ a young woman and mentor her, but I also don't want to bring someone to work here that David and the rest can sexually harass, demean and probably treat like their assistant as well. I know how they are with the secretaries and I don't want that for someone working with me. I've fought damn hard to be treated in a professional manner and, unfortunately, I think I need someone who will stand up for themselves.

The last candidate was a young man, Andrew. He was

something of a surprise, being quite young and very handsome – and, also, clearly gay. He's worked at Jenner's for a long time, working mainly in ladies' fashions, but he read Classics at uni and is an avid reader. We had quite the chat about Jackie Collins, Ovid, Kafka and Dennis Wheatley and got on famously.

Also, when David asked him – quite frostily, I could tell that he and the other men on the panel didn't like Andrew at all – how he thought "selling skirts to ladies" would qualify him for the job, Andrew gave him a brilliant smile and said that as middle-aged women were the biggest audience for books, he thought that understanding what they liked, and knowing how to talk to them, could only be a positive. When he said that, I knew I wanted to offer him the job. Partly because he's right, about women readers. And partly because of the way he looked David right in the eye when he replied, with a little arched eyebrow and a charming smile. I knew, right then and there, that Andrew wouldn't be easily bossed around by those dinosaurs. So, I insisted that he got the job.

David and the others grumbled about it, but since it's my assistant we're hiring for, and since I'm good friends with Sophie, the head of Personnel – and, rightly, pointed out to her that I detected some fairly obvious bias against Andrew at the interview – I think I'll get my way. I usually do.

'Ha! Listen to that.' Fred clapped his hands in delight. 'Oh, I wish I knew Gretchen better now. She sounds amazing.'

'She really is. She's the most forthright and confident woman I've ever known.' Lottie grinned. It was fun, sharing Gretchen's story with someone – and the journal was as entertaining as she'd expected. But, she was sure that Gretchen had seemed to be saying to her that the diaries contained some kind of deep, dark secret. Whatever it was, they didn't seem to have got to it yet.

'What's next? Right, listen to this.' She turned the page.

18 May 1986

I called Andrew to tell him he got the job. He sounded genuinely surprised, and then unexpectedly flustered. He thanked me profusely, and then asked why I'd decided on him. I was honest and said that the fact that David didn't like him very much was a huge feather in his cap, and I'd been impressed with his enthusiasm for books and the fact that he'd been able to stand up to that panel of misogynists. I warned him that there are lots of men at Hatch that like to throw their weight around, and that I see it as my job to disrupt their reign of sexism, racism and homophobia. Andrew just laughed and said, it would be my honour to help you with that, Miss Ross. And that was that.

Tonight, when I gave Stella her bath, we practised the alphabet and her numbers. She's as sharp as a tack. I hope that when she gets older, the world is a little easier to be in if you're not a white, heterosexual man.

'She must feel quite disappointed with how it all turned out,' Fred commented, leaning back against the sink. 'Modern life, I mean. Still so much inequality.'

'I don't know. I mean, things are definitely better now, I think she'd say that. Remember that AIDS was happening around then. People were *really* anti-gay at that time.'

'That's true. I guess I just wish even any instances of prejudice didn't exist. Living in a small village, you still hear stuff like that now, sometimes. People can be ignorant,' Fred remarked. 'It's just because they've lived here all their lives and never been anywhere else. I guess if you've never met a gay person... but then, that's really no excuse as there are gay people in Loch

Cameron. It's more and more diverse in all ways now, especially since the development on Gyle Head.'

'Yes, it's not bad at all. And at least we have the Gretchens of the world, fighting the good fight,' Lottie said.

'Indeed. Let's hear another one, then,' Fred said.

10 June 1986

Andrew's first day. I took him to lunch and introduced him around. He is already a delight – very efficient, excellent phone manner, good note taking skills. At lunch I asked his opinion about the synopsis for DH's new book and he made some excellent suggestions.

Most brilliantly, though, after lunch, we were back in the office and David came in for his weekly meeting. I hadn't mentioned to Andrew that I despise these efforts at micromanagement which are largely ineffective, it being his first day. Yet, fifteen minutes into the meeting, the door to my office opened a snick and I saw him look inside. As David was looking at his notes, I mimed a "bored, kill me now" face and, exactly as if he had read my mind, the phone rang and Andrew's voice called out 'There's an urgent call for you from Don DeLillo's agent, Miss Ross,' nice and loudly through the door, so that David could hear.

Of course, I excused myself from the meeting and David left. I picked up the phone and thanked Andrew, who, of course, did not have Don DeLillo's agent on the other end.

I think we will get along very well.

'I love that,' Fred chuckled. 'And Andrew sounds brilliant. Imagine working with those two.'

'I know. I can't wait to read the rest of the diaries.' Lottie set the book down on the table. 'Anyway, thanks for being interested. It's nice to share this with someone.' She felt oddly shy, though there was no reason to.

'Oh, not at all. It's fascinating. I want to hear all of it,' he said. 'I love finding out about people's lives from the past, you know? Like, I low key love those documentaries about family history and people finding their lost relatives. No one ever wants to watch them with me.'

'Oh! I would. I love that stuff.' Lottie chuckled.

'We're cut from the same cloth,' Fred said, and turned back to the washing up. He looked back at Lottie as if he was going to say something more, but his phone started to buzz on the kitchen counter next to the sink.

'Oh. That's Helen. I should get that,' he said, instead. He answered the phone, smiling apologetically at Lottie. 'Hey, babe. How are you? I didn't know you were going to call. No, I'm not doing anything. Just chatting to Lottie.'

Fred mouthed *sorry* to her, but Lottie waved her hands as if to say, *no problem.*

Fred had a girlfriend. She had to remember that, even if Fred's soft tone, talking to Helen, made Lottie feel a little sad.

It wasn't fair of her to feel sad. All that had happened between them was a couple of random, accidental moments. Fred wasn't in any way hers.

She'd been enjoying sharing Gretchen's diary with him, though. It meant a lot to her that Fred seemed genuinely into hearing about her project.

Lottie closed the journal with her finger marking the page she'd got to. She was impatient to read on and find out what this big secret was: the secret that Gretchen had implied was hidden inside one or both of these books.

20

Settled on her bed, Lottie flicked through the book containing the journal entries from the 1980s, but, while it was fascinating, none of it seemed like it hid a huge secret. Most of the entries were about Gretchen's work life, and Lottie was really grateful to have that insight: the journal was a historical document of a professional woman in the 1980s. That, itself, was incredible, and would be a huge help towards her project. She knew that her tutor would love looking at it, for one thing.

She opened the second journal. It seemed to contain entries from the early seventies as opposed to the eighties in the previous one that she had read aloud to Fred.

Lottie started to read.

2 September 1972

I sometimes think back to what Mother wanted for me, and I wonder if she wasn't right, after all. I remember Mrs Carstairs and her measuring tape and her not letting me out of the house wearing my tight pencil skirt. Mother thought universities were

*hotbeds of sin, and a girl didn't need a higher education. If I
was too clever, I wouldn't find a husband.*

*I never went to university, but I still didn't find a husband.
Yet, perhaps Mother and Mrs Carstairs knew something about
men that I had to learn the hard way.*

*I have been seeing Alex for a year now. There's an old
saying that goes: you don't know anyone until you've known
them through every season. There's something in that. And
there's also something in seeing how people react to bad news,
or big news in general. I'm about to see how he responds to
something unexpected. It's not something I want, and I hope
that he sees things in the same way as me.*

Lottie frowned, looking back at the date of the entry. 1972.
It was much earlier than the entries about work and Gretchen's
assistant in the eighties. These were a very different tone
altogether.

9 September 1972

*I don't want a child, but Alex does. Alex wants this baby that
we have made together.*

*Accidentally. I am pregnant, and it is an accident. I have
been dreading telling him ever since I found out.*

*When I told him – and, of course, I had to tell him, despite
the fact that he has hurt and frightened me recently – he looked
shocked for a moment, then caught me up in a hug. He had
tears in his eyes. This is what I dreamed of, Gretchen, he said.*

*And that would have been lovely – I would have reconsid-
ered my thoughts about not having a child, if I trusted him. But,
I don't.*

*I am trapped. I realised I was pregnant four weeks ago, and
precisely three days after he raised his hand to me for the first
time.*

Taking your time to get to know someone pays dividends, but you can never know what people will do. It might take years before they show you the darkest parts of themselves.

I told him that I couldn't have a baby with him. Incredibly, he wanted to know why. I said, because a week ago you almost snapped my neck in two and then threw your dinner plate at the wall and told me to clean it up. You terrified me.

Now that I'm pregnant with his baby, he seems to think I am his property. I cannot stay after what he has done. I know that women do stay with men like him. And, I know what happens to them.

But it is bloody murder on my heart. I am still in love with him. You don't just turn off those feelings overnight.

'Oh, no.' Lottie took in a breath as she re-read the entry. Gretchen had made allusions to the fact that things hadn't gone well with Alex, but this... this was quite a lot more serious than something *not ending well*. Her heart in her mouth, Lottie read on.

11 *September* 1972

I don't want a child with Alex. I don't want the life of being a stay-at-home mother in Loch Cameron. I don't know how I would keep my job and I've worked so hard for it. The hours are long. Have I really endured the Charlies of the world just so that I could give up now? Most of all, I don't want the child of an abusive partner.

Alex says I can work in the shop with him and have the baby and give up my job. I think that he thinks this is a delightful solution. To me, it sounds like a living hell. He wants me under his thumb completely. He has said things in the past couple of days like calling me "my little wife" and saying if the baby is a girl, he will treat her like the little princess she will be.

I do not want to raise a princess. I am incapable of it.

It's as if Alex knowing that I am pregnant has erased every-thing true he knows about me: that I love my job, that I am committed to my career. All he sees now is the baby inside me. I am nothing to him now except a walking uterus.

Again, it would be different, perhaps, if he hadn't assaulted me. But he had.

1 October 1972

I am refusing his calls. I am avoiding the shop. I have told Alex that it's over, but he won't leave me alone.

I will not raise any child with a man like Alex. I have told him that I won't, but he refuses to hear me.

Now, the decision lies with me as to what to do. I respect any woman who has a termination, but the thought terrifies me, and when I made enquiries at the local surgery, all I got was a rather sniffy attitude and told that terminations are for married women only. I could enquire in Edinburgh, but I'm also worried that I am actually further along than I thought, and therefore close to the end of the allowable time period.

Therefore, I have made enquiries about giving the baby up for adoption. Despite my mother warning me about what happens to women who have babies out of wedlock, I will end up doing exactly that. Time will tell if I end up at the edge of the graveyard in the chapel on the hill.

I just can't see another way out. I don't want to be linked to Alex, I couldn't manage to keep working with another child as a single mother. It seems like the only solution.

'Oh, Gretchen,' Lottie breathed. Her heart went out to her friend, though these entries were written so many years ago. What a terrible situation she had been in. Lottie couldn't imagine how awful it must have been for her friend, to be facing this decision alone.

4 October 1972

I have made contact with a good adoption agency. They will take the baby when it is born.

It tears my heart out to have to do this, but I cannot and will not raise any child with Alexander O'Connell.

7 March 1973

They have taken her. My baby. A girl.

They have told me that she will be adopted by a good family. People always want babies, that is what they've said.

My milk has come in, and the district nurse says it will go away again in a few days if I don't use it. She advised me to bind my chest until then or wear a tight vest, but it's too painful.

My heart is broken in two. My whole body yearns for my baby, but I had to give her away. It would be too easy for Alexander to find me if I kept her and if we moved away. He knows where I work, and he knows that I won't leave my job.

I keep reminding myself that I had to give her away. I had to do it. I had to do it to protect her.

But it aches. All of me aches, and I don't know if the pain will ever go away

Lottie started to cry. What she was reading was so incredibly sad that she couldn't do anything but let the tears course down her cheeks. Her heart was aflame with grief for Gretchen and her baby. And, she was also furious. How could the world allow men like Alexander O'Connell to do these things?

20 March 1973

Alex is furious about what I've done. I've stopped seeing him and made it clear that our relationship was over months ago.

I have gone back to Edinburgh but everyone in Loch Cameron knows, it seems. The gossips have had a field day with me being pregnant, but I can't control their malicious tongues. Mother and Father are mortified and can hardly leave the house for shame.

29 March 1973

He came to my flat tonight, trying to get me back, he said – but I know that he was trying to find out where the baby is. I had to call the police to get him to go away. Alex appears gentle and bookish to the general public. But he's a big man, and he really scared me tonight. He has been hammering on the main door downstairs, screaming that he wants custody of the baby. Luckily, my neighbours didn't let him into the building.

'Gretchen,' Lottie murmured as she read. 'Poor, poor Gretchen.'

Now, Lottie could see why her friend had given her these journals to read. If this had happened to her, Lottie thought that she wouldn't have been able to talk about it, either. It was too hard. This was Gretchen's way of telling Lottie that she trusted her with her whole story – even if Gretchen couldn't bring herself to voice all of it.

The local police came quite quickly when I called, in their defence. I think they could hear on the phone that I was scared.

They arrived while Alex was still there and told him to stay away from me and the flat. Nothing official was done: just a

*quiet word and a bit of strong-arming, as far as I could see.
Still, it worked.*

4 April 1973

*Alex knows he can't come around, but he's been phoning me
all hours of the day and night. I have had to unplug the tele-
phone altogether.*

Then, there was a longer gap in the dates between entries in
the journal. The next one said:

10 May 1973

It has been a month since I got any calls from Alex.

*Cautiously, I visited Mother and Father in the village to
see they were all right. They are gradually recovering from the
shock but I don't know if they will ever forgive me. Mother in
particular refuses to accept that I couldn't have married Alex.
She says he "seemed like a sensible fellow" and that "any man
would be upset in the same situation". She seems unable to
hear the facts from me: that he hurt me, that he has frightened
me, that if I had stayed with him and had the baby, I know that
I would have been sentencing myself and the baby to a life of
fear and pain.*

*While I was in the village, I had to pass the shop. I made
sure that I walked past quickly on the other side of the street,
but when I glanced over, the shop was closed. I dropped in to
see Dotty at the Inn – she is head of the Loch Cameron gossip
mill, but she has a good heart – and had a quiet catch up. It
seems that Alex has left the village and closed up the shop for
now. Dotty says that she has heard he has advertised for a
manager.*

If he is gone, I will be hugely relieved. The thought of being

*in any kind of proximity at all with Alexander O'Connell for
the rest of my days was intolerable. So, if Alex has at the very
least done me this small kindness of staying away from me, I
am grateful to him.*

18 June 1973

*Still nothing from Alex. With every day that passes, I heal a
little more.*

*I will miss the baby, always. The adoption agency has told
me that she has been adopted now by a good family, just as they
promised. My milk has dried up, but my body still yearns for
her. It's like we are connected by an invisible thread. I can feel
her, even though she isn't with me. I think I will always
feel her.*

*Tonight, the phone rang, but when I picked it up, no one
said anything. I could hear someone breathing. I said, Alex, is
that you? But there was no reply.*

*It made me feel paranoid; that he is still there, that he was
watching in some way. Even though I know he has left the
village, I don't know where he is. He might have moved to
Edinburgh. If he is on the end of the phone, then at least he
can't be outside the building, hammering on the door. Still, I
made sure my door was locked, and closed all the windows,
even though I am on the second floor.*

Lottie looked up from the journal, tears brimming in her
eyes. She had listened to so much of Gretchen's story, but she'd
had no idea that her friend had gone through something so
traumatic.

This was the secret, then: the thing that Gretchen had
wanted to tell her, but had found too difficult. Lottie could see
why. It was heartbreaking.

21

———

'Hey, Gretchen,' Lottie called out as she let herself in to her friend's apartment. She felt unsure of how to broach the subject of Gretchen's baby that she'd read about the night before in her diaries, but as she walked in and met Gretchen's friendly gaze, she saw in her friend's eyes that she knew.

'Good morning, dear.' Gretchen held out both her hands to Lottie. 'You don't think I'm a monster, do you? Please, tell me that you don't. I've been up all night, worrying what you must think of me.' She looked and sounded so uncharacteristically anxious that Lottie's heart – already full of sorrow for Gretchen – sank, even heavier with sadness.

'Oh, Gretchen. Of course I don't!' Lottie hugged her friend, remembering to be gentle. 'Gretchen. I'm honoured you gave me those diaries to read, and I just...' she paused, trying to find the right words. 'I guess I'm just amazed at how you managed to cope with such a difficult thing in your life. I'm so sorry you had to do that. And I'm so sorry for you. About Alexander.'

'Thank you, sweetheart. That means so much,' Gretchen said, in a small voice. 'You know, I've kept that to myself, for all these years. Some people in my past knew: it went around the village that I'd had a baby, despite my mother's attempts to keep it quiet. Alexander knew, of course. And the people at the adoption agency, and the people that adopted my baby. But I didn't talk to anyone I worked with about it, though of course they knew. I worked up to about a month before I had the baby, and I would have worked for longer, if I had been able to. And no one here knows. As the years went on, when I still lived in the village, fewer and fewer people knew. In the years after the baby was born, I didn't talk about her to anyone. It feels strange, to talk about her now.' She wiped a tear from her eye.

'Is it too painful to talk about?' Lottie asked. 'I mean, as far as the project goes, it doesn't have to be included, any of this. I only want to do what feels comfortable for you. This kind of goes beyond my project. We're friends, aren't we?' Lottie tilted her head to one side.

'Of course we are, dear. I didn't know how to broach the subject, but I wanted to tell you. And I remembered that I had the journals. So that was why I gave them to you. I haven't looked at them in years, so I don't remember exactly what I wrote. But, I'm guessing that you got the gist, anyway.'

'Yes.' Lottie nodded. 'Look, Gretchen. You were the victim in that situation. You have nothing to feel bad about. It's sad, but you did what you had to do. You made sure your baby was safe. As much as you could.'

'I know, dear. I've tortured myself, over the years, thinking, what if I'd kept her? And, of course, I adopted my daughter Stella, some years after. And I think having to give my baby up factored into that decision. I felt the loss of my first girl so much. It never really went away.' Gretchen let out a long breath.

'That's totally understandable,' Lottie said. 'Did you ever know anything more about the baby? Your daughter with Alexander?' she prompted, knowing that Gretchen had already told her so much. But, she was curious to know if Gretchen had had any contact with her child.

'No,' Gretchen said, bluntly. Her expression became stony again, just as it had before when Lottie had pressed her about her past. Having seen this reaction before, Lottie suspected that Gretchen wasn't exactly being truthful, but that for whatever reason, she didn't want to discuss it any more. 'Let's just leave it for a moment, shall we? I feel like we need some light relief.' Gretchen pointed to a framed photo on one of her bookshelves; it featured a younger version of herself with an attractive young man. They were in an office – Lottie guessed, Gretchen's – laughing at the camera. They looked very comfortable and happy in each other's presence.

'I insisted on having a young, gay male secretary when I finally became a publisher. Andrew. I knew as soon as he sat down in the interview room that I was going to give him the job.'

'I read about him in your journal. He looks like fun.' Lottie acquiesced to the change in subject, making a mental note to return to the subject of the baby later.

'Oh, he was. When he applied for the job, I could see that his CV was good, but it was his *joie de vivre* and his confidence that won him the job. I knew that he'd always be honest with me, and he wouldn't take any rubbish from the men with rather *antique* ideas we had to work with.' Gretchen stopped for a minute and stared at Lottie.

'What is it?' Lottie touched her face, feeling suddenly self-conscious.

'Oh... nothing, dear. You just remind me of someone I once knew. Every now and again, you hold your head in a particular way. The look in your eyes.' Gretchen made a dismissive gesture. 'What was I saying?'

'Who do I remind you of?' Lottie asked, curiously.

'Oh, just someone from a long time ago.' Gretchen shook her head. 'I was telling you about Andrew.'

'Hmm. Yes, he sounds amazing.' Lottie nodded, curious to

know who it was that she resembled in Gretchen's past. Were there more secrets that she was yet to reveal? However, she was learning that Gretchen could be evasive when she didn't want to talk about something, and Lottie was still working out how best to persuade Gretchen she could be trusted with her secrets.

'He was. Is. We're still good friends. He lives down on the south coast, in England, now. But he came up and visited me last year, bless his heart.'

'That's so nice.'

'Ha. He is nice, but he was just like me, too: a rebel. I just loved seeing the look on those stuffy old dinosaurs' faces when they had to make an appointment with Andrew to see me. I used to peer through the crack in the door from my office into Andrew's office, outside. I loved watching his sweet as pie expression with them, and then when they'd left or they weren't looking, he'd turn around and make a face at me. We used to laugh like drains.'

Gretchen smiled affectionately. 'That photo. 1990, a long while after I first gave him the job. We were a great team; Andrew was my assistant for years and years. I had a bob, as you can see, and Andrew was always telling me off for wearing mannish clothes. But that was the style, then. You've seen *Friends*.' Lottie went to the picture and picked it up, noting Gretchen's tan colour waistcoat and matching wide legged trousers. Andrew – a handsome, blonde young man with high cheekbones and deep brown eyes – wore a monogrammed dark blue shirt.

'I have. And you look lovely, anyway. Very elegant.'

'Well, thank you, dear. I always loved clothes. Spent far too much of my money on them, but then, I was single. Although a lot of my salary went on childcare for my daughter.'

'Stella. The librarian?' Lottie asked, gently.

'Yes. She died a few years ago, which is why I didn't want to talk about it the other day when you asked me,' Gretchen said, shortly. 'Sorry, dear. It's just still difficult, some days.'

'No, *I'm* sorry. It's perfectly okay if you don't want to talk about her.'

'Well, I'm happy to talk about her life, but I don't like to talk about her death too much, dear, if you don't mind. It was an accident, a few years ago. She had an allergic reaction while driving. Went into anaphylaxis. She was fifty years old.' Gretchen blinked.

'Oh, Gretchen.' Lottie reached for the other woman's hand and held it gently. 'I'm so very sorry.'

'Thank you, dear. That's kind. Beautiful girl. I raised her to love books.' Gretchen smiled gently. 'Everyone thought I was mad when I adopted her, being a single mother, unmarried, all that. But it just felt right. As I say, I was still mourning the loss of my first baby. Once your body has made a baby, it always sort of... yearns to be there for that child, I suppose.' She shook her head. 'I didn't get the chance to be a mother to my baby with Alexander, but the yearning didn't go away. So, when the opportunity presented itself, I made a decision. Again, it wasn't easy, but I knew it was the right thing.'

'How did that come about? If you don't mind telling me?' Lottie asked gently, and angled her phone towards Gretchen.

'No, I don't mind telling you about that. Stella's life is a source of joy for me. It's just her death that makes me sad.' Gretchen looked into the corner of the room for a moment, then began.

'It all began with a friend of mine at Hatch, Cathy. I'd moved over from Dunne's by then and got to know Cathy because she ran the cafeteria as it was then – all dry ham sandwiches and chips with everything, you can imagine. It was the mid-seventies. Anyway, I'd pop down there for a coffee and we'd end up chatting. She was a little older than me, one of those salt of the earth types. So, I liked to catch up with Cathy when I could, and if she wasn't too busy, she'd invite me into the kitchen at the back of the cafeteria and we'd have a cuppa and a cigarette out of the back door. Yes, I smoked then. I'm not proud of it, but everyone did, then. And you were allowed to smoke indoors, so you can imagine what the offices were like. And the cafeteria, come to that.'

'Eww.' Lottie made a face.

'Indeed.' Gretchen raised an eyebrow. 'Now, Cathy was from a large family. She lived with them still, very proudly working class. I could never keep up with all her brothers and sisters, cousins and whatnot, and she told such charming stories about them all, I felt like I knew them all. And they lived in a street where – a bit like Loch Cameron, I suppose – everyone knew everybody else, and there was always lots going on. Husbands cheating on their wives, gambling, husbands coming home at all hours drunk, beating their wives, their children, children playing wild games in the street, you name it.

'Now, one day, Cathy was telling me about the family next door to hers. Cathy's family were quite religious and well-behaved, but the family next door were the worst on the street and Cathy's mother was at her wit's end because of all the noise and the upset. The wife was always threatening to leave, and she was a drinker, and she'd do things like put the dinner in the oven for the kids, drunk, then fall asleep and it would burn, and there'd be smoke billowing out of the windows. Once, there was a chip pan fire for the same reason.' Gretchen paused for a moment, gathering her thoughts.

'Anyway, that family had a teenage daughter who was a frequent runaway. You can't blame the girl, can you? By the sounds of things, it wasn't a great place to live, what with her father beating her mother, and her mother drunk, and nobody in charge but chaos and sadness. And, the thing was, that she'd run away for a few months and come back pregnant.'

'Oh, wow.'

'Wow, indeed. At this point, when I had the chat to Cathy that day, the daughter had just come back pregnant again. I think she would have been about sixteen at the time and it was her second time pregnant. I never knew what happened to the other baby.'

'Her second, at that age?' Lottie asked, aghast.

'I know. But, as I say, no one was looking after anyone in that house. Anyhow, I went back to work, and got on with my week. But I kept thinking about that poor girl and that poor baby and the life it was going to be born into, and I hated the idea of it. I know that it was my own experience, having to give up my first baby, guiding me towards Stella. It was as though the universe – that's how you young people talk about it these days, isn't it – in my day, we would have said *fate* or *God*, but I suppose it's the same thing – the universe was giving me another chance. I'd never really got over having to say goodbye to that perfect little girl. And I suppose I just thought, this is an opportunity to make it right, somehow.

'A couple of weeks later, Cathy's family were having a big party – I think it was her parents' anniversary – and she invited me along. It was a jolly affair, more of a street party really, with bunting up on all the houses, cakes, things in aspic – that was a type of jelly that was popular then – sparkling wine, even, which was deemed very fancy at the time.

'I met the wayward neighbours, and the mother, Linda, was sober, and Cathy had whispered to me that she seemed to be trying to turn over a new leaf since her awful, violent husband had left. They all hoped it was for good. The daughter, Molly, was there too, and I talked to them both. Molly was actually a bright girl, but she'd been expelled from school a few years back due to excessive truanting. She didn't want the baby, but she was too far along not to have it by then, and anyway her mother hadn't let her consider anything else.'

'Was that even an option, then? This was the 1970s?' Lottie

frowned. 'I don't actually know when abortion became legal in the UK.'

'1968. David Steel got it through. Whatever you think of politics, whatever side you're on, that man saved women's lives. I'll always think the world of him.' Gretchen looked away for a moment.

'So, it was legal then?'

'Yes, but only just, and people's attitudes weren't exactly progressive. A lot of the time, like so many things linked to women's health, it was all about the doctor you had – usually a man – and what he thought was good for you.' Gretchen's expression darkened. 'That went for contraception too, and gynaecological problems. Don't even get me started on all of that.'

'That's awful. Imagine, if you got pregnant by accident then, or even before. It must have been so scary.'

'Hmm.' Gretchen frowned. 'It was. I had been pregnant, unmarried, remember. I wasn't given the option of an abortion either. Would I have done it? I don't know. But I do support a woman's right to choose, and at least I was older than Molly and had a job and was able to look after myself. She didn't have any of that.'

'So, Molly wouldn't have been able to have an abortion?'

'I doubt it was presented to her as an option, quite honestly. But she was five months pregnant when I met her.' Gretchen sighed. 'So, there wasn't an option left apart from having the baby and keeping it, or having the baby and giving it away. She wasn't particularly keen on either option, and I don't blame her. Babies are hard enough when you're a fully grown woman and you plan to have one, never mind being a child and it happening by accident. And despite the fact that she'd had to grow up fast, be streetwise – she was still a child.' Gretchen pursed her lips.

'Poor Molly,' Lottie said. 'It must have been really tough for her.'

'It was, poor lamb. She'd lost out on an education because no one ever made sure she went to school, and she didn't want to go because she was upset with life at home being, let's say, far from ideal, plus, I know that she found it difficult. I think, looking back, she was probably dyslexic, possibly neurodivergent. But in those days, if you didn't sit quietly and behave, schools labelled you the naughty or stupid child and you'd spend the day writing lines in the hallway, like as not. And, the school knew her family, and that she lived on the street that she did, so they just wrote her off. Nowadays, Molly would have had more help. But, then, she was on her own.'

'That's awful.' Lottie felt desperately sorry for Molly.

'I know. Well, that day we had a good chat and I told her about my job, and about working in books, and she seemed really interested. She later told me that it was the first time in her life she'd ever met a woman who made her think that she had options for her own life. I always valued that.'

Gretchen closed her eyes and rubbed them, then opened them widely again and blinked a few times. 'Dear. Could you pass me those eye drops, on the side, there? Wonderful. Yes.'

Lottie crossed the room to the small kitchenette, picked up a small bottle of eye drops from a shelf that was filled with other medication and returned to Gretchen. She couldn't help but notice some morphine there too, among the other varied and likely quite standard old lady drugs that were lined up neatly.

'Gretchen? Are you all right?' she asked as Gretchen put a couple of the drops in each eye. 'I don't mean to pry... you just seem to be suffering with your eyes a little. And... the morphine...' Lottie trailed off. She hardly knew Gretchen, so she felt like she was overstepping a little. But, on the other hand, she had got quite fond of Gretchen in a short space of time. She didn't like to think that her new friend might be suffering.

'Quite all right, dear. Just an antique body and its requirements. Honestly, it's dull as dishwater when you get to be my age. Enjoy your youth, is my advice.' Gretchen blinked her eyes a few times and then reached for a pair of glasses which were hanging around her neck. She pushed them up her nose, and then squinted at Lottie. 'Now, where were we?'

'Um. You were telling me about Molly and the baby. Was that Stella? Your daughter? The baby, I mean.'

'Yes. What happened was that I started visiting Molly and Linda. I'd take books for Molly – she was an avid reader, actually, even though she hated school – and we'd talk, Linda made dinner. Me adopting Stella was Linda's idea, initially. I was there at the dinner table, and Molly was very close to her due date. And Linda said, have you ever thought of having a baby yourself, Gretchen? And I said no. Because I didn't want them to know. I was ashamed of what I'd done...' Gretchen halted for a moment and moistened her lips. She sighed.

'You shouldn't have been,' Lottie said, quietly.

'Well, it's easy to say that now. But I still feel the loss. Even now, in my eighties, the resonance is there. The emptiness.' Gretchen blinked; it seemed to hurt, because she rubbed her eyes and winced. 'And, at the time, it was only a few years prior to all this that I'd given Alex's baby up for adoption. It was still raw, though I thought, at the time, that I was over it.'

'But you weren't?' Lottie asked, gently.

'No. I wasn't,' Gretchen said.

22

———

'The thing is that, after a while, your body recovers from childbirth. My milk went away, my nipples went back to normal, I lost the baby weight. My perineum healed. The body is an amazing thing. But, I didn't recover from it, mentally and emotionally. That took much longer.'

'I suppose it's such a deeply ingrained thing, motherhood,' Lottie said. 'And, though you had what was best for the baby in your mind, I can imagine that it was still incredibly hard to give her up.'

'It was. There were so many times I thought of getting in contact with her. I craved her. I wanted her back. But I knew that if I did go and try to get her back, not only would I have taken her away from her new family, but I'd be putting her in danger, too. I'd be putting her in danger of Alex, and that fear was what kept me from doing any of those things. But, yes. I missed her terribly. Like someone must miss a limb that has been removed.'

There was a silence. Lottie reached for Gretchen's birdlike, wrinkled hand. Two tears rolled down Gretchen's lined cheeks.

'So, anyway,' Gretchen gave Lottie a rueful smile and wiped

the tears away with the back of her hand. 'I was telling you about how Stella and I came to be mother and daughter. I was there for dinner one night and Linda said, "Molly and I have been talking and we wondered whether you might take the baby when she's born. Adopt her, so it's legal. But you can give her a much better life than we can. And Molly wants to go to college. She can still get some qualifications and make something of herself, like you did."'

'So, you said yes?' Lottie's heart was breaking for Gretchen. She had had such a hard time of it, and Lottie fervently wished that she could do something to help heal the pain that her friend still so obviously held close to her heart.

'I didn't at first, actually. It was such an outlandish idea that I had no clue what I thought about it or how I would even go about such a thing.' Gretchen's voice quavered, but she continued nonetheless. 'So, I asked if I could think about it, and they said yes. Now, there was such a thing as private adoption, then. Nowadays, it's a bit different. You'd have to be a member of the family to privately adopt a baby. Then, I just had to demonstrate that I was a functioning member of society and I could provide Stella with a good life, which I could. Just about. This was still in the days before I got to be the head honcho at Hatch, but I had a decent job as senior editor at this point, in the mid-seventies.'

'More people should adopt. It must be so awful for children not to have a home,' Lottie observed.

'Indeed. Well, anyway, I mulled it over. Looked into how I'd do it. And then, when Stella was born, I went to see her and Molly, and I fell in love. She was such a perfect little bundle. I'd been thinking that I couldn't ever be a mother because I wasn't married, and I had no intention of getting married, either. That I'd given up my one chance, and that was it. I could either have married Alex and kept the baby, and subjected both of us to a life of violence and intimidation, or I could stay an old maid forever. And then, when I saw Stella that day for the first time, I thought, what am I thinking? When had I ever let conventional thought stop me doing what I wanted to do? I never had. I'd moved to Edinburgh to work, against my mother's wishes. I'd worked my way up in publishing, despite the misogyny. They had decent maternity arrangements at Hatch. Not as good as now, obviously. But decent. I realised that the only thing standing in the way of being Stella's mother was me. So, I got out of my own way.'

'But there was a kind of... parallel... there. Between you and Molly. You knew what it was like to give up a baby, and yet you adopted Stella. I mean, I don't want this to sound like I'm judging you. Because I'm not, by any means,' Lottie said, hurriedly. 'I'm just interested to see what you think about that.'

'No, you're right, dear. And I don't mind you asking. I *was* very aware of that. I didn't ever want to feel that I'd taken advantage of a vulnerable young girl and taken her child away from her. The difference was that, because we did it as a private adoption, I could make sure that Molly and Stella still had a relationship. She was Auntie Molly to Stella when she was little, and I told Stella that Molly was her biological mother when she was older. Linda would come up and see us from time to time. It was a very different situation.'

'Did you feel as though... with Stella... I don't know. It sort of healed you from what had happened before?' Lottie asked, knowing that she was pushing for more than perhaps Gretchen wanted to discuss, but she was invested in the story and she wanted to know.

'Yes. In a way.' Gretchen nodded, though her expression was guarded. 'It was a healing experience in some ways for me, but it was also a really tough experience for me, being a mother.

'The nuts and bolts of being the mother of a baby weren't simple, and it didn't come naturally. Not to me, anyway.' Gretchen snorted. 'Not one bit. I wasn't the classic maternal type. I'm still not. I'd burn a boiled egg.' She raised an eyebrow at Lottie, who was glad to see that she hadn't offended Gretchen with her questions.

'Ha. I'm sure you were better than you're making out.'

'Well, I did it my way, which is all you can ever really do. I wasn't a traditional mother. We ate out of tins a lot and I can't say that the flat I had by then was always that clean. But I always read to her, and we played a lot. When she could talk, we talked a lot. I worked. I wasn't home all the time. But, I think she learned something good from that.'

'I'm sure she did.' It occurred to Lottie that, even though she had been spending a lot of time with Gretchen, there was still something about her that felt strangely familiar. Being around Gretchen just felt *right*, in an odd kind of way that she couldn't really explain. It wasn't any one thing – her voice, her way of speaking, her stories, the way she dressed – it was more that she just felt as though she had known Gretchen all her life.

'I remember taking Stella home to my flat in Edinburgh – I lived alone, by then, and realised how unfit for purpose the flat itself was. It was up eight flights of stairs, a lovely mansion block, mind you,' Gretchen continued.

'Beautiful large double doors, carved wooden pigeonholes for your post in the lobby where you came in, a carved wood banister on the staircase. But I hadn't carried a baby up eight flights of stairs before, in her baby carrier, and a baby bag, and two shopping bags full of nappies and formula and food for me. That was an eye-opening experience. Then, I realised that I was going to have to get a pram, and then a pushchair, and how was I going to get that up and down eight flights of stairs every time I wanted to go out? There wasn't a lift.'

'That must have been terrible,' Lottie sympathised. 'I can't imagine how mothers do all that. The heavy lifting alone, never mind the caring and the not sleeping and all that.'

'Oh, let me tell you, I had not thought it through at all. And, in those days, there were some books about how to look after babies, but they were not helpful at all. They all assumed the baby would just do what they were supposed to do. Stella didn't. I think the baby books are better, nowadays. But it's still intensely difficult. Give me a manuscript that needs a complete rewrite and a drama queen author to tame. I could do that, then. But Stella was a whole new world.'

'Did your parents help?' Lottie asked, thinking of her own mum, Emma, and how helpful she would probably have been if Lottie had been in the same situation. Her grandparents too, come to that. Her heart clenched for a moment, like it always did when she thought of her mum.

'Goodness, no. Mother had never really got over me getting pregnant the first time and giving up the baby, and Father had all but stopped talking to me after that. For a good while, anyway. They absolutely did not approve of me adopting Stella as a single mother. They did come to love her, over time – I mean, she was such an adorable child, it was impossible not to love her. But, no. I was on my own when it came to Stella as a baby. Linda helped a bit, but as much as we maintained a relationship, she couldn't allow herself to get too close to Stella as a baby. I think it would have hurt her too much.'

'That's understandable. Goodness, everything about this was so complicated, wasn't it?' Lottie shook her head. 'So many people's feelings to consider.'

'Yes. But I had to focus on Stella, so at the time I sort of just had to let all that stuff pass me by,' Gretchen said. 'I took a few months' sabbatical from work and got Stella into a bit of a routine. And then I found a lovely nanny, Elsie, and went back to work. That worked all right for about a year, but paying a full-time nanny isn't cheap. And I felt like I never saw Stella, which I didn't, really. Hatch were understanding enough about my sabbatical, but once I was back at work, they wanted me there full time. And that meant start at eight, finish around seven. It was tough.'

'Wow. How did you cope?'

'Well, fortunately for me, after Stella turned three, I got Jenny – my slush pile author turned megastar – to come with me to Hatch, and she brought in so much money that they promoted me again, this time to Managing Editor. So, I started to have more influence and power in the workplace. And that meant I could make demands, like doing some days working from home.

'At around this time, I lost both of my parents – they died within a couple of months of each other. It was heartbreaking, and the stress with having Stella, working and trying to cope with losing both parents and sorting out the cottage was intense. So, I made a decision. The laird – he's the landowner in that area, so, if you live there, he's your landlord – asked if I wanted to keep on renting the cottage, and so I said yes, and I moved me and Stella to Loch Cameron.'

'But that's quite a long way from Edinburgh. Isn't that where you said your offices were?'

'Yes. It wasn't easy, to be sure, but I arranged to go into the office two days a week and work from home the rest of the time. For those two days per week, Stella went to a lovely lady in the village who would take her for two overnights as well. So, I'd drop her off on a Sunday night, drive over to Edinburgh, be there for Monday and Tuesday and drive back late on the Tuesday night. In those days, I had the energy for that kind of thing,' Gretchen chuckled.

'Wow.' Lottie was impressed. 'That's pretty tough, Gretchen. Good for you.'

'Hmm. Well, it's hard, being a working single parent. I did it because I wanted to, I had an okay job, I made it work. But plenty of women – and men – have to cope with being single parents, not out of choice. It's far harder for some people.'

'I know.' Lottie nodded. 'Still, you know, Gretchen. You were a bit of a trailblazer.'

'Oh, goodness, dear.' Gretchen took off her glasses and rolled her eyes. 'I don't know about that. But, you don't need a man to do anything in life, that's what I found out as I went along. Stella didn't need a father, and I didn't need a husband. And we were just fine. So, if that's trailblazing, then, all right, I'll be a trailblazer for you.' She shrugged.

'You're an inspiration, Gretchen,' Lottie replied, and she meant it. Talking to Gretchen was fascinating, and sometimes it had been deeply sad, but it was also, in a way, life-affirming. If Gretchen could do all these difficult things, then maybe she, Lottie, could heal and move on from the difficulties in her life. If she could be anything like Gretchen she would be proud, Lottie thought, watching as her friend closed her eyes. She looked tired now, and Lottie wasn't surprised. They had talked a long time, and it hadn't been an easy talk for Gretchen, either.

Yet, Lottie was left wondering: was there still a part of her story that Gretchen wasn't telling her? And, if so, what was it?

23

———

GRETCHEN

I love talking to Lottie. I'm enjoying telling her my story, but the further I go in it, the closer I'm getting to the last big secret I have. I don't want to tell her that part of the story. Not yet, and maybe not ever. I was nervous that the diaries might give it away; I regretted giving them to her that day, after she left, but she doesn't seem to have noticed anything.

So far, I've hidden the truth in my story like a bookmark pushed down between the pages. It's there, but to an untrained eye, the pages look undisturbed.

Lottie wants to think of me as a trailblazing single parent, and I suppose I was.

However, "trailblazing" is not how I feel in Jenner's one Saturday with a bawling Stella in the pushchair, wishing I had stayed at home.

We have ventured out to Edinburgh's best department store because I have to buy a wedding present for one of the women in the typing pool. We still have a typing pool at Hatch; it will be years before this is a thing of the past.

The editorial office has had a whip round, and obviously it is me that gets dispatched to buy something nice for Elaine and her betrothed (despite now working with one other woman in the editorial team, for which I am very grateful), because I am nevertheless one of two women and my male colleagues joke that if they had to buy Elaine a wedding gift, it would just be an ashtray and thirty-two cans of Special Brew.

I am planning on buying some Edinburgh Crystal, but I am deeply regretting not bringing any snacks for Stella who started whinging on the bus, and by the time we get to the homewares floor of Jenner's on a busy Saturday afternoon, is wailing loud enough to shatter the crystal vases.

I crouch by the side of the pushchair and offer her sippy cup which only has water in it.

'Biscuit!' she roars, and I wince at the volume. I know that to her it's the most important thing in the world right now, and that aged two, Stella has absolutely no interest in being quiet for the sake of society. Plus, she is a bonny toddler, which is a nice way of saying that Stella is a ball of wilful muscle and nowadays can wrestle her way out of the pushchair if she wants to. Her verbal skills have always been advanced – I put it down to the fact that I have read to her every day, and always talk to her – and *biscuit* is definitely part of her vocabulary.

'I don't have a biscuit, sweetie,' I cajole her. 'Let Mummy get this one thing and then we'll go to the café and get a snack.'

I also dread the café in Jenner's which will be similarly packed, but if I don't get Stella something to eat soon, I won't be able to get her on the bus later.

In all of this, I am lonely. I adore Stella and I do not for a second regret becoming her mother. But, my life is lonely. I have work friends and acquaintances, but when I am at home, it is just Stella and me. When she is in bed, I try and work, but sometimes I stare at the walls and want to scream.

I pick up a crystal fruit bowl and check the price tag. There's enough money in the collection – in a brown envelope in my handbag – for this and something else. I decide quickly on a matching water jug and pick up a boxed version of both things, balancing them carefully on the top of the pushchair. I will Stella not to start thrashing around, and wonder if I have enough room in the shopping tray under the pushchair to get both items in that after I've paid for them.

I join the queue, which is interminably long and staffed by one middle aged man. Mentally, I roll my eyes. In my experience, the quickest and most efficient staff on a till is 1. A middle aged or older lady, 2. A teenage girl, 3. A middle aged man and 4, worst of all, a teenage boy.

'Biscuit!' Stella shouts again. I ignore her, and smile brightly at the woman in front of me in the queue who turns around to give us a withering look. She looks me up and down, then looks at Stella, then back at me. Her gaze stops on my hands which are steadying the boxes on top of the navy-blue canvas pushchair hood.

I can read this woman's thoughts, not because I am at all gifted psychically, but because this has happened to me so many times before. She is noticing that I don't wear a wedding ring, and she is noticing that Stella and I do not look very alike at all. Stella is, at this age, raven-haired, a messy frizz. Her eyes are dark, her skin is darker than mine.

'Nanny?' The woman nods to Stella, parrying her one-word question in the way that strangers do when they feel entitled to your attention. I know what she is asking. She is asking me if I am Stella's nanny, her childminder or caregiver, and not her mother, because that would explain my lack of wedding ring and my obvious difference of appearance to Stella. I know that if Stella and my colouring were reversed, then I would likely frequently be suspected of abducting her.

'This is my daughter, Stella,' I reply, loudly, knowing that my well-spoken voice will bring this officious woman up short at least a little. I raise an imperious eyebrow, showing this woman that I do not stand for her judgement. That I am not here to be pigeonholed by her narrow mindedness. And, that Stella and I are absolutely none of her business.

The woman simpers and turns away. I will Stella not to make more of a fuss, and, though she kicks a little, she is mercifully quiet for the rest of the time we are queuing.

I make a point of standing up to these women – and it is always women who will look down their noses at me – but it always hurts. Many times, I have considered buying a cheap gold band to wear on my wedding ring finger, just to make these comments and looks stop.

It's perfectly normal for a mother to be out with her child, running errands, without the father of the child. Everyone expects Father to be out at work in the daytimes. But, I am suspicious, somehow, and if it's not the lack of wedding ring, it's the fact that I am open about being a single mother by choice when I am asked.

When I take Stella to the playground or to the park on the weekends, other mothers will talk to me in the way that mothers do. They will ask me about Stella, all the usual things: how old she is, what she likes to eat, at what age she walked, crawled, talked. We swap anecdotes of the funny things our children say, albeit slightly competitively.

But when they ask – and they always do – what does her daddy do? I am honest and say, *she doesn't have a daddy*. Then, their brows furrow: I'm so sorry. They assume he is dead. And I could leave it there, and I could even invent a whole story to tell them about being a widow, about bringing up Stella on my own, against my wishes. What would be the harm? They are strangers; likely, I'd never see these women again.

But, I don't, because I am too stubborn. I didn't choose to be Stella's mother just so I could spend my life lying about that choice. So, I steel myself for the veil that will lower over their expressions when I tell them I am a single mother by choice. That I adopted Stella alone, and I expect to be alone forever.

I am not a trailblazer, or, at least, in those moments, I don't feel like one. I feel left out of the cosy wife club; I am not invited to other mothers' houses for tea and cake. I think they fear that I will steal their husbands, or perhaps that the taint of singledom will rub off on them.

I stand by my decision, and I know it was the right thing for me and the right thing for Stella. But, I am still hurt every time I get one of those looks like today in Jenner's, and every time another mother awkwardly distances herself from me at the playground or the park. I would like to have other mother friends. I like having those conversations in the park. It's nice to know that I am not alone, and that the odd things Stella does are, in fact, normal.

I am busy with work and with Stella, but I am still lonely at this time in my life. At work, I have to be hard, bulletproof, always on my guard. With Stella, I am always Mummy. I sometimes cry myself to sleep with the loneliness; the want of a good friend.

I want to lift Lottie up. Lottie is a good friend that I have now. I want to help empower her, inspire her to be the best she can be, because she is such a ray of light in a sometimes dark world. I'm not sure that she knows how bright and special she is, and I wish that she did. But, old women's wishes are thin on the wind and have little currency in the ears of anyone who would listen.

She has seemed brighter, lately. She is dressing better – no more shapeless, grey sweatshirts and saggy, pilled and ancient jogging bottoms. When she wears a dress, she looks lovely. Perhaps I am old fashioned – I am very definitely antique – but, whatever you wear, I've always thought that you should choose something that does the best it can for your figure, and reflects something of who you are. Your innate special-ness. And she is so very special. Lottie thinks I am inspirational. A trailblazer. The truth is that making your own decisions, based on the truth of who you are, is good for you. But, it isn't always easy. That is what I would like to tell Lottie, but I don't want to discourage her. I don't want her to know how hard life can be. I want to protect her, but I fear that I cannot protect her from what life really is. Perhaps, though, I can be her friend, and that is something.

But there is the one thing that I still cannot tell her, and if I can never tell her, will it make me a bad friend? Will I be a friend to her at all if I cannot or do not tell her this truth, which looms so large in both of our lives? I don't know if I can do it, and time grows ever shorter.

I know my days here are short, and the secret presses more and more heavily on me as each day passes. I knew that when Lottie arrived, I was being given an opportunity. A final chance to remove that weight from my heart that I had never dared hope would arrive.

But, now that it is here, I find myself holding on to that weight like a drowning woman holding a life-preserver. I suppose I have grown so very used to its weight, over the years. And I fear what will happen if I let go.

24

———

'And this is the mezzanine,' Fred said from above, holding out a hand to steady her as she climbed up the spiral staircase. 'I didn't show it to you last time. Take it slowly; it's safe for two people, but it's still a bit rickety.'

Lottie had been heading back from a walk around the loch and seen Fred through the window at Pageturner's, so she'd gone inside to say hello. Fred, who had been dusting book-shelves when she'd come in, had offered to show her the vintage copies of *Dracula* he'd mentioned at the quiz. The Folio edition had been quite something; Lottie had thought seriously for a minute about buying it, even though she had to be super careful in budgeting at the moment, being a full-time student for a year.

'Okay... wow. Oh, wow! This is amazing!' Lottie exclaimed as she stepped onto to the narrow walkway that comprised an intermediate tier of the shop floor. Where the staircase stopped, an ornate cast iron railing began, circling a thin walkway around the shop walls. Up here, the walls were still lined with books, as they were on the ground floor, but the books up here looked as though they were exclusively vintage.

Rows of leather-bound poetry, history and scientific books

nestled next to each other, some with worn spines, and some surprisingly bright and vivid, with gold lettering on the spine. 'Look! A whole set of Shakespeare. Oh, and look at this map!' Lottie pointed to a large tome that was displayed, open at a double page of South America. In the ocean, illustrations of sea serpents cavorted alongside sailing ships.

'Beautiful, isn't it? I love looking at old maps. You can see all the old names for countries. And, if you look at say, maps of Africa, all the boundary lines are different. Of course, the text in a lot of the old map books is a bit dated, to say the least.' Fred raised an eyebrow. 'But if you can look beyond the uncritical glorification of the British Empire, and the racism, then it's great.'

'Well, I don't think we should ever look beyond racism.' Lottie frowned. 'But yeah, stuff like this is really interesting from a sociological perspective.'

'Of course. I didn't mean to sound flippant.'

'You weren't.' Lottie smiled, and walked around the mezzanine, trailing her fingertips along the top of the iron railing.

'This space was sort of under-used when the previous owners were running the shop, but when Mum took it over she had builders come and put this back to how it was. Look.' Fred reached onto a shelf and took out a book titled *Scenes from Loch Cameron*, flicking to the middle section where there were a number of black and white photos. 'We found this book here, and it's got pictures of the shop from years ago. This was the mezzanine then.' He handed her the open book, and Lottie gazed at the sepia toned picture with interest.

'Isn't it pretty!' She peered at the man in the foreground of the picture. 'Who's that?'

'Yeah. That's Alexander O'Connell. The guy who wrote those diaries I found.' Fred raised an eyebrow.

'Oh, goodness.' Lottie peered at the picture, feeling uncomfortable at being suddenly presented with a picture of the man that had hurt Gretchen and scared and harassed her.

'He looks quite serious. Dashing, a bit, as well. Like Cary Grant,' Fred said.

'If you say so.' Lottie made a face. She would never think that Alexander O'Connell was *dashing*. Not now that she knew what she knew.

'No?' Fred looked at her face and closed the book, obviously picking up on the nonverbal cue that Lottie was uncomfortable. 'I thought it would be good news if working in a bookshop makes women think you're dashing.'

Lottie smiled politely, not quite knowing how to respond. Fred *was* a nice-looking young man – tall and athletic with curly dark hair which was slightly unruly on the top where it was longer. He wore glasses most of the time, but Lottie had noticed his warm hazel eyes. She also hadn't failed to notice his surprisingly muscular forearms, on display today because he'd rolled up the sleeves of his flannel shirt.

You could say that Fred was dashing, but he was also her housemate, and he had a girlfriend. They were friends. Lottie didn't really think of him as a man, in the sense of him being attractive and dashing. Fred was just Fred.

'No, it's not that. I just have... some knowledge about that man that... isn't very positive,' she said, not wanting to disclose any of Gretchen's secrets, but wanting to explain her reaction. 'Gretchen was really upset when I showed her his notebooks. And I can understand why, now.'

'Oh. I'm sorry. I didn't know.' Fred's forehead crinkled in concern. 'Did you want to tell me anything more about that, or should I change the subject?' he asked.

'Let's change the subject?' she suggested.

'Okay. What's your favourite part in *Dracula*?' he asked. 'Also, may I say, it's such a strange thing to meet someone else who loves that book as much as I do.'

'I know. People just know the films but they don't realise that the book is an epistolary novel,' Lottie said, remembering that they had discussed this fact briefly at the quiz. 'That's probably my favourite thing about it. I love letters and diaries telling a story. And Lucy's character, though she gets the standard bad treatment for being a sexual woman with needs.'

'Death. Right,' Fred chuckled. 'She definitely is more of an interesting character than Mina. At one point I think she says something about wanting to marry all three guys. Good on her.'

'*Why can't they let a girl marry three men, or as many as want her, and save all this trouble?*' Lottie quoted one of her favourite lines from the novel, chuckling, despite her earlier shock of seeing Alexander's photo. 'I always remember that, too. You sort of feel that Lucy would have been better off in modern times. She could have dated all three men. I mean, she did, really, but then she had to choose one to marry. She wouldn't have had that trouble now.' Still, this thought reminded Lottie of Tristan and his desire for an open relationship. She could recognise that, probably, there would be people out there doing a much better job of it than he had – much more ethical and caring – but the thought of dating three people at once, and knowing perhaps that all of your partners were seeing other people seemed a little much at best, and heartbreaking at worst.

They made their way back down to the ground floor.

'I can't believe you're such a Lucy fan. It was enough of a great thing about Dracula in the first place.' Fred touched her arm playfully, and, out of nowhere, Lottie felt a zing of electricity pass between them. Her eyes widened and her lips parted.

She stared up into Fred's brown eyes, not knowing what to say. But her body knew what it wanted, in that moment: to melt into his. To wrap her arms around his neck and kiss those full lips.

Fred cleared his throat and stepped backwards, letting his

hand drop to his side. It was as if an electrical current had been cut off.

'Hmm. Well, I better get back to it,' he muttered, looking away as the door opened and a tall, glamorous woman walked in, her heels clicking on the vintage parquet flooring of the shop. She was wearing high waisted jeans under long dark brown boots that looked expensive, a cream colour jumper with a high neck and her jet-black hair was tied up in a perfect ponytail.

Lottie wished she ever looked as effortlessly put together. She also didn't know what to make of the moment between her and Fred that had just happened.

'Okay, I'll have a look round and see if there's something I fancy. I'm sure there's something I'd like,' she said, her tone deliberately light and carefree. Lottie didn't want Fred to know that that little moment between them had shaken her so much. Not in a bad way, either.

'Twenty per cent discount for housemates.' Fred ran a hand through his tousled hair and grinned at her sheepishly. Lottie swallowed, watching the edge of his mouth as it pulled into quite a sexy grin. *Damn.*

'Sure. Thanks.' Lottie turned away, trying to collect herself. What had just happened?

'Not that I'm at all suggesting it's a slow day, sales-wise. Hey, Zelda.' Lottie could hear Fred chattering in his friendly way to the woman who had just walked in. She picked up a book on the table and pretended to look at it.

'Hey, Fred. I can help with that. It's Hal's birthday. What can you recommend?' she asked, tucking an equally expensive-looking handbag under her arm.

'Oh, amazing. I was just showing Lottie some of the vintage books for sale upstairs. He might like some of those,' Fred suggested. 'Do go up and have a browse. Or, alternatively, Faber have some great new music biographies. Or some cool new Folio Editions are out, over there.' He pointed to a shelf of hardback books in slipcases with gold foil on the spines and other elaborate illustrations and finishes.

'Thanks, Fred. Lifesaver,' she trilled. Zelda turned to Lottie. 'It's Lottie, isn't it?' she asked, unexpectedly.

'Err. Yes?' Lottie thought she would have remembered this glamorous American, but she was pretty sure they hadn't met before.

'Sorry. Didn't mean to give you crazy lady vibes, interrupting.' She held out her hand, smiling broadly. 'I'm Zelda Hicks? I'm a friend of Gretch. Gretchen Ross.'

'Oh. Hello.' Lottie shook Zelda's hand. 'Nice to meet you. Yes, I'm interviewing Gretchen for my university project. How do you know her?'

'We go back,' the woman said, in what Lottie thought was a broad New York accent. 'I came here for work and stayed at her cottage. I was doing a photo shoot for a newspaper I was working for at the time and we became friends. And then Hal and I fell in love and that was kinda all she wrote,' Zelda chuckled. 'I just got into town a few days ago and visited Gretch yesterday. She was telling me all about how she's loving telling her new friend her life story.'

'I'm loving hearing it,' Lottie said.

'Awesome. You should come up to the castle for afternoon tea someday, if you want to.' Zelda rummaged in her bag and handed Lottie a business card. 'I know, it's super lame and very *American Psycho*, but I still have a business card. That's my number. You should give me a call, we can chat about Gretch. I'm kinda worried about her. She seems frail.'

'Oh... all right. Thanks!' Lottie took the card. 'I don't think I've ever been invited to a castle for afternoon tea before. And, yes, I thought maybe she seemed frail, but you've known her longer than me.'

'She's definitely changed since I went to the States. And I haven't been away that long. About six weeks.' Zelda frowned.

'But, y'know, she's in her eighties now. I know this kind stuff is gonna happen, it's just that I love her. She's like family.'

'I get that.' Lottie thought of her grandparents, who weren't as elderly as Gretchen but were definitely slowing down. 'Of course you care.'

'Fred, come up for tea with Lottie, if you want. Are you an item?' Zelda asked, guilelessly. Lottie blushed. Had Zelda picked up on the moment they had just had?

'Oh, no! We just live together. As housemates,' she added, hastily.

'Oh! Okay. You just seemed... I dunno. I assumed. My bad.' Zelda shrugged. 'Come up anyway, Fred. Hal likes a chance to talk about books and we drink so much tea we could do with some kind of formal reason to do it. Plus, Anna, the house-keeper, makes these incredible scones if we tell her we're having visitors.'

'Ha. Well, I'd love to, if that's okay with Lottie. And you and Hal.' Fred looked pleased.

'Okay... when?' Lottie asked, feeling a little discombobu-lated because of what had just happened between her and Fred, but rationalising that it was nothing. *It was NOTHING*, she scolded herself. *Stop being so extra.*

'Tomorrow afternoon suits us, if that works for you,' Zelda suggested.

'Sure. I can close the shop for a couple of hours,' Fred said. 'Lottie?'

'Ummm... Sure, I can do that. I'm going to see Gretchen in the morning but I don't ever stay longer than a couple of hours.' Lottie tried to sound casual.

'Awesome. Come up at two, then.' Zelda nodded. 'Okay. I'm gonna go up to the mezzanine, Fred, but if I get my boot caught in the steps, you need to come and rescue me. It happened once before.'

'Oh. Okay.' Fred nodded, seriously. 'I'm here if you need me.'

Zelda inched her way up the ruinous metal steps and soon they heard her pottering along the upper level of the shop.

'Well, I guess that means we're going for afternoon tea at the castle.' Fred appeared behind Lottie and murmured in a low voice. She jumped, her heart pounding. Fred's low voice in her ear also wasn't helping. *Good lord,* she thought. *What is going on?*

'Does that mean we're part of some kind of Loch Cameron high society now?' Lottie whispered back, with a giggle.

'Maybe. Glad my grandma taught me bridge, now. You never know what we'll end up doing up there.'

'Maybe they're part of a cult. Wellness or yoga or something.' Lottie lowered her tone to be as conspiratorial as his.

'Maybe. Not sure where the scones fit in.' Fred looked thoughtful. 'So, I'll drive us up there, if you like? Should be fun.'

'Okay.' Lottie felt a warm excitement in the pit of her stomach. It felt like a treat, being invited to spend time at the castle which was usually only open to visitors at certain times. Lottie was also keen to learn more about Gretchen from Zelda: she knew they were close. But, if she was being completely honest, it was the thought of spending more time with Fred which was top of that list, even though she absolutely knew it shouldn't be. Fred had a girlfriend, and he was just being nice. He absolutely wasn't flirting with her.

Was he?

25

———

'Ah, yes. The bookshop in the village. It's been there for many years.' Gretchen nodded. 'Nice little place, isn't it? I haven't been in for a while. Not since the new owners took over.'

'It's lovely. My housemate Fred works there. His mum bought it as a retirement project, he says.' Lottie put down her bag next to her usual chair. She had come in and called out *hello* to Gretchen, who was lying on her bed as usual, filled up the kettle and put it on to boil. She had been chattering about the bookshop as she'd gone about her duties that were now second nature: put biscuits on a plate, set out the teacups and saucers on a tray.

She'd told Gretchen about the cute little mezzanine, about looking at the lovely edition of *Dracula*, one of her favourite books, and about Zelda popping in. But she hadn't mentioned anything about the awkward, chemistry-filled moment with Fred.

Because it was nothing, she scolded herself. What would there be to say to Gretchen? He had touched her arm. And Lottie had reacted like some kind of pathetic, sex-starved, atten-tion-hungry, desperate-for-human-contact freak.

'Oh, I see! Loch Cameron's such a small world,' Gretchen chuckled. 'Last time I went in, Ryan O'Connell was working there. Of course, he was a bit of a bad lad, as it turned out. Still, he was always polite to me.' She looked like she was going to say something more, and then shook her head.

'What?' Lottie asked.

'Oh, nothing. I just have a bit of... history with the shop. You know. Because of Alexander,' Gretchen said, quietly.

'Oh, no! Gretchen, I'm so sorry. It's thoughtless of me to mention it. You should have told me to shut up.' Lottie could have kicked herself, but Gretchen patted her hand affectionately.

'Don't be silly, dear. I lived in Loch Cameron for a long time after Alex, and I went in the shop all the time. I like books, so, after a while, it seemed daft not to go in.'

'How long did it take you to go back?' Lottie asked, gently. Gretchen shrugged and looked uncomfortable.

'I don't know, dear. When I came back to Loch Cameron I didn't know that he had left the shop. When I found out he'd gone, I still didn't go near it for a good year or so, just on the off chance that he might crop up again when he felt like it. But he never did. I would take Stella in to choose books. Alexander's family owned it for a long time, though, because Ryan was his nephew and he was just there a couple of years back. Then they sold it to your friend's mother, as you say.'

'That's right.'

'When you met Alexander – before the bad things happened. What was he like?' Lottie asked, knowing that it was a difficult question. But, she thought that she and Gretchen had talked about enough difficult things so far that it was at least okay to ask. 'I mean. What attracted you to him in the first place? I worry about whether I'm just always attracted to bad men. That there's some bad programming in me.' Lottie thought about her dad, leaving that day, and about

Tristan and the way he had left her. It couldn't be a coincidence.

'It was all a long time ago.' Gretchen stared at the corner of her room, looking slightly unfocused. Lottie had noticed her do that a lot recently, and wondered if her eyes were bothering her.

'Well, we had books in common, of course. That was how we got to know each other at first. I was always going in there, asking for books that had just come out. He'd order them for me. I went in there more than I really needed to, because I liked him, but he took ages to catch on. You know what men are like.'

'Not really,' Lottie confessed. 'I don't think I understand them at all.'

'Oh, dear. There's not much to know. If they ever do anything you don't understand, think of the most basic reason they could have done it, and that will be why. Most of the time men don't think about things in any great detail. Not like us.'

Lottie thought about Callum. Though he'd asked her out at the quiz night and taken her number, she hadn't heard from him, and it was bothering her. Had he had second thoughts? Was asking her out just a prank? Did he not find her attractive after all?

Initially, Callum's attention had made her feel *chosen*. Lottie wasn't really used to having men pay her attention, and the last time that one had, it had ended badly. Yet, the sensation of being noticed, of Callum complimenting her and asking her out, had felt good. If she was honest, she wanted more of it. It was nice, being flirted with. She didn't really think that the thing that had happened in the shop with Fred was flirting in the same way, but it had sort of been a moment, and it had been nice, if a little confusing.

Now that she hadn't heard any more from Callum, Lottie's anxiety had started to churn.

She thought of mentioning it to Gretchen, but she felt shy. Gretchen would probably think she was being silly.

'What was he like? Alexander?' she prompted Gretchen.

'Oh, handsome.' Gretchen blew out her cheeks and blew a raspberry. 'Don't fall for the handsome ones. That's my advice.'

'It's hard not to, sometimes,' Lottie said, feeling her tummy clench. She took in a deep breath and let it out. It wasn't time to think about Callum or Tristan or even Fred now: she should focus on Gretchen.

'Hm. I know, but they're trouble.' Gretchen played nervously with her glasses, which hung on a beaded string around her neck.

'Not always, surely. What else can you tell me about Alexander?' Lottie probed. She understood if Gretchen didn't want to talk about him, and she wouldn't push, if her friend really didn't want to open up. That was one of the key parts of interviewing anyone, especially elders. You had to just go with their stories as much as you could, and follow them wherever the twists and turns took you. Perhaps with a gentle nudge, every now and again. Yet, Lottie had to admit that she was curious.

'Oh, goodness. He was bookish, obviously. I liked that, and he liked hearing about the books I was working on, the authors, that kind of thing. He was one of those old school, stiff upper lip chaps,' Gretchen said, slowly. There was a pause.

'So, were you friends at first?'

'Yes, I suppose so. I was a customer for a long time. I'd come in when I was back from Edinburgh, visiting the folks. We got chatting a few times and he asked me out for a drink. Came to Edinburgh to take me out. I remember being impressed by that at the time.' She rolled her eyes and gave a snort. 'But, then, I was easily impressed when I was young.'

'You never really know people. Especially in those early days,' Lottie said, thinking about Tristan again. And, thinking that she really didn't know Callum at all, either. What if he was equally as bad as Tristan? What if her pattern was still alive and well?

'No, indeed.' Gretchen tapped her fingertips on the table next to her: she was sitting up in bed, wearing a blue knitted bedjacket around her shoulders, and her long grey hair was twisted up into a bun. She was wearing her glasses, as she often did, but now, she took them off, rubbed her eyes and closed them for a moment. 'Still. He wasn't right for me. I saw that in the end, albeit a little too late.'

'You always knew your own mind,' Lottie said. 'I wish I did.'

'Don't you? Of course you do.' Gretchen frowned. 'You're an intelligent woman. You're studying for your Master's degree! What is it, dear? You're mulling something over, I can tell. I'm happy to listen.'

'Oh, it's nothing,' Lottie began, and then stopped herself. It wasn't nothing. Her breakup with Tristan was still bothering her, and she'd never really told anyone about it. And, now, Callum's silence was bothering her more than it should.

'Well, actually. There is something.' Lottie let out a long sigh. 'I had a nasty breakup with someone and then something happened just recently, and both things have just made me feel like... I'm not enough for anyone. It's hard, being rejected.'

'Dear! Who would reject a lovely girl like you?' Gretchen took Lottie's hand. 'You must understand that you are more than enough. If someone decided that they didn't want to be with you, what they were saying was that perhaps you were too much for them, too good for them. Quite often, inferior men reject good women, because they just can't cope with us.' Gretchen tutted. 'Of course, they break our hearts at the time. Because we've fallen for them. Wrongly, we assign them much better qualities in our minds and our hearts than they really have, because we're trusting and loving people.'

'Well, that's one way to look at it,' Lottie mused. 'His name was Tristan. He sort of... swept me off my feet. He said he loved me. We had the most magical, beautiful moments together. We both loved being out in nature, so we'd go exploring – waterfalls, hiking up hills, finding natural springs, stone circles. We went to some of the most beautiful places I've ever been – in Scotland, Wales, Cornwall, even. We were always away, camping, staying in little holiday cottages, having adventures. I've never had that kind of relationship before. It was like a dream. And he was...' Lottie stopped herself, because her throat had tightened, and it was difficult to get the words out. 'He was so beautiful, Gretchen. I've never known anyone like him. I just used to look at him when we were walking along and feel so blessed to be with him. As corny as that sounds.'

'Ah. Yes. It's hard when they're gorgeous.' Gretchen nodded.

'Yes. I mean, I haven't had a lot of boyfriends anyway. But he really was. And at the risk of sounding even more corny, it wasn't even just a physical thing. I thought he had a beautiful soul.' Lottie let out a snort. 'I'm disgusted with myself for saying that out loud.'

'Darling. Don't ever be ashamed of what you felt for someone. Especially if it's coming from a place of love,' Gretchen began, slowly. 'What happened, after all the magical times?'

'He ended it with me. He was seeing another girl – we had an open relationship. He said he liked me a lot more when I didn't love him so much, and that she was more *chill* than me. He thought I wanted too much from him.'

'Oh, I see. One of those.' Gretchen rolled her eyes. 'Avoidants. Traumatised as children, and as adults they don't want to let anyone close to them because they're terrified of being hurt again. In doing so, they'll push you away, and never let themselves truly open up to anyone.'

'Oh. Did you date someone like that?'

'Yes. Lovely young man, but he was just the same. The first inkling that we were getting close, he ran for the hills. What was his name, now? Benedict, yes. That was it. Such a shame. He, too, was a beauty. Perhaps there's something in that. The really gorgeous ones are all emotionally unavailable.' Gretchen *hmph*ed. 'And I remember my assistant Andrew talking about this too. He had terrible trouble meeting someone. Then he found his long-term partner, but it took years.'

'Well, I think I've given up on dating,' Lottie said. 'This guy, Callum, asked me out recently. I gave him my number and he hasn't even bothered to call me.'

'Oh. Amateur.' Gretchen tsked. 'I hate that sort of thing. But, again, he's not worth your attention, sweetie. A real man would have called. A real man would recognise what a hot little ticket you were.'

'Gretchen!' Lottie laughed, despite herself. It was actually helping her anxiety over Callum, talking to Gretchen.

'Ha. I've learnt the terminology from social media now, dear. There's no stopping me.' Gretchen yawned. 'Now, dear, I think I need a nap. But, promise me one thing.'

'Of course. Anything.'

'Right. Promise me that you'll say to yourself in the mirror, every day, *I am more than enough for anyone. I am lovely, I am beautiful, I am talented.*'

'Oh. Really? I'd feel a little uncomfortable, saying that.' Lottie blushed. 'I'm not beautiful.'

'Yes, you are,' Gretchen insisted. 'Are you going to tell me I'm wrong? I'm never wrong.'

'No, but—'

'Exactly. You said you'd promise me anything.'

'I know,' Lottie acquiesced, reluctantly.

'*I am more than enough for anyone. I am lovely, I am beautiful, I am talented,*' Gretchen repeated. 'Now, you say it.'

'I am more than enough for anyone. I am lovely, I am beautiful, I am talented,' Lottie repeated, feeling embarrassed.

'Good. And remember. Avoidants and amateurs. You

deserve someone who will worship you, Lottie Fox. And as soon as you start believing in yourself as a beautiful, powerful woman, believe me, one will appear. They will hear your siren call.'

'All right. I don't quite believe it, but I believe in you, Gretchen,' Lottie sighed.

'You should, dear. I've got good instincts, for people and for books. Remember that. And, because I know you're thinking it, you *are* a beauty. I know that you don't think you are. But, both this Callum and this Tristan saw it, and I can see it too. Your golden hair and your gorgeous face are absolutely beautiful. If they were bad to you, it wasn't because of your looks. It was because they are scared little boys. And you are a goddess of a woman. If only you knew it.' Gretchen held both of Lottie's hands as she said this: her tone was serious. Their eyes met and Lottie felt as though Gretchen wanted to say more, but she just pressed Lottie's palms firmly, a light of zeal in her eyes. 'Promise me that you will believe that.'

'I promise, Gretchen. I'll try,' Lottie replied.

'You can do better than that,' Gretchen insisted. 'The only way for you to escape the cycle of these bad men is believing in yourself. Believe you are a queen, and you will be treated like one. I'm only saying this because I care, dear Lottie.' Gretchen wiped a tear from her eye. 'Because I care more than you know.'

26

'Come in, come in. Tea's waiting on the terrace.' Zelda Hicks stood in the grand stone entry of Loch Cameron Castle, her arms outstretched in welcome. She planted a kiss on Lottie's cheek and then on Fred's. 'Look at the weather, too! Sunny! The Celtic gods are smiling on us, I guess.'

'It's a beautiful day,' Lottie agreed. 'Thanks for inviting us! Fred took ages to get ready,' she teased her housemate, who had in fact agonised about whether to wear just a shirt, or a shirt and a jacket to the castle. Lottie had assured him that just a shirt was fine; it wasn't a formal event, even though they were going to a castle.

'I did not! I was ready before you!' Fred protested with a grin.

In fact, Fred looked very handsome today, in a crisp white shirt and dark jeans. When he'd walked into the kitchen at home earlier, fastening the cufflinks on his shirt, Lottie had done a subtle double take. She'd pretended that she hadn't, of course, but she couldn't help but notice his soft brown eyes, tousled brown hair and what looked like a surprisingly well-toned body under the shirt. She'd noticed his muscular forearms when she'd been at the shop the other day, but now she could see that it looked like Fred worked out.

Fred didn't seem like someone who would go to the gym. Lottie wondered what else she didn't know about him.

Lottie had studiously been avoiding making eye contact or doing anything that might have been even mildly construed as flirting since that day at the shop when she and Fred had had that moment of – whatever it was. She didn't even know. She didn't know if Fred had been avoiding her too, but he definitely hadn't been around as much as he usually was, and there had been a couple of nights that she and Celine were watching TV downstairs and Fred had stayed in his room.

'Oh! Ha. Fred, you look gorgeous,' Zelda flirted, and Fred blushed. 'As do you, Lottie, of course. Your hair is so pretty. I've always wanted to be a blonde, but you just can't with black hair.'

'Oh... thank you. I don't know what to say!' Lottie felt the familiar spectre of self-consciousness advancing, but pushed it away. 'I love your outfit. You always seem to look so smart.'

'Bless you. I just try and keep up with Hal, now that he's found tailoring and designer shirts. Lottie, you wouldn't believe it, when I met him, he dressed like someone's nerdy Scottish uncle. But he's such a natural smoke show I still couldn't take my eyes off him,' Zelda said as she led them into the castle and along a wood panelled hallway. 'Then, on one of the first days I met him I was doing a photo shoot here and the male model fell through at the last minute. I asked him to fill in for a wedding picture we were doing, for the castle website? Yeah. I looked up at one point and there he was, in full Highland dress. Jesus, Mary and Joseph.' Zelda crossed herself and stuck her tongue out like a thirsty puppy. 'I think that was it. I've been in love ever since.'

'Wow.' Lottie giggled as Zelda led them into a large, opulent drawing room with a huge, marble-topped inglenook fireplace and luxurious leather sofas and through the open wide glass patio doors at the front of the room.

'Yeah. He's so popular in New York. The girls – and the gays – adore him over there. And the thing is that he absolutely doesn't get how hot he is. Because he's such a sweetheart, and kind of a nerd,' Zelda said as she led them onto the patio, where Hal Cameron stood, with his hands behind his back, surveying the ornamental gardens lined with topiary trees and fragrant herb gardens that shelved away in front of them.

'What's that you're saying about me?' He turned with a smile. 'Hello, there. Lottie, I presume? And I know Fred, of course.' The laird of Loch Cameron shook both their hands enthusiastically.

'Lovely to meet you. And, we were just saying, thank you for the invite. It's a real treat to come for tea,' Lottie said, exchanging a wry look with Zelda.

'She's being polite. I was also bragging about what a hottie you are.' Zelda planted a kiss on Hal's cheek. He gave her a fond look. 'I have no chill. American. I get away with it here.'

'Ye get away wi' murder,' Hal said, affectionately. 'But I'm no' sure Fred an' Lottie want tae hear all aboot me. Please, sit – Anna's made her famous fruit scones an' we've got strawberry jam from the farm, an' clotted cream from one o' the local dairies. Ah love this stuff. Have tae watch it though, otherwise I won't be able to wear all my nice new gear, eh, hen?' He winked at Zelda. 'I'm her project, aye,' he said to Fred with a wry grin. 'I'm no' complainin'.'

'Absolutely.' Fred chuckled.

'Wow. The gardens are stunning,' Lottie said, taking a seat and gazing out over the bright bushes of violet and orange rhododendrons, the topiary trees dotted through the gently shelving gardens, and the steps leading down from the terrace, all the way to the loch below. 'Where does that lead to?' She pointed to the right at the bottom of the ornamental gardens where a pathway led into a wooded area.

'Ah. There's a private beach down there wi' a stone circle. Through the woodland,' Hal explained, and Lottie noticed that he exchanged a fond look with Zelda.

Lottie found herself feeling envious of Hal and Zelda: they were so obviously in love, they were both beautiful and glamorous and successful and had the perfect life. *What a thing it must be to be inside a relationship like that,* she thought.

'Back in the day, my father an' the laird before him that made the stone circle would let the villagers have their weddin's an' what have ye down there. We can walk down later an' have a look if ye want.'

'Oh, that sounds awesome. Yes, please,' Lottie said enthusiastically.

'So. How do you find Gretchen?' Zelda asked, reaching for a scone. 'She's a superstar, huh.'

'Yes. She is,' Lottie replied.

'I am a little worried about her, like I said,' Zelda continued. 'She's getting older and she doesn't like to accept help for anything. Thing is with Gretchen is that you can't make her do anything she doesn't want to.'

'What d'you want her tae do, hen?' Hal asked. 'She's in the care home, so she's bein' looked after. She's an auld woman. There isnae much ye can do aboot that.'

'No, I know that.' Zelda poured tea for everyone from a silver teapot in a knitted cosy. 'But I'm concerned about her eyesight and I told her she needs to ask the doctors there to check her out, but she says she doesn't want to bother them. I guess, because I love her – I think of her as family, you know? – if there was something wrong, I'd want her to see the best specialists that money could buy. I want her to stay with us for as long as she can.' Zelda's voice broke, and Hal leaned across the table and took her hand.

'I know ye love her, hen. I love Gretchen too. An' if she wants or needs anythin' then we'll be there. I've told ye that. But ye can lead a horse to water an' ye can't make it drink, as they say.' He patted her hand gently.

'I know. It's tough, though. She's getting really old now.' Zelda sighed. 'Sorry, guys. I just really care about Gretch.'

'Of course. That's understandable. Like you said, you've got a close bond,' Lottie said.

'You know, in the years since I lived at the cottage on Queen's Point, there's been a few different women that have stayed there and got their lives together. And, Gretchen helped every one of us,' Zelda mused. 'I sometimes think that might be because something was missing in her life. She had – still has – so much love to give, and I guess, apart from Stella, she never really had anyone to love. She's always been a bit of a lone wolf.'

'She's told me about Stella.' Lottie nodded, thinking about the rest of Gretchen's story and the fact that she hadn't even trusted Zelda with the truth about her baby with Alex.

'I remember Stella.' Fred looked sad. 'She was awesome. She worked at the library, while it was still open, and she was the kindest person. When I was a kid, I'd go along to the library and she'd help me choose books. When she died it was so sudden. Such a tragedy.'

'Yeah. I never knew Stella, but I know what happened, and you're right, Fred. It was a tragedy. And, I think Gretch has all this mothering in her, with nowhere to go. And that's why she wanted to help out the girls staying at her old cottage. She didn't have to. She moved into the care home pretty much when I got to Loch Cameron, but she wanted to stay the person who managed the lets for the cottage. And Hal let her, because he knew that it meant something to her.' Zelda squeezed Hal's hand. 'You've always been so sweet with her, Hal. I didn't realise it at first but you were always looking out for Gretchen.'

'Well, she's one o' the flock, as it were.' Hal shrugged. 'I'd do the same for any o' the community here. I'm the Laird. It's ma responsibility.'

'And we appreciate it,' Fred said. 'I'm sure Gretchen is grateful that you kept her involved with the cottage for as long as she could manage it.'

'Aye, well. I could see it mattered tae her, who lived in that cottage. The Ross family lived there fer years. Generations, actually, just like a lot o' families in Loch Cameron. They were tenants, so they never owned it, but ye live in a hoose long enough an' of course ye think o' it as home whether ye own it or not. An' I knew Gretchen had had it tough, losin' Stella. I lost my Maggie about the same time so I got it, y'know?' He smiled sadly for a moment.

'Maggie?' Lottie asked.

'That was ma first wife,' Hal explained. 'She died a couple years before I met Zelda. Illness.'

'I'm so sorry,' Lottie breathed. 'I had no idea. She was young, then?'

'Far too young. Aye,' Hal sighed. 'But, it meant Gretchen an' I always had a bond. We never spoke about it much but I felt like she understood what I was goin' through after Maggie died, an' vice versa.'

'I see,' Lottie said. 'I feel like I'm understanding more about Gretchen.'

'Aye. Losin' her daughter changed her, I think,' Hal continued. 'It'd change anyone.'

'Totally. But all the more reason for us to look after her.' Zelda sat forward, an intense expression on her face. 'I think we should agree that we'll look out for her. Like a special squad. What d'you think? I mean, I guess what I'm saying, Lottie, is I'd be so appreciative if you could keep me in touch, if anything happens. You know. You're there a lot, right? And I'm often away, these days,' Zelda explained.

'Of course. If I can help, I will.' Lottie nodded. 'You're her friend, more than me, but, sure.'

'Oh, I know that she thinks of you as a friend.' Zelda shook her head. 'So you'll help?'

'Of course.' Lottie spread some cream and jam on a fat white scone, studded with sultanas. 'Happy to.'

'Thanks. I appreciate it.' Zelda's expression lightened. 'Anyway. I'm excited to show you both the stone circle. It's super romantic.' She looked from Lottie to Fred, and then back again.

Fred looked like a deer caught in headlights.

'Oh. Errr... right,' he said, pushing his glasses up on his nose. Lottie also didn't know what to say – it was obvious that she and Fred weren't a couple, so she wondered why Zelda had said it in the first place. Had she noticed their awkward, yet electrical moment in the shop? Had she thought that they were seeing each other, because of it?

'Zelda. Stop it,' Hal chuckled. 'You're makin' them uncomfortable.'

'Oh. Guys. I'm just playing.' Zelda gave Lottie an impish glance.

'I have a girlfriend. She might like to come and see it,' Fred blurted out.

'Oh, do you now?' Zelda raised an eyebrow. 'Is she nicer and prettier than Lottie? Because you two would make a great couple. I thought you were a couple, being brutally honest.'

Well, that answered that question, Lottie thought. Zelda must have seen their moment of connection in the shop and made her assumption based on that. *Thank goodness no one else had been in the shop to see it, then.* Lottie felt mortified.

'No, we aren't... Well, she's... obviously, Lottie is very...' Fred stammered.

'Relax, Fred. I was messing with you.' Zelda grinned. 'I'm sure she's lovely, and Lottie is, of course, gorgeous. It was just the way you suddenly announced it. Like, well done for having a girlfriend, dude?'

'Lottie *is* gorgeous,' Fred said, shyly, and Lottie noticed a blush creep up his neck and onto his cheeks. She could only assume that it was because Zelda was making fun of him a little, and Fred was a gentle soul.

For a moment, Lottie wondered what it would be like to have a boyfriend like Fred. He was so different to Tristan's over-confidence; she'd never been out with anyone as gentle and kind as him.

Well, I guess Helen's a lucky girl, Lottie thought. *But, maybe I can find someone like that for myself. Maybe, one day, I'd get to have a wedding at a stone circle next to Loch Cameron, and be happy for the rest of my days, like Hal and Zelda.*

But, as Lottie's gaze flicked to Fred, she saw that he was looking at her, and there was something in his gaze that wasn't usually there: it wasn't the way he usually looked at her.

But it was exactly like the way he had looked at her in the shop, when he'd put his hand on her arm. When he had been looking at her in the eye and run his hand through his hair, giving her a sexy little grin. Then, he looked away, and the moment was gone.

Lottie is gorgeous, he'd said. Was he just being a good friend in saying that, or was there something else going on?

27

'Wow. This is stunning,' Lottie exclaimed as she walked onto the hidden beach.

They had made their way through woodland to get here, and a little pathway through a series of gates that led from the castle's ornamental gardens down towards the edge of the loch.

'Gorgeous,' Fred said, catching Lottie's eyes and grinning.

'It's so pretty, isn't it?' Zelda beamed. 'The first time I came down here, I couldn't believe it was here. A stone circle! I still love it.' She hugged Hal, who was standing next to her.

'Ma ancestors built it. Seventeenth century. I think it was initially the idea to entertain party guests, maybe, but there's also records of the previous lairds havin' the villagers up here tae do their weddin' vows. We've had some nice celebrations up here in the past years, aye,' Hal explained.

A grass lawn spread out alongside the loch, with the manicured gardens and topiary that Lottie had seen from the caste terrace when having tea, hidden behind a tall stone wall. From this spot, you would never have known that the castle gardens were there at all; instead, a forest of pine led the eye down to a narrow, white-sand beach. Willows dipped their branches into the loch, and a group of standing stones formed a circle on the narrow beach.

Hal made his way over the wet sand and reached out a hand to touch the arrangement of ancient-looking menhirs.

'It feels so magical!' Lottie exclaimed.

'It really is. Fairy tale-esque,' Fred agreed, as they followed Hal to the stones. 'I came here when you had your last May Day party, Hal. It was just beautiful, Lottie.' He turned to her, and Lottie had to return his grin; it was so full of a childlike joy that her heart warmed, too.

'I bet. I would have loved to see that.' Lottie gazed around her.

'Oh, Lottie. You would have loved it,' Zelda sighed. 'The first May Day I came to, there was this just otherworldly feel to it. I genuinely felt as though I'd been transported to the magical land of the Seelie Court. That's the Scottish land of the fairies,' she added. 'There was this lamplit procession through the castle gardens. There was a huge bonfire, fireworks – I was wearing a stunning dress, by the way – then Hal recited poetry, as if I wasn't already putty in his hands. Then, before I knew it, we were walking through the woods in the glittering evening, hand-in-hand. What girl could say no to that?'

'Pretty much no one,' Lottie chuckled. 'It sounds very romantic.'

'Oh, it was.'

'Time was, when the villagers used tae have their weddin's up here, they'd walk through the arch. Like a good luck charm,' Hal added. 'That first May Day party, we actually commemorated one o' Gretchen's ancestors up here. Here, I had their initials carved intae the stone.' Hal pointed out the initials *AM & RM* entwined in Celtic knotwork on one side of one of the menhirs.

'Wow. That's gorgeous. What was the story there? Gretchen hasn't mentioned it,' Lottie asked, curiously.

'Hal, you tell it. I can't remember all the details,' Zelda prompted him. Hal ran his fingers through his tousled hair and nodded.

'Okay. So, Gretchen's great-great-grandmother, Alice McQueen, fell in love wi' a local lad, Richard McKelvie, on a May Day night in 1854. There was a letter, or a diary, I think, wasn't there, hen?' he asked Zelda, who nodded. 'That's how we knew they fell in love. Anyway, Alice and Richard danced through these very stones that night. But then Alice got pregnant. They were nae married, an' Alice's faither didnae approve of Richard, so when he found out, he sent Alice away tae marry another fella up near Loch Awe.'

'Wow.' Lottie wished that she'd thought to put her voice recorder on: this was an unexpected extra part of Gretchen's story that she had no idea about. 'Harsh.'

'Aye. So, Alice married this other fella, and her bairn grew up with him as a faither. Alice had other bairns wi' him, too, I think. Then, many years later, her parents passed and Alice and her family came back tae live at Gretchen's cottage at Queen's Point. Sadly, Richard had died by that time, so they were never reunited. That's why I had their initials carved here in the rock.'

'That's such a thoughtful gesture, Hal,' Fred said. 'I remember that party now, but I must say it all takes on greater significance now that Lottie and Gretchen are so close.'

'It really does, huh,' Zelda mused.

'I think it's important tae remember our ancestors, an' I wanted tae put that story right, at least a little,' Hal said. 'It's always been important to me that the Camerons look after the community here. I know that the fact we own the land is an outdated kinda idea, in a way. At the very least we have a responsibility tae look after the people that live here.'

'That seems fair,' Lottie said. 'I know that Gretchen thinks very highly of you.'

'Ah. She's a wonderful lady.' Hal smiled warmly.

'Since we've been renting out the castle as a wedding desti-nation it's been hugely popular,' Zelda explained. 'And one of the really popular features is the stones. People like to have the ceremony here, just like people did in the old days.'

'Wow. I can imagine that would be beautiful,' Lottie sighed. The idea of her own wedding seemed ridiculously unlikely at this point in her life. She wondered whether she would ever get married; her heart warmed at the thought of doing something so romantic. There had been a time when she would never have believed that was something that would happen for her, but now she found herself thinking *why not? It could happen.*

'There's similar stories about communities in other parts of the UK usin' standin' stones fer ceremonies of different kinds. There's that one in the south where people passed their babies through the hole in the centre of the rock for good health.'

'That's really cool.' Fred, standing next to Lottie, reached past her and laid a hand on one of the menhirs. 'I'd love to do that one day. If I got married.'

Lottie turned her body towards his, instinctively, and met his eyes. Without thinking, she said, 'I'd like that too.'

A moment of heat passed unexpectedly between them. Fred was standing close to her, and Lottie felt a sudden and overpowering desire to be in his arms. He looked so handsome in his white shirt and dark jeans; since they'd been at the castle, Lottie hadn't been able to stop darting little glances in his direc-tion. And, this close, Lottie could catch a little of his aftershave, which smelt good: clean, woody, manly.

Before the moment in the bookshop recently, Lottie had thought of Fred as *just Fred*; her friend and housemate. She hadn't looked at him as a desirable man. But, now, something had changed. Now, Lottie was truly aware of Fred as a man and not just a friend.

Fred looked deep into her eyes for a long moment; there was an unreadable expression there. Lottie gazed up at him; time seemed to stand still. She was very aware of the width of his shoulders and the strength of his arms. And, other than that, she could feel the masculine aura around him, and realised that she was drawn to it.

She wanted him to touch her again. She wanted him to wrap her up in his arms and to rest her head against his chest.

Fred blinked and cleared his throat.

'I mean. I don't have any plans to at the moment. Or for a long time,' he added, quickly. 'I don't know why I said that.'

He stepped away from Lottie, looking uncomfortable. She felt the warmth between them evaporate, and felt silly. It was just a moment; it was the romantic setting, maybe.

Whatever it was, Lottie definitely couldn't be attracted to her housemate. That really wouldn't be a good idea, regardless of how good he looked in a clean white shirt.

Zelda caught her eye and gave her a knowing look. Lottie blushed and looked away.

'Well, I'm ready for another scone,' Zelda said, brightly, and took Lottie's arm. 'Shall we go up?'

'Good idea,' Lottie said, and followed Zelda's lead as they began to walk back up the beach and through the forest.

'What was that, girl?' Zelda asked quietly as they walked up. 'Don't think that I didn't notice something between you and Fred just then.'

'Oh. It was nothing, just a bit of a weird moment,' Lottie said, hoping that she sounded dismissive.

'Hmm. I thought it looked like more than that, but okay.' Zelda shot her a curious look. 'After I saw you at the shop together, I did actually think you were together. He's a nice guy, you know. And he likes you. I can tell.'

At that moment, Lottie's phone notifications dinged. Out of habit, Lottie took the phone out of her pocket and looked at the screen. She had a text from Callum.

Hey, gorgeous. Sorry it's taken me a while to get back to you. I'd love to take you out this weekend if you were free?

Lottie stared at her phone. *I guess it's true, what they say about watched pots,* she thought with incredulity. She'd been waiting for Callum to contact her for over a week now.

When she'd been sitting alone in her room, wanting him to call: nothing. Now that she was busy, having a lovely time at the castle with friends – and talking to Zelda about Fred – *now,* Callum chose the moment to text. As if he knew, somehow, that she wasn't thinking about him at all.

Finally, she thought, frowning. *Better late than never.*

'You okay?' Zelda asked, looking at Lottie's phone, and then at her.

'Oh. Yeah. Fine.' Lottie nodded and put her phone in her pocket. 'I'll reply to that later.'

She considered not replying at all, but, anyway, it would do Callum good to wait for a reply.

'Okayyy. So. Back to you and Fred.' Zelda raised an impish eyebrow. 'I can see it. That's all I'm saying.'

'Zelda. We're just friends. He has a girlfriend!' Lottie hissed. 'He doesn't like me. Not in that way.'

'Well, what do I know?' Zelda shrugged. 'All I'll say is that I can read body language. And when you were both standing next to the stones just now...' she raised an eyebrow. 'Hot.'

'Zelda!' Lottie shushed her. She definitely didn't want Fred to hear this; fortunately, he was ahead, walking with Hal.

'Your secret is safe with me, babe,' Zelda whispered. 'What happens at the stones, stays with the stones.'

Lottie rolled her eyes.

'Zelda. There is nothing going on between me and Fred, and there will never be anything going on between me and Fred,' she repeated.

'Okay, okay.' Zelda held up both hands in a defensive

gesture. 'For the record, though, you guys look great together. I'm totally shipping this.'

Lottie stared at Fred's back, watching the muscles in it move slowly as he walked along. Something *had* changed between them; there had been a moment, just then, something definite, something she was unable to deny, like the first time which she could have written off as just one of those things. Suddenly, Fred wasn't *just Fred* anymore, and she didn't know what to do with that.

28

'The thing is that I suppose I was always very mindful of what happened to unmarried mothers in Loch Cameron.' Gretchen was looking paler than usual today, and Lottie was concerned for her: she resolved to have a word with one of the care home staff on her way out, and let Zelda know that she was right: Gretchen did seem under the weather.

'There were various cautionary tales that used to be whispered about, when I was younger. I still vividly remember being with my mother at the chapel, up on the hill, and her telling me about why there were some women buried up there in a special place, apart from everyone else.' She raised an eyebrow. 'Unhallowed ground.'

'What women?' Lottie frowned.

'Women who had had babies outside of wedlock.' Gretchen rolled her eyes. 'I know. Terrible, isn't it? And don't even get me started on the "old maid" business. At least Liz over at the distillery did something to address that.'

'Did what?' Lottie's phone screen lit up. It was a message from Callum, confirming their date. Lottie's resolve not to reply had weakened after an hour or so of getting back from her castle trip with Fred. She had replied to Callum and said, yes, she was available.

'Oh, of course. I forget you're new to the village. Well, Liz – she actually runs the distillery now with her husband, she really saved that business, let me tell you – she saw these gravestones up at the chapel that just said OLD MAID on them. And she was rightly appalled, that was what these poor women were being remembered for. Their marital status and lack of children. So, she chose three of those women, and *me*, if you can believe it,' Gretchen chuckled, 'to name four new whiskies after. She did a wonderful job of researching our life histories and publicising them, all in a bid to remember some lost women's histories. It was marvellous.'

'That's super cool. So, there's a whisky named after you?'

'Yes, indeed. The Gretchen. It's rather smoky, and, some would say, bitter, but I rather like it. I got a few free bottles for being the poster girl. And the only living one, at that.'

'Ha. Gretchen, you're so awesome.' Lottie shook her head. 'I want to be you when I grow up.'

'Oh, don't wish your life away, dear,' Gretchen tutted. 'But what I was telling you about was this horrible stigma I grew up with, about being an unmarried mother. It was always seen as something so terrible. There was this one story, which I remembered from childhood, and then, funnily enough, Liz chose that same woman that it was about to be another one of the four old maids. Evelyn McCallister.'

'And what happened to Evelyn?' Lottie asked.

'Well, you know, when I heard the story as a young woman, I didn't hear all of it. That's the first thing to say. Often, when we demonise women in these gossipy stories, we leave the woman's side of the story out.

'Anyway. As my mother told it to me, there was a girl in the village who was a disrespectful, wilful little miss, who got pregnant out of wedlock, and brought shame on her poor family.

Her poor father had been off fighting in the war – this was World War One – and when he came home, he was a sight to behold. Half dead, flea bitten, feet half rotted off. You can imagine the kind of thing. I don't doubt that was true.' Gretchen stopped talking for a moment to cough; Lottie watched, concernedly.

'Are you all right, Gretchen?' she asked, gently.

'Fine. This medicine disagrees with me.' Gretchen made a dismissive gesture.

'Anyway, this fellow was the Master Distiller up at the distillery at the time, and Evelyn, his daughter, had been holding the fort while he was away.'

'As the distiller? What is that, exactly?' Lottie asked.

'Yes. It's the overseer of the whole distillation process, basically. It's a very skilled job, and she was then – and I believe still is – the only woman to have held that job up at Loch Cameron Distillery.' Gretchen nodded. 'Now, Evelyn actually did that job for many years. She wasn't just a stand-in for her father. But, the story my mother told me was all about how wicked little Evelyn had got herself knocked up and brought shame on her poor father who had been away risking life and limb in the trenches. And, then, she was sent away to have the baby, and had to give it up for adoption. And that was very much presented as just what had to happen. Her baby was taken away, because who would trust such a wicked, wilful miss as that?' Gretchen hissed. 'You know, even to this day, it makes me angry.'

'I can see that. And I get it. It's a horrible story.'

'Yes, it is. Especially when you know the truth, which is that, of course, young Evelyn wasn't wicked and wilful. She was taken advantage of by her boss, the owner of the distillery at the time – actually, the current owner's ancestor. She was just a naïve girl, and he was a predatory older man. Makes your skin crawl.'

'Ugh. Poor Evelyn.' Lottie grimaced.

'Indeed. Imagine. And, imagine what it was like, growing up, listening to these cautionary tales about supposedly evil girls – not even women, girls – and believing that you were in some way wrong and evil by nature, just like them.'

'That's awful. It still happens, too. With the media. You see it in the news sometimes, about how girls who have been the victims of sexual abuse or harassment are judged for what they were wearing at the time, or for their behaviour,' Lottie said, thinking about all the times she'd read that kind of story in the newspaper or seen it on TV, and felt even more self-conscious about her body, and vulnerable about being a woman.

'Exactly. When I grew up and started thinking for myself, I realised what nonsense it all was. I knew that it was wrong, that those women were kept apart in the graveyard, as if they were unclean. I knew that story about poor Evelyn was probably rubbish, and then, when the Old Maids thing happened, I realised who she was and that I really had heard the wrong story, all those years. And I knew that it wasn't wrong of me to adopt Stella on my own, and I'll always be glad I did.' Gretchen finished her story with a sigh. 'Ah, but I do miss her. My darling little girl. It won't be too long before I join her, though. Some days I think about that, and it makes me glad.'

'Gretchen! You'll be here for a lot longer! Don't say that!' Lottie exclaimed, taking Gretchen's gnarled hand. But Gretchen just smiled tiredly, closing her eyes.

'Nobody lives forever, darling,' she said. 'And I've had a long and very good life. I miss Stella. It brings me comfort to think that I'll join her, wherever she is. One day.'

Lottie didn't know what to say, so she held Gretchen's hand.

'You know, Lottie,' Gretchen said, dreamily, as if she was half asleep. 'Sometimes I hear her, talking to me. Do you think that's possible? Like she's an angel, keeping me company, until I can be with her?'

'Of course,' Lottie replied, softly, feeling her eyes brim with sudden tears. Suddenly, she realised that Zelda was right to be concerned. Gretchen seemed preoccupied – not herself.

'My angel,' Gretchen said. She kept her eyes closed, and Lottie sensed that she had dozed off. She sat quietly, holding Gretchen's hand for a while, and then, sensing that Gretchen would be asleep, she got up quietly and left the room.

As she walked down the corridor, Lottie couldn't shake a sense of unease about what Gretchen had said. Of course, being in her eighties meant that Gretchen was elderly and frail, and, while some people might carry on into their nineties or even to a hundred, many didn't. Gretchen was right: she had already had a long and enjoyable life. But, still, the idea that she might pass away upset Lottie. She felt like she'd found a good friend.

In Reception, Lottie waved at Kimberley, who she remembered from her introduction to the care home.

'Hi, Lottie. How's the project going?' Kimberley came over, rubbing some sanitiser on her hands.

'Good, thanks. Listen, I wanted to ask you about Gretchen. Does she seem okay to you? I was just with her and she was kind of talking about... you know. The end,' Lottie lowered her voice.

'Oh. Well, she's got a check-up due next week, so we can see what's going on then,' Kimberley said, looking at some notes on a clipboard. 'But I'd say, try not to worry. It's normal for people of their age to get a little vague sometimes, or to think about their loved ones that have passed on. It's part of that stage of life.'

'Her friend Zelda asked me to keep an eye on her. I guess I was just wondering if there was anything we should know. If that's possible,' Lottie said.

'As far as we know, Gretchen Ross is as healthy as she can be.' Kimberley held up her hands. 'She's got angina and arthritis, like many of our residents, but of all of them, Gretchen's one of the livelier ones, which I'm sure you've noticed.' Kimberley smiled. 'We'll check her over and of course we'll let you and Zelda know if there's anything to be concerned about. Okay?'

'Okay.' Lottie was somewhat reassured. 'Thanks, Kimberley.'

'Not at all. I can see that you care,' Kimberley replied, kindly. 'That's what we're here for. Give me a heads up again if you're concerned.'

'All right. Thanks.' As she walked out to her car, Lottie still felt anxious about Gretchen, but she also felt glad that she'd been recording her new friend's life stories: it felt right, whatever happened next.

29

———

Lottie walked downstairs feeling self-conscious in the outfit she'd chosen for her date with Callum. After he'd admired her in the wrap dress, she'd bought another online and it had arrived yesterday. This one was a dusky pink with small black polka dots: it was knee length and the crossover part of the wrap wasn't too low, so she didn't feel like she'd be pulling at it self-consciously all evening. The material was a lovely, thick, silky stretch jersey and when she'd put it on and curled her hair, she had to admit she felt really pretty.

Lottie was trying to adopt a more "Gretchen" attitude towards herself, remembering all the pep talks she'd been given about her looks. Before she came downstairs, she'd looked at herself in the mirror in her room.

'I am more than enough for anyone. I am lovely, I am beautiful, I am talented,' she'd told herself, looking at herself in the eye, just like Gretchen had told her to. She felt silly, saying it out loud; paranoid that Fred would hear her, even though she knew he was downstairs and Celine was out with her bird-watching club. 'I am lovely, I am beautiful, I am talented,' she repeated, trying to believe it.

'Oh wow!' Fred looked up from the sofa; he was watching TV and eating pizza. 'You look amazing. Glamour girl from the movies vibes.'

'Thanks. It's new.' Lottie did a very self-conscious twirl, and then felt embarrassed. 'I'm going on a date with Callum,' she added. Ever since that day at the castle, she'd been slightly avoiding Fred; she didn't know what to do in his presence. She felt awkward around him, now that she had started thinking of him differently. As a man, not just a friend. Now, standing in front of Fred in her new dress, she found that she both wanted him to see her as a woman, and also worried about the same thing. They were supposed to be friends. She was being silly to think about anything else.

'Oh. Where's he taking you?' Fred frowned slightly, and then his smile returned. Lottie wondered why the mention of Callum had changed his expression – wasn't Callum his friend? Fred had been the one that had introduced them in the first place, and they'd seemed friendly at the quiz.

'We're going to this place a few villages over. He says it's got crazy golf and AR darts and axe-throwing.' Lottie hadn't been sure about the axe-throwing part, but when Callum had texted and suggested it, she'd written *sure, sounds good!* She had done her mantra, but she still wanted Callum to like her. Axe-throwing wouldn't necessarily have been her choice, but surely, it was better to be agreeable on a first date.

For a moment, Lottie was suddenly reminded of that day when she'd hung onto her Daddy's trouser leg and begged him not to go. The sudden wave of emotion hit her, making her tummy clench again. A terrible emptiness filled her chest; a terrible loneliness. *Don't make a fuss, or Daddy might not come back at all.*

You had to be agreeable, otherwise people left and never came back. These thoughts about her dad always crept up on her when she was feeling her most vulnerable.

'Well, I'm sure you'll have a brilliant time,' Fred said. Was she imagining a note of something off in his voice? 'I've got a big night in with a pizza.'

'Looks yummy.' Lottie sat down beside him; her stomach growled. She wasn't sure if it was hunger or anxiety.

'Have some, if you want.' Fred pointed to the box on the table. 'It's too much for me anyway.'

'Thanks.' She sat down. Lottie looked at the time on her phone: Callum was fifteen minutes late.

'That's for you, by the way.' Fred pointed offhandedly to a carrier bag on the kitchen table.

'What is it? she asked, curiously. 'Oh!' When she saw what was inside, she stopped dead.

'Fred. Is this... from you?' she asked, holding up the Folio edition of *Dracula* in her hands. It was the same one Fred had shown her in Pageturner's – the one she'd wanted, and hadn't been able to afford.

'Staff discount is large.' He shrugged.

'Fred! You didn't have to... it's still expensive...' Lottie was flabbergasted. 'It's not my birthday, or anything.'

'I know. I just thought, no one else in Loch Cameron is ever going to buy it. It's likely just going to sit on the shelf, slowly decomposing. You might as well enjoy it.' He was being tremendously self-effacing, Lottie knew, but she could also see a twinkle of amusement in his eyes.

'Fred, this is... it's very kind of you, but I don't know if I can accept it,' she said. She was confused about why Fred had bought her this present at all; it was so thoughtful and generous.

'Of course you can. I'd just like someone to enjoy the book, that's all,' he said. 'I like to give people books I know they'll enjoy. We're a bookshop, sure, but sometimes I just think a certain book belongs with someone. This one belonged with you. It's not a big deal.'

'Well... if you put it like that, then, okay. It's very thought-ful, Fred. I don't quite know what to say.'

'Say, you'll read it.' Fred smiled.

'I'll read it.' She returned his smile. 'This is so nice. I don't think anyone has ever given me a surprise present like this before.' Lottie's heart felt soft and melty for a moment.

'It's nothing,' he repeated, but he looked pleased.

'So, how's Helen?' she asked, also feeling a little uncomfortable that Fred, a man with a girlfriend, was giving her thoughtful gifts. Yet, her thoughts returned to what Zelda had said, up at the castle: did Fred like her, more than being a friend and housemate?

'Oh. All right. I haven't seen that much of her recently, she's been busy at work.' Fred shrugged. Lottie didn't want to be rude and ask too much about their relationship, but she'd only met Helen that one time at the pub quiz. Yet, she was curious.

'How did you meet?' she asked.

'Dating app. The usual,' he said, semi apologetically.

'Oh, I hated them.' Lottie nodded. It had been how she'd met Tristan, but she didn't say that. 'You hear such stories, too. Narcissists, abusers, men cheating on multiple women... it just puts you off forever.'

'I bet it's awful being a woman on the apps,' Fred sighed. 'That's what Helen and Celine tell me, anyway. I mean, it's not great as a guy either, but at least I don't have to deal with men.'

'They're not wrong. How long have you been seeing Helen?' Lottie asked.

'Just a couple of months. It's going okay.' He cleared his throat. 'So...' he looked like he was about to say something, and then the doorbell rang.

'Oh. That's him, I expect,' Lottie said, somewhat awkwardly.

'Better go and get it,' Fred said, with what sounded like a slightly forced jolly tone. 'Don't keep him waiting!'

'He's fifteen minutes late.' Lottie raised an eyebrow, getting up from her seat.

'Lottie?' Fred looked up at her, his face open. 'I just wanted to say…' he paused, and made an awkward face.

'What?' she asked. The doorbell rang again.

'You look really lovely. I hope you have a good night,' he said, and cleared his throat. 'Say hi to Callum from me.'

'I will. And, thanks.' Lottie felt a blush stealing onto her cheeks. She wasn't used to compliments, and didn't know how to take them. Her instinct was always to assume that the person was wrong.

But, Fred was her friend. He had no reason to lie; his sight was normal, as far as she could tell, and Lottie had met Helen. Helen was an attractive girl, so Fred didn't have abnormally bad taste in women. So, she had to come to the even more uncomfortable conclusion that Fred might be sincere, and, in which case, it would be bad manners to throw the compliment back in his face.

She pushed the other thoughts about Fred to the back of her mind: yes, he was attractive, and they'd had a moment of some kind, up at the castle. But it was just a moment. It didn't mean anything.

And, when she opened the front door and saw Callum's face light up with a wide, goofy smile, she felt something she hadn't felt in a very long time.

She felt chosen. And it was lovely.

30

————

'You got it! Awesome job!' Callum high-fived Lottie as she threw her final dart at the board, and hit the triple twenty. 'I'm impressed. I thought you said you hadn't played darts before? Are you a ringer?' He grinned.

'Well, I've played. Just not for a long time.' Lottie shrugged, grinning back. 'Beginner's luck.'

'Nah. You've got a real eye for it, I reckon.' Callum shook his head. 'I'm gonna have to start bringing my A game.'

'Oh, you weren't doing that already?' Lottie countered, her eyebrow raised.

'Nah. I was going easy on you.'

'Oh. Because I think I beat you by... hmm, a hundred and thirty points.' She put her fingertip to her mouth in a thoughtful gesture. 'So...'

'A ringer, ladies and gentlemen!' Callum went to the doorway of the private room where they were playing augmented darts, and shouted to the people in the bar beyond it. He turned back to her, still grinning. 'And a very pretty one!' he added, still in a loud voice. Lottie blushed.

Callum went to the board, took the darts from it and,

without warning, planted a kiss on her cheek as he came to stand next to her.

'Can't say I usually have such a distracting opponent. That's why I'm off my game,' he said, meeting her eyes playfully. Lottie instinctively stepped away from the line of sight of people in the bar; Callum's very vocal compliment was way outside of her comfort zone. She didn't want people to look inside the room, expecting some kind of centrefold model, and see her instead.

'I'm sure that's not why,' she muttered, wrapping her arms around herself self-consciously. She wished she'd worn jeans and a T-shirt, or something less pretty; she felt overdressed.

'I would.' He threw his darts at the board, making it light up and flash. 'So, do you like it here?'

'Yes. It's really fun,' Lottie replied, truthfully. She'd never have chosen to come to a place like this, but, apart from Callum making her feel self-conscious just then, she was having a lovely time.

The Pitch n' Putt was about half an hour's drive from Loch Cameron, and, though Lottie had felt shy when she'd opened the door to Callum, he'd chattered easily to her through the whole drive, so by the time they'd pulled up in the Pitch n' Putt car park, she'd felt much more at ease. Callum didn't seem to mind that Lottie was a little quiet. He didn't ask her many questions, but kept her entertained with a stream of anecdotes about the food truck and his friends and family. She didn't mind: he was funny, and surprisingly sweet when talking about people he obviously loved.

Inside, there was a sports bar hung with various framed photos of athletes and sporting events from horse racing to athletics and tennis; these alternated with cool neon light decorations with slogans like *Hole in One* and *Mine's a Cocktail*. A wide set of doors led to an outside, covered crazy golf course, and there were a number of private rooms where customers could play augmented darts. Lottie hadn't quite understood what that was, but it seemed that it was a game where you threw real darts at a dartboard, which had sensors under it so that your score could show up on a big TV screen next to it. Plus, there was a smaller screen connected to it where you could choose all manner of fun games to play using the darts – highest scores, accuracy games, where you had to aim your darts in particular areas of the board to win.

'So, tell me about your course. I've been nattering on about myself all night so far. You're doing an MA, right?' Callum passed the darts to her.

'That's right. It's in Sociology but I'm focusing on elders and intergenerational work. So, I'm doing a project, collecting life stories from people up at a care home.'

'Wow. Old people. My nanna's in one of those places. I go now and again but the smell really gets me. It's really...' he pulled a face. 'I dunno. I don't love it, so well done you for going.'

'I don't think the place I go to really has a smell.' Lottie frowned. 'Or, if it has, I haven't noticed. People there are generally quite active, so it's not a nursing home, more of an elderly village. Maybe your nanna's somewhere different,' she said, diplomatically.

'Maybe. Isn't it quite boring, listening to them go on and on about, like, the war, or something?' He threw his darts and the board lit up. 'Hey. That's more like it.' He took them from the board and handed them to her.

'No, not at all. These are people who have lived fascinating, full lives.' Lottie thought of Gretchen and the sheer depth of experience she had had; even though they'd been talking a while now, Lottie thought that she probably still hadn't got anywhere near through all of the highlights of Gretchen's life. 'If I was bored by listening to elders, I wouldn't have chosen to do this project.'

She threw her darts, but she wasn't really focused, and one of the darts hit the floor.

'Whoops.' Callum retrieved it for her. 'See, I knew it was just beginner's luck.'

Callum seemed to find her project boring and a worm of disappointment wound into Lottie's heart.

But Callum asked you out, and brought you here, and you're having fun. Stop overthinking, Lottie cautioned herself. *He doesn't have to love everything you love. You don't have to be the same. Opposites attract.*

That was true. People in successful relationships were always talking about their funny little differences. She and Callum didn't have to be too similar to like each other.

She stopped herself for a minute and analysed her train of thought, wondering what Gretchen would say about that. *People in successful relationships. That's a bit of a leap for a first date, dear,* she imagined Gretchen saying, kindly. *Why don't you just have fun, enjoy yourself, and stop thinking you're over-dressed. You look lovely.*

All right, Lottie thought. *Why don't I just relax a bit?* She went to the little table where a waitress had put their drinks, and took a sip of her margarita. It was spicy and delicious, so she took another sip.

'How is it?' Callum came over to where she stood and took a long draught of his pint of lager.

'Really good. I hardly ever have cocktails, but I love how tangy this is.' Lottie took another sip and felt a warmth fill her belly. 'Want some?'

'Sure.' He took the glass from her and took a sip, then, putting the glass back on the little table, gently leaned in to kiss her.

His lips were delectably soft, and brushed hers with a light touch. She wasn't expecting the kiss, and it caught her off guard.

'Mmmm,' he murmured, and she wasn't sure whether he

meant the kiss or the taste of lime and salt on their lips. 'Delicious.'

Delicious.

Callum kissed her again, then, and his hands found her waist. The kiss was still soft, but she felt herself melting against his strong chest; he was taking his time, savouring the moment. Lottie felt something in her heart flutter, wild and suddenly awake: there was something in his touch, his presence, that made her feel at once safe and deeply aroused. Chosen.

And the feeling of being chosen, for Lottie, was very seductive.

Gently, he pulled away from the kiss and stroked her cheek.

'Better get back to it. Or they'll be turning on the sprinklers to put the fire out,' he murmured. Lottie made some kind of half-nonsensical reply: *uh-huh, okay, haha.*

But, inside, she was thinking *what the hell just happened?*

31

When Lottie got to the care home that afternoon, she met Kimberley in the corridor.

It had been a few days since her date with Callum, and she had been trying not to watch her phone for a message from him, but she wasn't doing very well. Shouldn't he have texted by now, though, she wondered? She didn't want to seem too keen, but she'd messaged him the day after their date with a short thank you note – it only seemed polite. But, since then, she'd heard nothing.

It was making her really anxious. What had she done wrong? Why didn't he want to see her anymore?

She'd checked her phone and put it in her pocket as she entered the care home, her tummy feeling unsettled. But, Lottie had got used to masking her feelings when she was little. *Don't make a fuss, or Daddy might not come back at all.*

'Oh, hi, Lottie. You headed in to see Gretchen?' Kimberley stopped in the hallway and held out her hand to stop Lottie for a moment. 'Now, Lottie. Don't be alarmed when you go in there, she's fine. But she had a bit of an accident a couple of days ago,' Kimberley said, carefully.

'Oh, no. What happened?'

'Well, I think she got up in the night and put the kettle on. She said she couldn't sleep, and she wanted to make a cup of tea. But, unfortunately, she managed to scald herself with the hot water. Missed the cup and poured it straight on the back of her hand and her thumb.'

'Is she okay? That sounds terrible!' Lottie stared at Gretchen's door, down the hallway.

'Well, obviously, it's a nasty injury. She managed to press the alarm button after she did it, so we managed to get to her quickly, but she went into shock and we had to call the ambulance. They were able to treat the burn and the shock without taking her into hospital – they thought, as she's so frail, we'd be better off keeping an eye on her here and avoid the stress of a hospital visit. The district nurse has been out to see her a few times, but obviously, if she takes a bad turn or the wound doesn't heal up, then we'll take her in.'

'Oh, my. Poor Gretchen,' Lottie breathed, her tummy clenched with anxiety. 'That must be so painful for her.'

'Yes, it's really sore, bless her. The doctor's been out too and prescribed her some pain medication, but of course you have to be super careful with the elderly with this kind of injury. Or, any injury, really. They just don't have the immunity and the strength and healing capabilities a younger person has.' Kimberley looked concernedly at Lottie. 'Are you all right, sweetheart? It's upsetting, I know, but Gretchen's a tough one. She'll be okay. We've run various tests as well, by the way, just because you were asking when you were here last. We'll get the results in a week or so; it is confidential, this kind of thing, so if there is anything, it would still be up to Gretchen to tell you.'

'I understand. I just don't like to think of Gretchen suffering.' Lottie felt tears well up in her eyes, and blinked them back. 'We've become quite close over the past few weeks.'

'Aww. Bless you. Well, I know she's loving talking to you.

She talks about you all the time.' Kimberley gave Lottie a kind pat on the arm. 'She's okay. Just be prepared for a big bandage, and she might be a little more tired than usual.'

'All right. I'll let you know if there's anything different about her.' Lottie paused, thinking for a moment. 'In fact, she's complained about her eyesight quite a few times now. She seems to get tired sometimes, takes her glasses off, rubs her eyes, that kind of thing. Maybe it was that she couldn't see properly in the night? Why she scalded herself?'

'Hmm. She hasn't mentioned her vision to anyone on the care staff, as far as I know.' Kimberley looked thoughtful. 'I'll check her notes. And maybe we'll get her eyes tested as well, then. I mean, she's old, and goodness knows I can't see that well when I get up in the night, never mind being in my eighties.'

'Sure. It might be nothing, but you never know.' Lottie nodded. 'Anyway. I'd better go and see how she is, then.'

'Of course. Have a good chat, that'll do her the power of good.' Kimberley nodded.

Lottie walked up to Gretchen's door and knocked, her heart hammering in her chest. She was nervous about seeing her friend injured and frail. She never wanted to think about Gretchen that way, but the truth was that she was elderly, and prone to falls and illnesses and all the things that befell you when you were – in Gretchen's words – an antique.

'Come in,' Gretchen's voice called, and Lottie turned the handle. Whatever she felt, she had to put on a smile for her friend. Distract her, entertain her, be a good visitor. That was what was required, and that was what she would do.

'Hello, there.' Lottie brightened her voice as she walked in, noting the fact that the curtains were still pulled mostly closed, and there was a stale smell in the room. 'I hear that you've been up making tea for your boyfriends in the night, Gretchen. Is that true?'

'Oh. Ha. Yes, I had Chris Hemsworth and Jason Momoa up

here for coffee,' Gretchen chuckled, but her voice sounded thin. 'Unfortunately, things got rather heated.' She held up her left hand, which was completely mittened in a thick white bandage.

'Oh, Gretchen.' Lottie went to the curtains and pulled them, opening a window and letting in some fresh air. She went to sit carefully at the edge of Gretchen's bed. 'Kimberley told me what happened. It sounds so painful.'

'Yes. It's not my favourite thing that's ever happened, I must admit,' Gretchen sighed. 'I feel like a silly old woman. Which, of course, I am.'

'You're not silly at all. It was just an accident,' Lottie replied. 'Is the pain relief working?'

'It's quite good, yes. When you're ancient, they have to be careful about what they give you, but it's mostly making it bearable. I'm dreading the nurse changing the dressing, though,' she shivered. 'Darling. Now you're here, could you make tea? I can't manage it, for obvious reasons.'

'Of course.' Lottie got up and started busying herself in the kitchen.

32

———

Hey. U up?

The message flashed up on her phone at around 11pm. Lottie *was* up, but only because she was behind on transcribing Gretchen's interviews and trying to catch up. She frowned and picked up her phone. The message was from Callum.

Her heart started to race.

They'd been on a date, it had gone well – or, so she'd thought – and then there had been absolutely no contact for weeks. And, now, at 11pm, here he was, not even with a full sentence.

Lottie might not have been the most experienced woman when it came to dating, but even she knew that *Hey. U up?* sent late at night was a booty call.

She watched as the three dots pulsed in the body of their message chat, indicating that Callum was writing something else.

Sorry I haven't been around much. Busy with work. Would love to see you again.

Lottie didn't reply. Who wasn't busy? She was busy: she had to submit her final project in the next two months and she had mountains of interviews to transcribe as well as a critical theory essay to write. *Being busy* wasn't a good excuse. She watched the screen for a minute, and, when she didn't reply, the dots appeared again.

I'd really love to take you on another date and make it up to you, Lottie. I'm free tomorrow night if that works?

Lottie bit her lip and sat up, taking out her ear buds and pressing stop on Gretchen's interview. The truth was that she did still really want to see Callum again, but he'd really hurt her feelings by not calling after last time.

She'd thought that they'd had a good time. So, why had he just ignored her for weeks? There was no real explanation in the messages he was sending her now. No real apology. And the very act of messaging late at night didn't feel very respectful.

Please, Lottie.
   Please don't make me beg.

You absolutely should beg, she replied, despite her better judgement. She knew that she should ignore him: he'd ghosted her once. What was the likelihood that he would do it again? But, she couldn't resist. She really liked Callum. She'd really enjoyed their date, and when he'd kissed her... well, that had felt special. The little girl inside her, the little girl that had to deal with her daddy disappearing and never paying her the attention she needed – that little girl wanted this attention very badly. Even something partial, probably insincere, noncommittal. It was a breadcrumb and she was desperate for anything.

I will. Please, please forgive me, Callum replied immediately. *I was an idiot.*

Yes, you were.

So, can you make tomorrow night? I'll take you somewhere lovely.

Where? she asked. She already knew she was going to say yes, and she felt a pang of guilt about it. Was she rewarding bad behaviour? Probably. She knew that she should ignore Callum, or at the very least, not reply to him until the next day and refuse him the satisfaction of getting what he wanted instantly.

But, her heart wanted what it wanted. She wanted to see Callum again. Maybe, sometimes, there were these bumps in the road in relationships, she rationalised. Maybe it was OK to give him a second chance.

The Fat Hen. It's a nice restaurant in the village. Have you been? he wrote.

No.

So? Have I grovelled enough? he messaged, with a smiley face emoji.

I wasn't aware you'd started.

Dearest goddess, please bestow your forgiveness upon me. I am but a lowly worm and not deserving of your attention, but if you would do me the great honour of allowing me to take you to this fine food establishment, I would be eternally grateful, he wrote.

Cheesy. But OK. I suppose so. Lottie felt a burst of butterfly wings in her tummy.

Great. I'll see you there. 7.30pm? For a moment, Lottie felt a stab of annoyance. He wasn't intending to pick her up. But then, she dashed the thought aside. It wasn't required. She was a modern woman. She didn't need to be picked up.

So, instead, she just wrote, *See you there!*

Maybe I shouldn't have responded, she thought, her fingers hovering over the phone screen. *Maybe it sends the wrong message, by going out with him again. But,* she rationalised, *everyone deserves a second chance, and it was cute, how he begged me to go out with him. Worst case scenario, I get to go out for a nice dinner.*

She checked her messages again to see if he had responded, but he hadn't.

Lottie went back to her transcription, but gave it up after half an hour. It was late, and she wasn't concentrating. *You're tired,* she thought. *Go to bed.*

But, as she brushed her teeth, flossed and washed her face, she knew that she'd become distracted from her work by Callum, not the fact that she was tired. She was excited to see him again.

It took a long time for Lottie to get to sleep, because of the butterflies in her stomach. She lay awake for a long time, wondering what to wear. Wondering why Callum had left such a long gap between now and the last time he'd been in touch. Did he like her? Or was he just filling time with her because he had nothing better to do?

Don't go for the ones that give you butterflies in the beginning. You think it's love, but it's a lack of balance, Gretchen had said. Lottie didn't want to believe that.

Butterflies aren't bad, she told herself, as sleep started to pull her under. *Butterflies are beautiful creatures. Surely, feeling butterflies is a good thing. It's better than not feeling anything at all.*

33

'Hello, Lottie. Don't mind Kimberley, she's just leaving,' Gretchen called out as Lottie let herself into her room the next day. Gretchen seemed in better spirits than when she had left her the last time, which gave Lottie a sense of relief. Today, Kimberley was in Gretchen's flat when Lottie arrived. As Lottie put her bag down and began the now-familiar ritual of making tea, she was taking Gretchen's blood pressure. Gretchen still had one hand bandaged up, like a paw.

'Hi, Kimberley,' Lottie said, turning on the gas hob and filling up the kettle.

'Hello, Lottie. Just finishing up here. How's the project going?'

'Good, thanks. Still lots to do, but Gretchen's been amazing,' she said, arranging the tea cups on the tray and opening the fridge to find milk. 'I started off talking to a few of the ladies here, but, honestly, it's really become the Gretchen Ross Show.'

'Ha. I bet. I'd love to read that when it's finished.' Kimberley took the blood pressure cuff from Gretchen's arm and patted it. 'There you are, Your Grace. All done.'

'Thank you, dear. Now. It's time for This Is Your Life, so, if you don't mind...' Gretchen shooed Kimberley away.

'I'll be back tomorrow to change the dressing.' Kimberley picked up her bag and gave them both a little wave. 'Good to see you, Lottie.'

'And you.' Lottie waved, and set the tea tray down on Gretchen's bedside table. It had been a long time since Gretchen had sat up in one of her easy chairs during her visit, and, now, when Lottie came, Gretchen was always propped up in bed. 'Are you all right, Gretchen? Well. As all right as you can be with that terrible scald.'

'Right as rain, dear.' Gretchen picked up her china cup and blew on the tea that Lottie had poured for her. 'Don't worry. I hardly notice it.'

That was definitely a lie, but Lottie nodded.

'Kimberley said you were having some tests,' she prompted. 'Have the results come back?'

'Oh, she told you that, did she?' Gretchen frowned, giving Lottie a gimlet stare. 'Yes, I've endured the ignominy of being poked and prodded. No results yet, but I really don't see the point.'

'Will you tell me, or Zelda, if there is anything? She's worried for you.' Lottie wondered if she'd said too much, but she wanted Gretchen to know that people were thinking about her. That they'd noticed she didn't have quite her usual sparkle.

'Oh, pffft. I've told you, dear. There's nothing to worry about. I shall tell Zelda the same thing,' Gretchen scolded Lottie. 'Now. Let me tell you about my assistant Andrew. I thought we'd talk about him today. Is your recorder on?'

'It is.' Lottie pressed the button on the voice recorder app obediently; she guessed that was as much as she was going to get out of Gretchen, who, she'd learned by now, was as stubborn as an ox.

'Right. Well, I've told you a bit about how Andrew started

with me. He made quite the impression at interview. Well, we got on extremely well from day one.' Gretchen smiled. 'Initially, there was a stream of girls from the typing pool who suddenly made it their business to come up to my office to ask for one thing or another. Obviously, word got around fast that there was a new attractive young man in the building, and they came to sniff him out. I'm not sure if he ever explicitly told them that he was gay, at the time. But I think that they realised fairly quickly that there weren't going to be wedding bells for anyone.'

'Did Andrew mind that? It must have been a bit demoralising, in a way.'

'I don't think so. Bear in mind that these were polite young ladies, not the entitled, aggressive young men I worked with then. Yes, they were curious, and they might well have been hunting for a husband. But they weren't rude. I think he thought it was rather amusing.'

'So, how did you work together? Were there some favourite times you had?' Lottie prompted.

'Well, Andrew was my assistant, so he took calls for me, organised my diary, booked lunches and dinners with authors, worked up editorial schedules sometimes, looked over contracts with me. I trusted him implicitly. Obviously, it took a while for us to get used to how to work together, but he really was marvellous. Always had my coffee ready when I got into the office, learned how I liked it and what sandwiches I liked from the deli around the corner.'

'That sounds good. I wouldn't mind having an Andrew in my life,' Lottie chuckled.

'Ha. Indeed. Now, in terms of a favourite time... I mean, there were so many. We had some lovely times at literary festivals, for instance. Sometimes we'd go to support an author, make a little jolly out of it. I knew that my colleagues used to gossip about us, but I really didn't care. There used to be the rumour, for instance, that Andrew and I were secretly sleeping together. Which is utterly hilarious, of course. And, frankly, even if Andrew had been faintly interested in sleeping with me, I wouldn't have, because I'm a professional. Unlike most of the men I worked with, who were sleeping with their secretaries, assistants and, sometimes, authors.'

'No way! The authors?' Lottie gasped. 'Isn't that... very much against the rules?'

'Oh, a hundred per cent, yes. Didn't stop them, though. Terrible business.' Gretchen clicked her tongue. 'So, it was very much about me being tarred with the same brush. They thought it was normal and acceptable so they assumed I was doing it too. Which I absolutely was not.' She shook her head. 'I did date a few writers, over the years. But none that we published, or had any likelihood of publishing. It's unethical.'

'Quite. I mean, now I really want to know who you dated.' Lottie raised an eyebrow.

'Oh, I couldn't possibly say. But there's a row of their books on that end of the shelf.' Gretchen nodded to a nearby book unit.

'These?' Lottie got up and went over to where Gretchen pointed.

'To about the middle.' Gretchen smiled and closed her eyes.

'Goodness.' Lottie read out the names of a number of well-known authors, and some that she hadn't heard of. 'You dated this guy?' She held up a bestseller written by an author who had specialised in mafia crime novels.

'Oh, yes,' Gretchen chuckled. 'He was good fun. He knew a lot of good restaurants.'

'Italian, presumably,' Lottie said.

'Naturally.'

'And this one?' Lottie held up a nonfiction book about steam trains.

'Oh. He was quite charming, actually, despite the terrifically dull book.' Gretchen reached out for it and opened the book, showing Lottie a handwritten inscription of poetry on the title page. 'He had the soul of a poet, but a poet who was also obsessed with The Flying Scotsman.'

'Oh.' Lottie started to giggle, and put the book back on the shelf. 'Just what every girl dreams of.'

'Well, you know, he would have made a very nice husband for someone.' Gretchen held up a finger on her good hand as if to rebuke Lottie. 'Just, not me.'

'I wondered if you had any boyfriends. After Alex,' Lottie said. 'Sorry, I didn't mean to mention him again. I don't want to make you uncomfortable.'

'No, I never allowed myself to fall in love, after Alex. But I dated. I wasn't a nun.'

'Gosh. Dating.' Lottie put the books back and returned to her seat. 'How do you do that, anyway? I've been asked on a date with someone, and I want to go, but last time he kind of hurt me, so I want to sort of... you know. Turn my heart off, so I don't get hurt again.'

'Oh. Who is this, then? The one that gave you butterflies, before? I told you about that. No good will come of it,' Gretchen said.

'Callum. We went on a date once, he ghosted me for a few weeks after that, and he got in contact again last night and asked me out for tonight. He did apologise.' Lottie could hear in her own voice that she was making apologies for Callum, and she didn't like the feeling of having to justify his actions to Gretchen.

'And you want to go?' Gretchen asked. 'Really? After he was so inconsiderate?'

'It might not be inconsiderate. People get busy.' Lottie knew it was a poor excuse, but she wanted to see Callum, and she didn't feel like being judged for it. Not even by Gretchen.

'They do, dear, but, generally, if a man likes you, he will be in touch.' Gretchen raised an eyebrow.

'I know, I know. But I still like him. I guess I don't feel like I'm done with him. I want to give him a second chance.' Lottie shrugged, feeling defensive. 'Can't you be a little more supportive?'

'I am being supportive. In my experience, dear, when they've shown you who they are, believe them. But I also know that the heart wants what it wants,' Gretchen sighed. 'The thing with men like that is to be aware, and make decisions accordingly. Think about what you want, and don't put him first. And, remember. Don't prioritise someone for whom you are not a priority.' She wagged her finger at Lottie. 'That's the sum total of my advice on the subject.'

'I won't. You're talking to me as if I'm a child. I'm not.' She was irritated.

'I know you're not, dear. Don't be cross.' Gretchen looked pensive for a moment. 'I wish I'd had someone around to say all this when I was seeing Alex, but I had to learn the hard way with him,' Gretchen said. 'After he wooed me, and we were sleeping together, he started with this kind of behaviour. Cancelling plans last minute, going silent on me for days at a time. Then, he wouldn't leave me alone when I walked away from the relationship. Trying to manipulate and control me. It didn't work.' A dark look crossed her face for a moment.

'It must have been difficult,' Lottie said. She was wary of talking about Alex; she didn't want to upset Gretchen. 'But the situation with you and Alex was quite different to me and Callum. I mean, I don't know, but I'd hope that Callum wasn't...' she trailed off.

'A domestic abuser?' Gretchen interjected. 'Darling. I would very much hope, for your sake, that he isn't. But, my point is that you won't know until you know. And, sometimes, that's too late.'

'Are you saying I shouldn't date, because all men have the

potential to abuse me?' Lottie asked. 'Because that seems unfair at best.'

'Of course not. I'm not going to tell you they aren't out there, because they are. Every year, the names of the women killed by domestic abusers gets read out in the House of Commons. It's over a hundred women every year. That's just the ones that are killed by men. Not including the women that survive, which probably counts in the thousands.' Gretchen grimaced. 'And I include myself in that. No, dear. Perhaps it's just that I feel protective of you and I don't want you to go through the same thing as I did.' Gretchen reached for Lottie's hand; hers felt frail and small. 'You have free will in all of this. See Callum if you like. Just be prepared. See the red flags when they come up, and if they do, run. Protect yourself. That's all I'm saying,' she said. 'I care about you, Lottie. Perhaps, more than you know.'

Today, she was under a blanket, and her bandaged hand lay on top of the covers. Lottie hadn't mentioned it, but she could imagine that the scald must be very painful.

Lottie felt bad for being cross with Gretchen. 'I'm sorry, for being a little short with you just now. I didn't mean it.'

'You don't have to be sorry, dear. Just protect yourself with these men.' Gretchen squeezed her hand.

'I will.'

'Good. And if this Callum tries any more funny business, I'll send a couple of big fellas around to teach him a lesson.' Gretchen coughed for a moment, and gave Lottie a weak smile.

'Well, I hope we don't need to do that.'

'Neither do I. But, like they taught us in the Guides. Always be prepared,' Gretchen said. 'Words to live by.' She coughed again. 'Of course, I was a terrible Girl Guide.'

'I can't imagine you being much of a one for rules.' Lottie chuckled, though she was still concerned about her friend.

'Oh, I wasn't. I never got any badges,' Gretchen said. 'But

that's another story,' she sighed. 'Now, listen, Lottie. There comes a time when you know that you... might not have long left,' Gretchen said, quietly. 'It's been nice, talking to you, since you've been visiting. In a funny kind of way, I feel like it's come just at the right time. I got to tell my story.'

'Gretchen! You're not going anywhere! You'll be here for ages yet,' Lottie exclaimed, her heart twisting at the thought of losing her friend. 'Please don't think that way. You had an accident. That's all. It's going to happen now and again, at your age.'

'Hmm. I'm eighty-six, dear. It's a good age to have got to, but I'm not sure that I want to get much past here.' Gretchen gave Lottie a tired smile. 'I haven't been feeling so good, recently. Tired. Things aren't working as well as they once did.'

'Well, you should see the doctor, Gretchen. If you're not feeling well.'

'I did, my dear girl.' She held up her bandaged hand.

'You know what I mean. About other things, if they're bothering you.'

'Hmm. I might do. But what will they do, now? I'm already at the Last Chance Saloon. That's this care home, by the way. Although there aren't nearly enough cowboys for my taste. No one is that invested in prolonging life at this stage, and neither should they be. I've had a good life.'

'Gretchen. I don't like to hear you talk this way.' Lottie frowned.

'I know, dear. And I'm sorry. But you're young, and the idea of death scares you because it's such an unnatural beast for you. And, so it should be. But, at my age, the beast is a comforting bear that you realise you've been walking steadily towards for many years. On and on, through the forest. Leaving all the chaos and darkness of the woods behind you, and, finally, resting your head on his big, strong chest. In a sunlit, dappled glade.' She smiled, and closed her eyes. 'That's how I think of it, anyway. *Waldeinsamkeit.*'

'Waldeinsamkeit?' Lottie repeated the unfamiliar word.

'It's a German word. It means feeling at peace in nature,' Gretchen explained.

'I don't know what to say, to that,' Lottie said. 'I don't like hearing you talk like this.'

'There's nothing to say, dearie. Live your life well, because one day, you'll find the bear in the forest, too. And you need to be ready for him.' Gretchen smiled, her eyes closed. 'And, learn from me. Don't make the mistakes I made. Remember, if he gives you butterflies, it's not love. It's unease. Real love makes you feel peaceful.'

'Did you ever find that kind of love?' Lottie asked, thinking about Callum. Callum gave her butterflies. And Tristan... well, Tristan had broken her heart.

'No. After Alexander, I didn't allow myself love again, because... I suppose I didn't trust myself,' Gretchen said. 'I didn't trust my own heart not to fall for another person who would hurt me,' her voice broke as she said it. 'Because of Alex, I had to give that baby away. And I've hated him every single day for that. I still hate him. I will never, ever forgive him for hurting and scaring me, but, worse than that, I have never forgiven him for making me give my baby up. For her own safety. I would take him hurting me a thousand times over if that was all it was. But not her.'

'Oh, Gretchen.' Lottie could only imagine the terrible pain that her friend was feeling. 'If I was there I would never have let him hurt you, either.' She hugged Gretchen awkwardly, avoiding her bandaged hand. 'I'm so very sorry for what he did to you.'

'I know, dear. So am I. But, don't forget, I had Stella, and then, she had a son. My grandson. And I poured all my love into them. And that was my life.' A tear leaked out from her eyelid, and rolled down her cheek. 'It was a good life, Lottie. It was better than I ever expected.'

Lottie held Gretchen's hand. She still didn't have anything insightful to say, but she stayed where she was.

Lottie sat on the side of Gretchen's bed for a long time, and, finally, Gretchen opened her eyes again.

'I'm tired, dear,' Gretchen said. 'Could you come back another day?'

'Of course. I'll come in a couple of days' time. Let you rest up.' Lottie stood up, and, instinctively, bent down and kissed Gretchen on the cheek. 'I want you to know how much I've enjoyed coming to talk to you, Gretchen. I feel like we've become good friends. And... it's helped me a lot, talking to you.'

'I'm glad, dear. I've enjoyed our talks, too.' Gretchen's eyes crinkled as she smiled, through her tears. 'I've always enjoyed the company of the young. I've been fortunate to have many young friends, over the years. You young women today are marvellous. Never forget how beautiful and gifted you are. How clever and creative and kind. You're the future, and I'm so glad. I'm glad to leave this world in your hands.'

'You're not leaving this world, Gretchen. Not yet.'

'Ah, but I will, one day. And at least I can say, hand on heart, that I did something to improve it. Even though I had to make some difficult choices, and I'll always wonder whether I made the right ones.' She waved her good hand at Lottie. 'Go on, now. I'll see you soon.'

'All right. Sleep well, Gretchen.'

Lottie let herself out, closing the door behind her quietly. She couldn't help but feel uneasy about what Gretchen had said about dying, but as she walked along the corridor, she rationalised that Gretchen was tired, probably not feeling her best.

She'd do her best to lift Gretchen's spirits, next time she saw her. Gretchen was her friend, and Lottie was so grateful to have her in her life.

34

GRETCHEN

Time moves on so quickly as you get older. When you get to my age, a day can sometimes feel like a matter of minutes. Especially if you doze through it, as can often happen.

A body gets tired; a mind gets confused. Sometimes, as we get old, we dwell on the past. Some of us at the care home live *only* in the past. Looking at the present, with our dilapidated bodies and reduced horizons, who can blame us if we retreat into our memories?

My time is coming. I can feel it. I have been walking slowly into the forest for a while, now; like I said to Lottie, I don't fear death. I imagine it as a bear, waiting for me. Waiting to enfold me in its grasp. *Waldeinsamkeit.* The feeling of being at peace in the forest.

I am not sad. I walk towards my loved ones who have gone before me, and I know they are waiting. I have missed them so very much. The forest is my heart, and I have held them in there for so long.

I have been in my memories rather a lot, lately, though. Telling my story to Lottie has been freeing. Even the difficult parts of the story that still have sharp edges: those, I have still managed to tell. And, in the telling, I have begun to let those painful memories lose some of their bite.

I have spent my life in the business of telling stories. I know what their nature is: I know the transformation they can bring. I know that, in a fairy tale, children enter the forest and bravely face the perils there. But, children can defeat the bear or the witch in the woods. Old women, if they are not the witch themselves, must submit to the bear and know that they will not walk out of the forest.

But, there is still one part of the story I have not told. It is the most remarkable part of it, and it is part of my story that I never expected to happen. An ending I had forsaken; a conclusion unlooked for. It is something amazing, but, since I came to know it, I have not known how to tell it to Lottie. For Lottie is the listener of my story, but she has no idea that she is also an intrinsic part of it.

Yet, as I walk further towards the forest, my worries about telling her my last secret fall away. What power do secrets have when you are clasped in the arms of the bear, and can hear the sweet voices of your loved ones close by?

I am being given a last chance, before the bear takes my final breath. I will find a way to tell Lottie what she needs to know. And what I need to release, so that I may find peace in his arms.

35

When Lottie arrived at The Fat Hen, Callum was already there, waiting at the table. He stood up as she walked in.

'Hi, Lottie. You look fantastic.' He grinned, and gave her a kiss on the cheek. 'Thanks for coming. I wouldn't have blamed you for standing me up.'

'I'd never do that,' Lottie said, taking off her cardigan and putting it on the back of the chair. Tonight she was wearing a full white cotton skirt with a wide brown leather belt and a white, short-sleeved blouse. Celine had helped her curl her hair, and Lottie had taken care with her makeup. She'd got a few appreciative glances on her walk to the restaurant, which, on one hand, was nice, but overall she felt self-conscious around Callum. His compliments made her feel uncomfortable, and she wasn't sure why. Fred's compliments never made her feel that way.

'I'm glad. Because now I get to have dinner with the prettiest girl in Loch Cameron,' he said as Lottie sat down.

'Oh, goodness. I wouldn't say that.' She blushed.

'I would, and I did.' Callum gave her a long, lingering look. 'I mean it, Lottie. You're stunning.'

'Let's look at the menu,' she said, not knowing what to do with the compliment. There was something about the way Callum looked at her that made her feel objectified, as if he was only interested in her body. 'Have you eaten here before? What's good?'

'I have, and everything's great,' he said. 'I mean, maybe avoid anything with a tomato sauce. You don't want to spoil that white dress.'

'Hmm.' Lottie scanned the menu, feeling nervous.

'Drink?' He signalled to a waitress, who came over for their order. 'Could I have a pint of lager please, and, Lottie? What do you want?'

'Just a coke, please,' she said.

'You walked up, right?' he asked.

'Yes.'

'Put something in it, then. Rum? Vodka?'

'Oh. Well, I don't really drink that much,' she said.

'Aww. Come on. Do you good to loosen up a little,' Callum said, in a persuasive tone.

'Well, I'd really just prefer a soft drink,' Lottie said.

'You don't want to kick back a little? Have a good time?' He grinned.

'Well, I don't really drink very much,' she repeated, feeling uncomfortable.

'You do you.' He shrugged, but his tone suggested that he was disappointed. Lottie felt self-conscious with the waitress standing there.

'All right. Rum and coke, please,' she said to the waitress, who nodded and went to the bar.

'Good girl,' Callum said, approvingly. Lottie blanched at the comment, and slightly regretted asking for an alcoholic drink when she didn't really want one. She'd felt pressured.

'So, how's your project going?' he asked, not seeming to sense her unease.

'Umm. Yeah. Really well, thanks,' she replied, rationalising that one drink would hardly hurt her. *You're being oversensitive,* she cautioned herself. 'I'm mostly interviewing one woman at the care home and her life has been really fascinating. She worked in publishing and she's been telling me all about the sexism she had to deal with. And her gay assistant, and her relationships with men. It's all very eye-opening.'

'Sexism? Like, how?' He frowned.

'Oh, well. You know. In the seventies and eighties. Well, until now, really. In the workplace, in life in general.'

'Well, not now, surely?' He laughed. 'I mean, I know it happened a bit in the past.'

'Err... very much now, too.' Lottie frowned. *A bit in the past?*

'Really? I thought we had laws and that, nowadays,' he said, smiling at the waitress as she brought their drinks and set them on the table. 'Cheers to you, anyway, Lottie.' He picked up his pint of lager and took a long drink.

'We do, but that doesn't stop bad things happening, a lot of the time. It's a cultural issue. History still affects us,' she said, slightly concerned that she might be on a date with a man who didn't think sexism was a problem for women nowadays.

'Hmm,' Callum said. 'I expect you know more about it than me.' He picked up a menu. 'Shall we order food? Do you know what you want?' he asked.

'Sure, I'll have a look.' Lottie picked up her menu.

'I like a woman that knows what she wants.' He smiled, looking at her from under his long eyelashes. She knew he was trying to charm her, but Lottie couldn't help comparing their conversation to the chats she'd had with Fred. Fred wouldn't have brushed off sexism in a conversation, and she felt like he'd been a lot more interested in her chats with Gretchen than Callum had.

But, Fred had a girlfriend. And, Fred wasn't here, now.

Callum *was* here, had asked her out on a date, and was flirting with her. She had to remember to focus on the good things. If Callum didn't see the world in quite the same way as her, that wasn't necessarily a bad thing. They could still have fun.

~

'Well, this is me. Thanks for walking me home.' Lottie pulled her handbag up onto her shoulder, feeling awkward and a little nervous.

They'd chatted easily for the rest of the evening, and, over-all, she'd enjoyed herself at the restaurant. After a bit of a diffi-cult start, Callum had been attentive and sweet, and asked her lots of questions about herself, appearing to pay attention to her answers. The food had been lovely. Lottie's initial nervousness about Callum had receded, but, now, as they stood outside her front door, it had returned.

This was the moment where he would kiss her, if he was going to.

'You're welcome,' he said.

'Well, thank you for a lovely evening,' she said, not quite knowing how to end the moment.

'Thank *you*,' he replied, a smile tugging at the edge of his mouth.

There was a pause. They met each other's eyes, and Callum chuckled.

'I'd like to kiss you now,' he said, and touched her gently on her waist. 'If that's all right with you.'

'Okay.' Lottie swallowed hard. The butterflies in her stomach weren't so much fluttering now as stampeding.

'Okay.' He smiled, and pulled her in towards him.

The last time Callum had kissed her, he had said she was *delicious*. And, when Lottie had thought about that kiss – and she had thought about it, many times – she had thought about

Callum's soft lips on hers, and the sweet, heady desire the kiss had provoked in her.

Tonight, the kiss was just as soft, but, as she felt his lips brush hers with the same maddening slowness, she felt his grip on her waist tighten. He pressed her to him with intensity, and she let out an involuntary sigh.

The kiss deepened; his mouth grew more urgent on hers. Lottie kissed him back, desire flowing through her body as though someone had flicked a switch. Callum smelt *good*; of clean, fresh cotton. It was a nice smell; it made Lottie want to relax into him. She pressed herself against his broad chest.

They had spent the evening talking, laughing, being polite and courteous to each other. Callum hadn't even reached for her hand as he'd walked her home. But, now, a fire had been lit between them, and Lottie didn't care that it was consuming her. In that moment, she didn't care about anything except being inside this feeling.

'Lottie,' he said, in a low voice that was part growl. One hand stayed on her waist, and she felt the other on the back of her head, gripping it. He made a gentle fist of her hair – not hurting her, but using it to pull her head back slightly, kissing her more deeply. His breath grew more ragged.

She wrapped her arms around his neck and kissed him back, fiercely. There was a moment when she almost didn't recognise herself; she felt like a different woman. Callum's kiss – the way he touched her, held her, with the threat of strength under a sweet tenderness – made her surrender completely.

She felt wild, untamed. She wanted to wrap her legs around him and not let go.

Callum kissed her back, and then his hand relaxed on the back of her head. He broke away from the kiss, still holding her in his arms.

'Well... that was uhh... something,' he murmured, his voice husky.

'Do you want to come in?' She looked up into his eyes, the feeling in her stomach – in the whole of her – hot, wanting, needing him – intensifying. She would never usually do something like this, but she wanted Callum. She wanted more of that kiss, and, more than that, she realised how lonely she'd been since Tristan had dumped her. She wanted to be loved, and held, and touched. It was a basic human need. She didn't need to feel ashamed of that.

'Are you sure?' he asked, meeting her eyes.

'Yes.' She kissed him, gently this time. 'I'm sure.'

'Then, yes. I want to.'

Lottie took his hand and led him to the door. He followed her in, and she put her finger to her lips, leading him up to her room. She wasn't sure if Fred and Celine were in, but, if they were, she wanted to avoid a situation where she would have to explain what was going on.

She didn't want to have to explain what Callum was doing there, because she didn't really know, herself. But, she was sure of what she felt.

The heart wants what it wants, Gretchen had said. And Lottie's heart – and her body – wanted Callum, now.

She led him into her room and closed the door. Without saying anything, he took her back into his arms and kissed her softly, touching her face.

'We won't do anything that you don't want to,' he said, quietly.

'All right.' Lottie led him to the bed, and pulled him onto it.

'Do we need to be quiet?' he asked, and she nodded. She didn't want Celine and Fred to overhear anything, if they were in, or if they came back. The idea of having to be silent excited her.

'All right, then,' he said. She knew that he had seen the excitement flare behind her eyes. Gently, Callum took her wrists in his large, strong hands and pinned them firmly to the bed. Lottie let out a long sigh of anticipation. He leaned down towards her, kissing her.

'Quiet, remember,' he whispered in her ear. And, in that moment, Lottie finally forgot about Tristan, and succumbed to the pleasure she never thought she would feel again.

36

Hey. How are you? Last night was amazing.

Lottie messaged Callum the day after she had slept with him. He had left in the middle of the night, explaining that he had to get up early the next day. Lottie had felt all right about that, though she would have liked him to stay. However, when it got to mid-afternoon of the next day and she hadn't heard from him, she started to get an uneasy feeling in her stomach.

Surely, he wouldn't ignore her a second time.

She could see that he had read the message, but he didn't reply to it.

Lottie waited three more days, but there was still no reply.

Hi there, haven't heard from you, hope you're okay? she messaged on the fourth day. No response.

She waited another two days; she could see that he had read the message, but there was no reply.

Clearly, Callum was alive and not lost at sea without any mobile phone reception, so the only conclusion that she could come to was that he was ignoring her.

After she had given herself to him. After they had shared

what she had thought was a beautiful night of passion and intimacy. Because it had been beautiful. Callum had been attentive, sensual and had made her feel like a queen that night.

And, now, nothing.

Lottie had spent days and days feeling worse and worse. She kept checking her phone to see if he had replied – anything at all, an emoji, a single word reply, but there was nothing. She was hardly sleeping, she felt sick and couldn't eat.

She felt the familiar nauseous anxiety roil around her and consume her like a storm. She was anxious that she had done something wrong.

In desperation, she called her grandparents. She didn't know what else to do.

'Hallo, my little pigeon,' her grandfather answered the phone. 'It's a nice surprise tae hear from ye.'

'Hello, Grandpa. Is Grannie there?'

'Naw. She's oot shoppin'. What's up?'

'Oh.' Lottie let out a long sigh. She'd really wanted to talk to her grannie, who always had something sensible and grounding to say.

'Can I help, hen?' her grandpa sounded concerned. 'What's wrong?'

'Nothing. I was just feeling a little low,' Lottie said.

'Ye can talk tae me,' he said, in a kind voice. Just hearing anyone be kind right now was enough to make Lottie want to burst into tears.

'Oh... I don't know, Grandpa. It's just about this boy I went on a date with,' Lottie said.

'Oh, aye.' An edge entered Graham's voice; Lottie could imagine him raising his eyebrow. 'I hope he's bein' a gentleman, whoever he is.'

'Not really, no,' Lottie muttered.

'Want tae tell me aboot it? I know I'm an auld fella now, but I still know a few things about relationships,' her grandpa said.

'Well, it's just that we… saw each other, and now he seems to be ignoring me,' Lottie said, skating over the details. She didn't want to go into the nitty gritty about having slept with Callum in a conversation with her grandpa.

'Oh, I see.' Graham made a disapproving noise in the back of his throat. 'An' how is this makin' ye feel?'

'Not very good,' Lottie admitted. 'Anxious. Like I did something wrong. Like I'm not enough.'

'Well, I can tell ye that's wrong, for a start,' Graham snorted. 'Ye're a stonkin' young woman. Any young man should feel like a king, takin' ye out.'

'Then what happened? I don't understand,' Lottie said, her voice breaking. 'Why does this always happen?'

'It won't always happen, poppet. But, listen. This is what I know. The only thing ye have control over is how ye react tae this kinda thing. Now, unfortunately, the world is full o' terrible people. I wish I could wrap ye and yer grannie up in cotton wool an' protect ye all from all o' it, but I can't. What I can do is tell ye that the best thing ye can do fer yourself is say *no* tae this kinda crappy behaviour. Will it stop it ever happenin' again? No, probably not. But ye don't have tae stand fer it. You can say no, cut him off, refuse tae engage anymore. An' that is the best gift ye can give yerself, ma little crow princess. Because you demonstrate tae yerself that yer puttin' yer foot down an' protectin' yerself.'

'Oh.' Lottie blinked, somewhat surprised to be getting relationship advice from her grandpa.

'Aye,' he said. 'I know that sounds a little tough, but, believe me, if I was a younger man, I'd be askin' fer this chancer's address an' goin' round there tae have a word,' Graham said, tersely.

'Grandpa. You can't do that,' Lottie said, with a little chuckle.

'Aye well, in ma slightly younger days, I would, pigeon,'

Graham said. 'But, ye know. Since your mum passed, grannie an' me have tae keep an eye on ye. I don't like hearin' ye sad.'

'I know, Grandpa,' Lottie sighed. 'And you're right. I just don't understand what goes through men's heads. Like, how can Callum think it's OK to just ignore me like this?'

'I know, hen. Truth is, most of the time, there isnae much goin through their heads.' Graham hummed a simple childhood nursery rhyme. 'That's what there is. Just a little happy song.'

'I refuse to believe that,' Lottie said.

'Aye, well. Some o' us have brains. But you women are the thinkers. I've learnt that in life at the grand old age of eighty-somethin'.'

'So, I guess I'll never know why, then.' Lottie walked to the window of her bedroom and looked out.

'No. An' my advice is, don't waste yer time tryin' tae work it out. Concentrate on yerself, ma little pigeon. Don't be wastin' any more mental energy on these boys. An' then you'll leave space fer a kind man tae come along.'

'Hmph. Chance would be a fine thing.'

'Ah, we exist. Just, there's a lot o' idiots lettin' the side down.' Graham chuckled. 'You'll get there, hen. Will I tell grannie tae give ye a call when she gets in?'

'Yes, please. That would be great.'

'Ye take care, Lottie. I love ye,' her grandpa said, tenderly.

'I love you too, Grandpa.'

'Ye know ye can call us whenever ye need us.'

'I know.'

'Have I helped?' he asked, gruffly.

'Yeah. I just needed someone to talk to,' Lottie sighed. 'I'll be okay.'

'Oh, I know ye will, hen. You've been so resilient these past years. Losin' yer mum wasnae easy. We know how hard it is. How hard it was fer you as a little girl too. But we always want ye to know how much we love ye. Okay?'

'Okay.' Lottie felt tears spring to her eyes.

'Right, then. I better go. You'll be all right wi' this Callum now?' Graham sounded concerned.

'I think so,' she said. Lottie did, in fact, feel clearer about the situation than she had.

Callum. I don't want to believe that you're ghosting me after we had such a special night together, because that would be very bad behaviour on your part. There must be some reason you're not in contact with me. I can see that you read my last two messages. I don't think I did anything wrong. Please explain your lack of consideration for my feelings.

She sent the message not expecting a reply. However, she felt that he at least deserved to hear what she had to say.

Hi, Lottie. Sorry, I've been busy. Catch up soon.

The message arrived hours after she had sent hers, when Lottie was doing some grocery shopping on the high street. She'd only looked at her phone to check her shopping list, and she stared at the notification in slight disbelief.

Good to hear that you're not dead, at least. Can you understand that it's really hurtful for me that we slept together and now you're just ignoring me? I don't sleep around. That wasn't usual for me. She tapped out the message angrily, and pressed send.

She watched the screen for a moment, but the delivery notification of the two ticks going blue remained grey.

Fine. Whatever, she thought, and put her phone back in her bag.

~

'So, how's it going with Callum?' Fred asked, drying his hands on a tea towel.

'Oh. It's not, really,' Lottie confessed. 'He hasn't called. I messaged, but... nada.' She shrugged, trying not to appear bothered. 'I guess that's that.'

'No way. I'm sorry to hear that, Lottie,' Fred sounded genuinely surprised. 'He's an idiot, then. I wouldn't let a girl like you go.'

'Okay...' Lottie didn't quite know how to respond to that.

'All I'm saying is, if I was him, I'd have called you the next day and set up a date.' Fred went to the fridge, opened a microwave meal, stabbed the cellophane with a knife, and slid it into the microwave. 'It's just crappy behaviour to leave you hanging. And, if he didn't want another date, then he should tell you that too. Just a nice, straightforward *hey, it was fun, but I'm not really feeling it – best of luck out there* text.'

'Well, he might have a reason,' Lottie argued, and then realised it looked like she was taking Callum's side again, just like she had when she'd talked about him with Gretchen. The truth was that she was *furious* with Callum, but she felt embarrassed. She didn't want to admit to Fred and Celine what had really happened, because they would either pity her or think she was some kind of slut for sleeping with Callum on the second date – and, especially after he had ghosted her the first time.

As far as her housemates knew, Lottie and Callum had gone out for a nice meal, and that was that. She hadn't been sure if either of them were home that night, but, as it turned out, Fred had been at Helen's and Celine had gone to stay with a friend for the night. So, neither of them had witnessed Callum tiptoeing down the hallway and down the stairs at three o'clock in the morning and Lottie kissing him goodbye at the door.

Only she knew that. But Callum and she had been so intimate. She had made herself so vulnerable, and now, she felt sick with loss and mortification.

'What reason could he have for ghosting you? Unless you're out in the field with UNICEF, without wifi, providing vital life-saving immunisations, or you're in a coma, I don't accept that there's a reason for not texting after a date.' Fred pressed the timer button several times and the machine began whirring. 'He lives in the village. It's not like it's far away. He could pop by, even. Old school.'

'Perhaps there's something wrong with his phone,' Lottie said, too embarrassed to admit what had really happened.

'Like what? What actually happened?' Fred washed his hands.

'He read all the messages I sent. I could tell because the ticks went blue, but he didn't reply. Then, the last one I sent, the ticks didn't go blue. They still haven't.'

'When did you send it?'

'Earlier today.'

'Hm. I mean, he might still read it, but the other possibility exists that maybe he's muted or blocked you,' Fred said, making an awkward face. 'I mean, what was the last thing you said?'

'Umm. The general gist was that I wasn't impressed,' she said, not wanting to go into details.

If she had been more experienced with men, then maybe this would never have happened. Lottie felt mortified that she hadn't seen this coming; she'd got carried away in the heat of the moment, and she shouldn't have. Not with a man who had already shown her who he was, as Gretchen had said.

'Hmmm.' Fred raised an eyebrow. 'It's not great behaviour, is it?'

'Not really,' Lottie sighed. She felt really betrayed, and all of the confidence she'd started to feel about herself now seemed a distant memory.

'I mean, I text Helen after every date and arrange the next one with her,' Fred said.

'Well, aren't you just the model boyfriend?' Lottie snapped.

'No. But I know how to treat someone with basic decency.' Fred blinked, obviously hurt by her tone.

'Sorry. You're just being nice, I know. It's just that I'm really upset about it,' Lottie confessed. 'Helen's a lucky girl.' She met his eyes for a moment, and then looked away. 'Sorry,' she said, again.

'It's okay.' Fred got a plate out from the cupboard. 'But listen. You don't have to wait around for him to text you. Why don't you go and see him? It's Tuesday, right? The Shrimp Shack should be on the High Street. Ask him what's going on.'

'Yeah. I could do that.' Lottie considered it. She imagined striding up to the food van and demanding Callum tell her why he hadn't called her. Especially after she and Callum had slept together.

'Do what?' Celine walked in and threw her hoodie over one of the kitchen chairs. 'Oh, I'm starving. Fred, are you cooking?'

'Microwave meal for one. Sorry,' he said.

'Ugh. Where is my 'usband to cook me dinner every day?' Celine groaned. 'Is it so much to ask? All I want is dinner on the table every day and the laundry done and a nice pretty boy to cuddle up with at night.'

'I was just saying to Lottie that she should go down to The Shrimp Shack and have it out with Callum,' he said.

'Oh. Why? Has that boy been mean to you?' Celine frowned.

'They went on that date, remember. And he's been ignoring her ever since,' Fred said. Lottie wasn't enjoying her love life being the topic of conversation between her housemates, and wished she hadn't told Fred.

'No! This was a week or so ago?' Celine blew out her cheeks. 'Didn't it go well?'

'He hasn't texted her since,' Fred interjected. 'It's been days.'

'Oh, thanks,' Lottie groaned. 'Tell the world, why don't you?'

'It's Celine. And it's not like she wasn't going to find out,' Fred said, patiently.

'That is terrible. Why are men such pigs?' Celine snorted.

'We're not all bad,' Fred protested.

'Ugh. Do not give me the *not all men* speech, Freddie,' Celine snapped. 'This is not about you.'

'Fine. Sorry.' He shrugged. 'But I still think you should go down there and confront him.' Fred took his meal out of the microwave and poured it out onto the plate. The savoury smell of spaghetti and meatballs made Lottie's stomach rumble.

'Ooo! Great idea.' Celine clapped her hands together. 'We will give him *what for*. As you English say.'

'I don't think anyone has said that since 1948, but okay,' Fred muttered. 'And, don't pretend that you aren't just going to see Tom, Celine.'

'What happened between you and Tom?' Lottie asked, remembering the quiz night where Celine had flirted unashamedly with Callum's friend.

'We kissed after the quiz. We've been sexy texting.' Celine shrugged. 'Maybe tonight we try it for real, eh?'

'So, you've been in touch a lot, then?' Lottie asked, mentally comparing her utter silence from Callum. The thought made her even more cross than she'd been already.

'Well, you know. Here and there. Most days though. I have been busy at work.' Her housemate grabbed her hoodie from the chair where she'd slung it.

'Lucky you,' Lottie muttered.

'I cannot believe Callum hasn't texted you. You are a goddess. That is bull*shit*,' Celine cried. 'Okay. In which case, we are going to go down there looking fabulous and make him regret it. Go and put something nice on, Lottie. *Vite, vite!* I'm hungry.'

'I don't need to change to go down there,' Lottie protested, and then looked at what she was wearing – an oversized Snoopy T shirt that had gone grey in the wash and jeans – and realised that Celine was right. She didn't want Callum to see her like this, if she was going down there like an avenging angel. She needed to make him see what he had lost. She let out an exasperated sigh. 'Fine. I'll be two minutes.'

She ran up to her room and changed into a more fitted top – she'd bought some new things at the boutique shop in the village, Fiona's Fashions, and the top was adorable. It was strappy, cream coloured, with gold buttons and faux pockets in the style of a Chanel twinset. When she'd tried it on in the shop, she'd been surprised how well it fitted: stretching comfortably around her bust and pulling her in at the waist. Paired with the same jeans, which sat nicely on her waist and showed off her bottom, she was transformed from shapeless to – as Gretchen might say – shapely.

Quickly, Lottie undid her hair which had been in a long plait all day, and shook out her hair which now fell in shiny golden waves down her back. Hastily, she put on a light makeup, and ran back downstairs to the kitchen.

'All right. Now I'm ready,' she announced, a little breathlessly.

'Girl. *Jolie madame.* You look *tres chic,*' Celine gushed. 'This is exactly the vibe. We make him regret the day he ignored you, *oui?*'

'All right. I guess.' Lottie rolled her eyes. On one hand, she didn't want to leave the house. She wanted to hole up and hide away. She was mortified; she hated men and she never wanted anything to do with one ever again.

On the other hand, she was livid. And it was that anger that made her get dressed, do her makeup and pick up her handbag.

If Callum wanted to use her and then throw her away, then he had another think coming.

Fred, now sitting at the kitchen table with his dinner, looked up and widened his eyes.

'Wow,' he said, and then started to say something else, but coughed instead. He cleared his throat repeatedly, eyes watering. He took a gulp from a glass of water next to him.

'All right?' Lottie clapped him on the back.

'Fine. Went down the wrong way,' he spluttered. 'You look lovely, Lottie.'

Once again, Lottie was reminded of the moment she and Fred had shared at the castle. Zelda had seemed sure that Fred liked her, but Lottie hadn't believed her. She still didn't, not really: she wasn't used to the idea that she could be attractive to him.

'See? You almost killed Fred, eh. With your beauty.' Celine took Lottie by the arm and propelled her towards the door. 'Don't wait up for us, Fred. We are beautiful women, taking back our power, and the town by storm.'

'Good luck.' Fred gave them a wave. 'And, I won't be offended if you bring me back a fish finger sandwich,' he called out, after them. 'Since you're going.'

Walking out of the door, Lottie thought for a moment that Gretchen might be proud of her. She was proud of herself, in that moment. She felt as though she was doing something positive. She looked good, and she felt powerful, for the first time in a long time.

'Ugh,' Celine repeated as she closed the door after them. 'I love Fred, but he needs to work on his timing, eh?' She put her arm around Lottie's shoulders. 'Come on, Lottie. I'm here for you, okay? Let us be queens.'

37

'I'm having the crab mac n' cheese.' Celine hugged her arms around herself as they stood in the queue for The Shrimp Shack. 'It's so good. I'm addicted.'

'Hm. I'm not sure what to have,' Lottie said. Her stomach was churning. 'I'm not sure that I'm actually hungry at all now.'

She was in two minds about Callum. On one hand, she didn't want to see him if he obviously had so little respect for her. But on the other hand, she was curious to see what he'd do if she turned up in front of him.

What would Gretchen do? she thought, idly, but she knew without thinking about it very hard. Gretchen would definitely come down to confront Callum, looking great, and ask him what the hell he thought he was playing at.

Gretchen would ask him, straight out, what he thought he was doing, taking her out for a date, kissing her, making love to her, and then not calling her for over a week.

Gretchen would not be taking any of Callum's – as Celine said – bull*shit*.

She had walked down to the high street with Celine feeling like a queen. She knew that was how Gretchen wanted her to feel. It was how being with Gretchen had taught her to feel about herself, but it was also hard to keep a hold of that feeling and not fall back on her habitual negative self-talk.

'You have to eat, *cherie*,' Celine said. 'Look. You can tell me. Was it just a date, or was there... something more?' she raised an eyebrow. 'I would never judge you, if that is what you are worried about. I have slept with men on the first or second or tenth date. It does not matter. If you feel it, you should do it. We are modern women, eh?' She nodded at Lottie. 'Whenever we sleep with them, it does not give them the reason to be little shits. A man who is a man will treat you like a queen regardless of when you sleep with him. He should be grateful that you do it at all.'

'We did. I didn't plan it, but it just sort of... happened. We were safe,' Lottie said. She'd insisted on that.

'You had a good time?' Celine asked.

'It was really good. Romantic. I thought...' Lottie trailed off. 'I guess I got taken in just like women always do.'

'Ugh. I am so sorry.' Celine gave her a big hug. 'When we find him, I'm going to give him a piece of my mind too.' Celine added some choice swear words onto the end of her vow, which seemed incongruous in her French accent.

'Thanks, Celine,' Lottie sighed. 'I just... maybe we shouldn't have come.'

'Nonsense. We absolutely should. Men should not be allowed to get away with this kind of behaviour,' her housemate scoffed.

With every step she took towards the front of the queue, Lottie became more and more nervous, and also more and more hyped up. Celine was right. She didn't deserve this bad behaviour, and she shouldn't feel mortified or embarrassed. Callum was the one that should feel ashamed.

When she and Celine got to the front of the queue, though,

Tom was serving in the van with a girl that hadn't been there before. He grinned when he saw Celine.

'Oh, hi, you,' he said. 'Come down to see me finally, then?'

'Oui, *cheri*. We came down for dinner, no? And maybe a little dessert, later?' She raised a flirtatious eyebrow. Lottie watched as Tom nodded bashfully: it was clear that Celine had him exactly where she wanted him.

'Sure,' he said. 'We close up in about an hour, if you want to hang around. We could go for a drink after?' He stammered over his words a little, and it was hard to tell exactly because the van was probably hot, but it looked as though Tom was blushing a little.

Well, at least Celine had a man in the palm of her hand. Which was more than Lottie felt she could say about Callum.

'Hey, Tom. Is Callum around?' she asked, casually.

'Ah, yeah... he's just nipped out for something. Not sure when he'll be back,' Tom said, vaguely.

Lottie's heart sank. She'd hyped herself up to be giving Callum a piece of her mind, and now he wasn't here.

'Oh. Okay.' She tried to sound breezy, but she thought it must be obvious that she was disappointed. Then, she had an even worse thought: what if Callum had seen her arrive, and snuck out to avoid her? Her heart sank.

I shouldn't have come, she thought. *What was I thinking?* She felt embarrassed all over again.

But, then, her anger spilled over. *How dare he avoid me?* she thought, her feelings boiling. *If that's what's happened here, then Callum is even more of a worm than I thought he was.*

Celine gave their order, and they stood to one side to wait for it.

'Suspicious that he is not here, no?' Celine said. 'What do you think? Shall we wait?'

'I don't know. Let's wait for our food and then decide.' Lottie felt anti-climactic. 'I mean, it could be perfectly innocent.

I guess he does have to run errands like everyone else. Bad timing, maybe.'

'Hmm. Maybe.' Celine raised an eyebrow.

'He didn't know I was coming,' Lottie argued.

'No. But maybe he got the sense from your messages that you were angry, and he is laying low. Like a worm.' Celine stuck out her tongue.

'Maybe. I don't know.' Lottie lowered her voice so that Celine had to incline her head to hear. 'Who's that girl, do you think?' She nodded towards the girl who was helping Tom serve customers. She was attractive, maybe in her early twenties, with black hair in two cute plaits and wore pink dungarees with a white crop top underneath.

'No idea. She's pretty, though, eh?' Celine said. 'I'll ask Tom later, if you like.'

'No, it doesn't matter.' Lottie looked away; the girl was one of Callum's team, that was all. And even if it wasn't all, what business was it of hers? Callum probably knew a thousand pretty girls. Perhaps he was on a date with one of them now.

Lottie felt stupid now for having dressed up; she wished she was still wearing her Snoopy T-shirt and hadn't put any makeup on. At least it wouldn't look so obvious that she'd made an effort for Callum, who wasn't even here. At least he wasn't here to see her. That was something.

Tom called out their number and Celine collected the food.

'Look, Celine, I'm going to head home. I'll take Fred's back for him if you want to stay,' Lottie said. She felt completely deflated; mortified she had come all the way down here, and disappointed that she hadn't been able to give Callum a piece of her mind.

'Sure. If you are okay?' Celine looked at her concernedly. 'Don't worry that Callum isn't here. It does not mean anything, no? And even if it did, he doesn't deserve you. All he deserves is a good telling off, eh?'

'I know,' Lottie said, taking the two food boxes from her friend. But, she felt awful. 'I just want to go home.'

'Okay, sweet.' Celine gave her an unexpected kiss on the cheek. 'You take care, though. Okay? This is not your fault. You did nothing wrong.' Celine held both of Lottie's arms, looking her firmly in the eye. 'Okay?'

'Okay.' Lottie nodded.

'All right. I will see you later. Or, maybe not, eh?' Celine winked.

'All right. Have fun.' Lottie walked off, up the high street, wanting to put as much distance as she could between herself and the food truck.

She genuinely hoped that Tom was a nicer man than Callum, but she also knew that Celine was fierce and could look after herself. Still, Lottie walked away, feeling less than enthusiastic about any man, in that moment. She hoped Celine would have a fun evening, but, as far as her love life went, she was pretty much done. A life of celibacy and cats looked pretty good to her right now.

It wouldn't be so bad, Lottie thought as she walked along the high street, back to Gyle Head. *A peaceful life, without men.* But, the thought made her deeply sad, and she started to cry. She wanted love. She wanted companionship. There was nothing wrong with that, was there? So why was it that everyone she tried to get close to, broke her heart? Why was it so difficult?

38

GRETCHEN

Men are perilous. This is something I learned in life.

Not all men, as the saying goes. But, some, and those men are often enough to put a woman off them for life. I have seen it, again and again. I read, on social media pages and groups and threads and chats, over and over, women saying, *I have given up on love. I have given up on looking for a relationship. It's too toxic out there. I choose to protect my peace and stay single.*

And I understand that. As lonely as it can be, I understand it totally. And, I don't think men are any worse now than they were in the past; a lot of them are much better. It's just that women now have the choice to be independent. In the past, you had to get married, and then you had to stick with what you had, for better or for worse.

On the internet, I once watched a video of a psychologist talking about evil. And he said, what produces trauma in people is not physical pain or even fear, in itself. Trauma comes when people fully witness the soulless evil which exists in the minds of others. When you are exposed to that kind of cold, inhuman violence; that desire to hurt, that complete lack of humanity, you are traumatised.

It is not pain that hurts you in the long term. You can break your arm, and it will heal, and it will not traumatise you in particular. It is not pain that dims your light and makes you fear connection with others. It is being in the terrifying presence of a human who has become dehumanised enough to hurt and horrify you in ways you never knew were possible.

This is what Alex did to me. I saw what was underneath the veneer of niceness and respectability he wore as a mask, and it frightened me so much that I never put myself in the position of being vulnerable with a man again.

I had dalliances; I was fond of some of them. Some of them stayed as friends. But I never, ever let anyone as close to me as I had Alex, and I certainly never put myself in a position where I would have to protect a child from them.

Have I been lonely? Yes. Should I have tried to open my heart again? Perhaps. If I was younger now, I might have seen a therapist. That would probably have helped a lot.

But, I didn't. I did the only thing I knew how to do: protect my peace and close my heart. And it cost me love; yes, I know that it did. But it also saved me.

When we are children, we can walk into the forest with a carefree heart, and be brave enough to fight the monsters that might wait there.

But when we grow old, we grow weak. And my heavy heart made me afraid.

'You're home early.' Fred looked up from the sofa in surprise as Lottie walked in. She handed him the box containing his fish finger sandwich wordlessly and turned to go upstairs. She'd been trying to stop herself from crying all the way home, mostly unsuccessfully, and as soon as she'd got in the front door, she'd felt her control of her emotions loosen. At this point, she wanted nothing more than to climb into bed, pull her curtains closed and sob her heart out.

Lottie was aware that it wasn't just the Callum situation that was upsetting her. This state of being in no contact, after she'd let herself open up to Callum, was triggering her memories of Tristan. It was Tristan who had broken her heart; Tristan who had pulled it out through her chest and shot it to pieces with a machine gun. That was how she felt.

'Lottie? Are you okay?' Fred turned around to look at her properly. 'What's happened?'

'Nothing. I'm taking this upstairs,' she said, flatly.

'Lottie. Something's wrong, I can tell. Talk to me.' Fred tapped the sofa next to him. 'Come on. If you need to talk, I'm here.'

'I don't need to talk,' she said, her voice breaking.

'Are you sure?' he asked, softly, and something in his voice made the tears spill down her cheeks. She couldn't hold them in anymore. 'Oh, Lottie. What is it?' Fred stood up and came to where she stood in the doorway, and put his arms around her.

'Careful of the box,' she mumbled into his chest; he was in danger of squashing it.

'Sod the box. Give it here.' He took it and put it on the coffee table, then came back to where she was standing. 'Now. What's happened? Where's Celine?'

'She stayed. She's going out with Tom.' Lottie wiped her eyes. 'It's nothing, really. It's just that... I thought he'd be there. I got all dressed up. And he wasn't and now I feel stupid. And used.'

'Callum? I thought you'd be able to see him and have a talk. Sort everything out.'

'No. Tom said he'd popped out to do something. It's okay, whatever.' Lottie shrugged.

'It's not okay, Lottie. He's treating you badly. All right, he couldn't have known you were coming to see him today, but he could message you. If I'm honest, I think you could do better. Just stop letting him upset you. Block and move on.'

'I don't know why you care so much,' Lottie lashed out. The truth was that she didn't want to think about blocking Callum, or the possibility that there might not be a future in whatever this was, with him. Something in her wanted to believe that it would work out. That there was a happy ever after out there for her. She so rarely had let herself feel anything for anyone, and she hated the fact that, apparently, the ones she let herself have feelings for were the ones that would hurt her.

'Because you're my friend, Lottie,' Fred said, steadily.

'You don't know that he doesn't have a good reason for calling. I just caught him on a day he wasn't there. It's not his fault,' she heard herself excusing Callum, and, in a sudden flash of insight, she remembered her mother saying exactly the same thing about her often-absent father. *It's not his fault. He has to be away, working. He loves us.*

But, *he didn't love us*, Lottie thought. *He had a second family, all those years. He was never there because he was with them. And, then, finally, he left us for good.*

But it wasn't wrong of me to need my dad, she thought. *And it was his fault that he chose to leave me.*

She had never admitted it to herself, but there was another buried feeling in there, under the abandonment, under the sadness. And it was anger. She was angry at her mother for saying *don't make a fuss*. It felt like such a terrible betrayal.

'I just think you could do better, and you shouldn't waste any more time on Callum,' Fred repeated. 'You're lovely, and there are a million guys out there who would be over the moon to be with you.'

'Right. They're queuing up as we speak.'

'Well, they would be if you put yourself out there at all. I mean, literally, have you gone on any dates other than with Callum? All you do is hang out at the care home, working on your project – and I'm not criticising that, by the way, because I think it's awesome – but you're hardly going to find love among the eighty-plus community. With the best will in the world.'

'I know that. I'll put myself out there when I'm ready. And I don't see how it's any business of yours,' she argued back.

'It's not. Whatever. Forget I said anything.'

'Fine. I will.' She turned away and stomped up the stairs to her room. Slamming her bedroom door, she burst into tears. She wasn't angry at Fred. She was angry at Callum and Tristan, but mostly at herself. She'd let Callum get to her, and she shouldn't have.

And, it was a horrible feeling to also realise that she was angry with her mum – the person she had loved most in the whole world. But it had been Emma that had said *don't make a fuss, or Daddy might not come back.* It wasn't even true. The fact that Lottie's dad had left them was nothing to do with whether she made a fuss or not. He had already gone, in his heart, when Lottie was small. She could see that now. And, it wouldn't have been because of her. She was old enough to know, now, that adults had their own reasons for making the decisions they did; none of which were ever because a child had been a little needy, now and again.

She hadn't even been *needy*. She had just been a normal child.

However, regardless of the reasons, her dad *had* been unavailable – literally and emotionally. Did that mean that now she was always going to be attracted to emotionally unavailable men? Men that were mostly physically absent from her life? Did that somehow feel "right" to her, even though it hurt her?

Lottie curled up on her bed and hugged her pillow, wiping the tears from her cheeks.

She tapped her phone and found the therapist's channel she'd been watching on social media. She'd been finding it helpful, and, at this moment, she felt like she needed something. Some kind of logic, a way to understand what was happening.

The video that popped up was about avoidant attachment styles. Lottie played it, remembering that Gretchen had mentioned the same term in one of their conversations. Typical of Gretchen to be aware of the most current conversations on social media.

The emotionally avoidant partner will end the relationship as soon as things get real, the presenter began in one of his many videos. *Quite often after a holiday or meeting your family, they will start to feel threatened by the relationship and end it without warning.*

The avoidant never received love as a child or was taught that their feelings were unacceptable, so, to avoid the pain of having their heart broken by being rejected, they close off any attempts at love or intimacy.

Was this what Callum was doing to her, all over again? If so, how was it that Lottie was attracting these guys, one after the other? Did she have some kind of beacon within her that was drawing them to her? And if so, how could she turn it off and attract someone nice, that loved her, who didn't want to run away at the first sign of love?

Lottie stopped the video and stared at the ceiling.

She'd pushed her feelings about Tristan to one side for a long time.

They will often give excuses for the ending of a relationship such as "right person, wrong time" or that they need to work on themselves, that they aren't ready for a relationship. Sadly, few avoidants will actually do the personal work required after ending a relationship. Rather, the ending of a relationship returns them to a feeling of safety and they will usually distract themselves with hobbies or new, casual relationships and not allow themselves to feel anything at all.

It's likely that months after the breakup, however, the avoidant will relax their guard over their emotions and allow themselves to miss you. It is at this stage that they are likely to reach out to you.

Be aware that, if you take them back, you would be well advised to put some firm boundaries in place before attempting to have a relationship with the avoidant, who is most likely not to have done the emotional work required to overcome their difficulties in relating to others and becoming more able to be relaxed in intimate relationships.

But, was it also possible that she was the one avoiding intimacy because of what had happened to her with her dad? Was there a reason she'd stayed single for so long? Had she "chosen" Callum and Tristan because, on some level, she'd known that they would leave her?

If so, what kind of crazy person did that make her?

Lottie rolled over in bed and groaned.

Maybe I'll just give up on men altogether, she thought. *I don't think they're worth it. This isn't worth it. I just want to be happy.*

But, how could she make herself happy? She had never known how to do it, and it felt like there had always been a man in her life who was in the process of abandoning her. How was she supposed to feel grounded and whole in the midst of this kind of next level messed up relationship? Gretchen had lived a life on her own terms, taking lovers when she wanted, having a child when she wanted and never compromising herself for a man. How had she achieved that kind of confidence?

How do I get to be like that? Lottie wondered. Was it really just a case of putting down firm boundaries and sticking to them? She couldn't get over the fear of abandonment – *don't make a fuss, or Daddy might not come back.* Firm boundaries meant that men like Callum and Tristan definitely wouldn't come back.

Maybe, she just had to somehow become okay with being alone, because that seemed to be the choice available. Take bad behaviour because you loved them, or thought you did, or raise your standards and be alone, either for a while or forever.

She was alone now, but she wouldn't have been if Tristan hadn't ended it. She'd spent six months missing him, but what if he'd done her a huge favour by ending it? And, despite the fact that she felt heartbroken all over again by what Callum had done, what if the same could be said for him? What if both men were echoes of the abandonment she had felt when she had lost her dad to his second family – and what if she could heal it by being conscious of it, and making different choices?

The sudden realisation that she could make herself happy hit her, like a secret door opening into a colourful garden. *You don't need a man to make you happy,* she thought. *You chose to do the MA, you chose to move to Loch Cameron, you found new friends, you started to feel good in your own body. None of those things involved a man. Sure, if a nice one comes along, then that would still be nice. But what if, for your whole of your life ahead, you dedicated yourself to making you happy? What about that?*

40

Lottie was typing up some of the entries from Gretchen's diary when something fell out of the diary.

She picked it up. It was loose page, by the looks of things. The paper was a little more aged at the edge than the rest of the pages in the book.

Curiously, she turned it over and scanned the few lines it held.

20 June 1973

The agency allowed me to leave her with one gift, so I chose a locket. It belonged to my mother: a beautiful thing, a cameo. Inside, I put a lock of my own hair for her. I know it's silly and sentimental, but I wanted there to be some kind of link between her and me. There is the invisible link of love, but, now, there is also the locket.

Lottie reached for her own locket which hung at her throat, like it always had since her mother had given it to her. It too was a cameo; it too contained a lock of hair. Was that a remarkable coincidence?

It could be. But, how likely was it that she should be reading about Gretchen bestowing her baby with a locket – a link from a mother to a lost daughter – when she too owned the same thing?

Lottie stared at the page, and then flicked back to the dates of the entries in Gretchen's journal when she gave up the baby. June 1973. *It couldn't be.* Could it?

She found the page where Gretchen said that the baby had been born, and looked at the date. The closest was 7 March 1973.

Her mother's birthday was 3 March, and she had been born in the same year. If she had still been alive, she would have been just fifty-one years old.

Lottie stared at the journal for a long moment, holding the spare page in her hand, her mind in a whirl.

She had thought that Gretchen had given her the journals to read because she couldn't bear to voice what had happened with Alex. But, it seemed that Gretchen might have had another reason for giving them to her. Lottie thought back. There had been a couple of times – after they had discussed Alex and the pregnancy, and Gretchen giving up the baby – that Gretchen's demeanour had suggested that she was still holding something back. Was this what it was? Her final secret?

The coincidences were too great. There couldn't be any other explanation: Gretchen Ross's baby – the one that she had given birth to in March of 1973, the one that she had given away and the baby that Gretchen had given a locket to with a curl of her own hair inside – had to be her own mother, Emma.

Emma's birthday was 3 March, 1973, just four days before Gretchen wrote the entry saying that she had had her baby and was giving her baby away. Emma was adopted, Lottie knew that – Sharon and Graham, Lottie's grandparents, were not her biological family. To Lottie's knowledge, they'd never told

Emma anything about her biological mother. To Lottie's knowledge, they'd never known anything about her. Emma had certainly never said anything.

Gretchen had commented on her locket; had reached for it and held it, and Lottie remembered feeling slightly odd about how she had done it. Like she *remembered* the cameo. Gretchen had stroked the curl of hair which was inside: no wonder, then, if it had been her hair. Her baby that she had given away, with one small memento of her that the baby would never truly understand.

If this was true, then, as strange as it was to think it, Gretchen Ross could be Lottie's biological grandmother. Could it really be true that the woman she had been sitting next to for months, recording her stories, was related to her in such an important way? That she, Lottie Fox, was a descendant of Alexander O'Connell and Gretchen too? What kind of strange fate had brought her to Gretchen's care home, and to Loch Cameron, a tiny Scottish village that she had no reason to visit, but that had felt oddly like home ever since she had lived there?

Lottie's breath caught in her throat. It was too late at night to call Gretchen and tell her that she had read the journals. But she would go over there the next morning and ask Gretchen if it was true. She had to know for sure; she had to hear it direct from Gretchen.

All this time, she had been talking to her grandmother, and she hadn't known it. It was a strange feeling, but, at the same time, there was a chamber in Lottie's heart that had known. That there was something about Gretchen that felt familiar; something that felt like home. Every hour that they'd spent together, Lottie had felt a love growing for Gretchen Ross.

Since her mum, Emma, had passed away so unexpectedly and so young – she was only in her late-forties, and Lottie herself was only twenty-five at the time – there had been a yawning hole in Lottie's life and her heart. She would never get over the loss of her mother, and her grandparents had been amazing. But, the idea that, suddenly, she had someone who was family where she hadn't before – that there was someone who might come in and fill that yawning hole in her heart – it filled Lottie with joy.

She held the journals to her heart. What had guided her here, to Gretchen? She had no idea, but she offered up a prayer of thanks to whatever angels had brought her here. She had found family, and that was more than she could ever have expected.

41

———

'It's cancer.' Zelda didn't even say hello as Lottie answered the phone. She was in the car, heading over to the care home to see Gretchen.

'What?' Lottie's heart clenched; it was like she'd been punched in the chest. She'd hardly slept since reading Gretchen's journal the night before and discovering the unbelievable link from her mum to Gretchen. In the light of day, it hardly seemed real. Yet, the coincidence was at the very least notable. Lottie had to know; she had been tossing and turning all night, waiting for it to get light so she could get up and talk to Gretchen.

'Gretchen got her test results. The home called me just now.' Zelda started sobbing. 'Oh, Lottie. I don't know what to do! That's why her vision's been impaired. It's in her brain. It's in her organs... just everywhere. She's... she's really sick.'

'Oh, no,' Lottie breathed. 'Zelda... I... I can't believe it.'

'It's horrible. I'm going over there soon, Hal's going to drive me, I can't...' Zelda trailed off, and Lottie's heart ached for her, listening to her sob. 'I just wanted to let you know.'

'Oh.' Lottie was driving along one of the country lanes

outside Loch Cameron, and had to pull sharply to the side of the road as a tractor passed her, sounding its horn; she'd veered into the middle of the narrow lane without realising. She pulled on the handbrake and sat there, heart pounding, staring out of the windscreen in shock.

'Lottie? Are you okay?' Zelda asked, her voice broken. 'Lottie?'

'I'm actually in the car, heading over there now,' Lottie said slowly, feeling strange. Her voice sounded weird in her own ears, as if she was underwater. 'I was... going to talk to Gretchen about something.'

'They said she can't talk to us, honey.' Zelda took a deep breath and let it go. 'She went downhill really fast, apparently. Kimberley said as soon as they told her, she kind of... let go. She's mostly unconscious. Kimberley said she'd done amazingly well to last as well as she has... it's everywhere, she said.' Zelda's voice hitched. 'I'm still going. Even if I can't talk to her, I want to hold her hand.'

'Sure, of course,' Lottie said, vaguely. She was feeling faint.

'Are you still going to go?' Zelda asked. 'If you're on your way, I'll see you there, maybe?'

'Yeah. I guess so.' Lottie cleared her throat. 'Sorry, It's... kind of a shock, that's all.'

'I'm so sorry, to be the one to tell you, Lottie,' Zelda said, brokenly. 'I'll chat to you later, okay?'

'Okay. Thanks for letting me know, Zelda.' Lottie ended the call and stared across the field from the car where she sat. On the horizon, a slate grey cloud was rolling in, despite the fact that the spot she was sitting in was bright.

'Oh, Gretchen,' Lottie said out loud, her heart contracting, feeling as though it wanted to fold onto itself. She crumpled over the steering wheel and started to sob, her head on the top of the wheel.

She'd known that Gretchen was old, and that she seemed to

be getting frail. Yet, she'd thought somehow that her friend would live much longer. At least, she couldn't believe that she had just found out about her own mother possibly being Gretchen's baby – and, now, Gretchen was too ill to talk to her about it.

It felt to Lottie as though she'd been given a wonderful gift, only to have it snatched away.

I have to see her. Even if she can't talk to me, Lottie thought. *I have to go.*

She started the car up again, wiping her eyes, and resumed the journey to Apple Orchard Care Home, full of dread and a tension that she might somehow be too late.

Please. Please let me see her, Lottie begged whoever was listening. She hadn't been brought up religious, but now and again she would ask the universe, an angel or an ancestor for a favour. It wasn't that she didn't believe in those things, it was more that she'd never been a part of any religion or had the particular inclination to join one.

But, in moments like these, she needed something, like so many people did. And so she prayed, as she drove along, that she wouldn't be too late. That she would at the very least be able to hold Gretchen's hand one more time, just like Zelda had said. And tell her that she loved her.

42

Lottie sat with her back to a tree in some woodland on Gyle Head, overlooking Loch Cameron. She had bought a sandwich and a coffee from the food truck next to the playground, but she hadn't wanted to go home. Somehow, it felt better to be outside for a while and breathe in the cool, calm air of Loch Cameron.

She had just got back from Apple Orchard Care Home. She and Zelda had sat at Gretchen's bedside for a couple of hours, watching her sleep. Kimberley had told them not to expect much; Gretchen had been put on morphine for the pain, and it had made her very sleepy. They had both gently held one of Gretchen's hands, not saying much to each other. Zelda had cried, quietly. Hal had stood at the window for most of the time they were there, looking out, as if he was letting Lottie and Zelda have their moment with Gretchen. Yet, he too loved her, just like so many people in Loch Cameron. When they'd left the room, finally, Hal had bent and kissed Gretchen's forehead very gently.

Lottie had wondered whether to tell Hal and Zelda what she'd discovered in Gretchen's journals, but the moment hadn't seemed right. She didn't want to mention it before speaking to

Gretchen; it felt disrespectful. And, what if she was wrong? She didn't know for sure that her mother Emma was Gretchen's biological daughter.

So, she'd driven home, and now she felt terrible. The weight of worry sat on her heart like a brick. She had come to love Gretchen so much in a short time; she wasn't ready to say goodbye yet.

Then there was the mystery of what she had found in the journals. Lottie had gone to see Gretchen for clarification, and she hadn't been able to get it. There was nothing that could be done about that, but the not knowing was hard. It was like being shown a beautiful garden through a door, but not being allowed to walk through it.

Lottie ate a little of her sandwich and stared across the loch. At least being here was in some way restful; she had no desire to go back to the house and hole up in her bedroom yet.

The sound of voices to her left made her look up. She was partially hidden in the little circle of trees: strong oaks surrounded her but opened at the front so that her view of the loch was unimpeded. However, she was otherwise protected from view.

Peeking around the trunk of the tree she was sitting against, she realised that the voices she could hear belonged to Fred and Helen. Instinctively, Lottie shrank back against the tree. She didn't feel like being recognised; she'd had a terrible day so far and she didn't want to have to explain why she was where she was or what was happening with Gretchen. Still, she attuned her ears to Fred and Helen's voices, curious to hear what they were talking about.

As they grew closer, Fred's voice became clearer. It was otherwise quiet up on Gyle Head apart from the wind in the trees.

... glad you see it that way, Fred said. When Lottie peeked again, she could see that Fred and Helen were walking through

the wooded part of Gyle Head, holding hands. Lottie didn't catch the beginning of what he had said.

Yeah, I get it, Helen replied. *I feel the same way.*

We've always been on the same page, he replied. *Peas in a pod.* They both laughed. Then, they stopped walking, and Helen snuggled up to Fred as he wrapped his arms around her and kissed the top of her head.

Lottie looked away. It was clearly such an intimate moment between them that she felt like she was trespassing; they didn't know she was there, and it felt weird, even though they weren't doing anything particularly outrageous.

Still, it was a personal, private and intimate moment, and it made Lottie more lonely than she expected.

After they had walked off, she examined her feelings. Fred was her friend; he was a good person who she liked. She was happy that he was happy with Helen.

So, why had seeing them together made Lottie feel even more terrible than she already did, today? Was she really that much of a grinch, being upset by seeing other people happy?

Or, was it more that she was jealous of what Fred and Helen had? That they had a happy relationship, and she, Lottie, had totally failed to find one with anyone who wasn't a narcissistic, dismissive avoidant?

A grey glumness nestled in Lottie's heart, like a cloud, and she felt it worm its way through her chest and down into her feet. *It's not fair*, she thought. *Why not me? Why do I have to be alone?*

She rested the back of her head against the tree trunk, breathed in a long breath of that clean, cool Loch Cameron air and let it go in a long exhale. *Don't be so hard on yourself*, she thought. *It's been an awful day. It's no wonder you don't feel all that positive about anything.*

So, Fred and Helen are perfectly matched, she thought. *Peas in a pod.* That's what Fred had said, just now. *So what?*

So, you want that, her internal voice said. *You've always wanted that. Your best friend. Your ride or die. Someone you could trust with your heart utterly and completely. Someone who wants to go on crazy adventures with you and cuddle up on rainy nights. Someone sweet and caring who makes you laugh and would never, ever consider not texting you after a date.*

She wanted a Fred, Lottie realised. She wanted a decent, honest guy who had wanted to listen to her read Gretchen's journal, who had listened to her complain about Callum, hugged her and told her she could do better. Who told her she was beautiful. Who would do things like kiss his girlfriend on her forehead as they took a romantic walk in the woods.

Well, you can't have him, she thought to herself, cruelly. *You can have someone like him, but not Fred. And goodness knows how rare Freds are because you've never met one before.*

Lottie shook her head and stared out across the loch, feeling more and more awful. It had been a bad day from the start, and now she felt doubly awful for being so envious of Fred and Helen. If she was having thoughts about him – which were entirely not okay – that was her fault, and meant she was a bad person. She didn't want to be that kind of girl. The kind of girl that got crushes on other people's boyfriends. That wasn't who she was.

That day at the castle with Fred, she had been attracted to him. Zelda had been right: there had been something between them.

But, just like when she and Fred had gone up to the castle and had tea with Zelda and Hal, Lottie also felt a hard pang of envy in observing Helen and Fred. And the emotion behind it was, *why can't I have that? What's wrong with me? When will it be my turn?*

Maybe it won't ever be your turn, she thought sadly to herself. *Maybe you're destined for a life alone, just like Gretchen.* And, while Gretchen seemed to have made the best of it, Lottie wondered if it really had been the happiest life imaginable, or whether Gretchen had been putting a positive spin on things in telling her story. When Lottie had been listening to Gretchen talk, she'd felt inspired and uplifted. But, the journals told a different story.

She might never know, now. That was the truth of it. And, she might never know who Gretchen really was to her: friend, or grandmother?

She stayed by the tree until it got dark, not wanting to go home. Not wanting to face Fred and Helen and their perfect, happy relationship. When it was late enough, she snuck into the house and went straight to her room, wishing she had never come to Loch Cameron in the first place. She had come to escape heartbreak, but she'd ended up finding it again.

Lottie got into bed and pulled the covers over her head. She didn't want to get out again. She opened one of the social media apps on her phone.

The video that started playing – just a series of animated text on the screen – was oddly relevant.

Choosing myself was one of the most liberating experiences of my life.

No longer extending my hand to those who won't do the same for me.

My worth isn't defined by how much I give to or compromise for others.

I put my needs first.

I put boundaries in place that protect me and my mental health.

I believe in me and trust the decisions I make that are not trying to please others.

I let go of the people who aren't holding me as tight as I need them to. The people who don't have my best interests at heart.

> *I am happy to be alone. I'd rather be in my own company than with someone disrespectful.*
> *I choose myself.*

I choose myself. Lottie mouthed the words. What would that even look like?

It was all very well, wanting to be chosen by somebody else. Her dad hadn't chosen her; he'd chosen his other family, and she'd felt abandoned all of her life. So much so that she was apparently willing to accept the slightest bit of attention from Tristan and Callum.

But, in her whole life, Lottie had never considered the radical possibility of being the one to choose. She hadn't ever realised that was an option.

I could choose to be alone, she thought. *I could choose to be happy.*

The thought bloomed in her heart, shyly hopeful. Before she had met Gretchen, Lottie would never have dared have the confidence to put her own happiness first, or believe that she could spend time alone and be happy, and not feel a terrible emptiness. But, Gretchen had given her the inspiration to concentrate on making herself happier.

I could choose to be happy.

And, that was a gift, even before Lottie had known that Gretchen might be so much more to her than a friend.

43

———————

Hey.

It was late, again, and the message flashed up on her phone.

It was Callum.

Lottie stared at the phone in complete disbelief. She'd assumed that she wouldn't hear from Callum again after him completely ghosting her.

Are you actually kidding me, she thought, watching as the three little dots flash for a moment.

How are u?

Lottie picked up her phone and wondered what to reply. She had been feeling so low for the past few days, after the news about Gretchen and seeing Fred and Helen, that she'd hardly got out of bed. Celine had tapped on her door a couple of times, asking her if she wanted anything from the shops and if she was okay – presumably, she'd heard the news about Gretchen – but Lottie hadn't had the energy to chat.

She was devastated with the news about Gretchen, like

Zelda was. Even though she knew how old Gretchen was, and she'd known that Gretchen had had some tests done, she still hadn't quite believed that her friend wasn't indestructible.

Gretchen had done so much, been through so much in her life, was such a tower of strength, that seeing her in her bed, so small, all of a sudden, and so weak, not herself – it was more shocking than Lottie had expected.

That was the thing that was really upsetting her. Seeing someone so close to death had also brought back Lottie's memories of her mother's sudden death.

Since seeing Gretchen, it had all come flooding back. Lottie had done nothing since but cry for days, curled up in a ball. She missed her mum terribly. She'd missed having a mum. Having someone to go to with her problems, to talk to, and do all the things they'd loved to do together. The simple things. They were all lost. Her grandparents were lovely, but it wasn't the same.

Now, she'd found Gretchen, and they'd found their simple routines. Without realising it, Lottie had come to look forward to and then almost rely on her visits to Gretchen. And, now, it was being taken away. Again.

In the meantime, she was looking at her phone in the middle of the night as Callum texted her *hey, u up?*

He couldn't even be bothered to write "you", Lottie thought.

Still, the surprise of Callum's attention was a spark of light in an otherwise deep greyness within her. She realised that she was tempted to reply.

I missed you. I keep thinking about the night we spent together he wrote, when she still didn't reply.

Callum was paying her attention now. But it was so little attention. A breadcrumb. A message because he was bored, probably.

I doubt that Hal Cameron ever texted anyone "hey, u up" in the middle of the night, Gretchen's voice popped into Lottie's head. *Don't respond to that, Lottie. That isn't the behaviour of a man that wants or respects you.*

Gretchen Ross might have been in her final days or weeks, but Lottie had learned a thing or two from her. And, the voice was right. If Gretchen had taught her anything, it was to have confidence in herself and not settle for less than she was worth.

Really? You've ignored me ever since it happened Lottie replied, finally. She ignored her urge to be agreeable and nice. Yes, a part of her wanted Callum's approval. His love. But she also realised that love was not what was being offered here.

I can choose myself, she thought. *I can choose myself by saying no to this.*

I've been busy with work he replied, quickly.

It's not even a different excuse, Lottie thought with incredulity. *And, it's amazing how quickly he's replying now, all of a sudden. When he wants something.*

And we all know what he wants, Gretchen's voice said in her mind. *It's fine to want sex, dear. You enjoy it. But, on your terms. And, ideally, when the other person treats you like the queen you are.*

Callum, that is a terrible excuse Lottie replied.

You deserve the best, Lottie Fox. And as soon as you start believing in yourself as a beautiful, powerful woman, believe me, one will appear. They will hear your siren call, Gretchen had said.

Part of that believing in herself was saying no to anyone like Callum who tried to treat her like anything less than a queen.

I'd love to see you again, Lottie he wrote.

I bet you would, Lottie thought. *You're horny. You want to fulfil your needs. But what about my needs?*

The temptation to say yes was strong. Because, in person, Callum was charming and attractive, and the sex between them had been wonderful. Lottie was willing to admit that.

But, it wasn't enough. Callum had ghosted her twice now, and Lottie wasn't about to let him do it for a third time.

I don't think so she wrote.

Lottie. Please. Do you want me to beg? He added a smiley face, and Lottie stared with mounting anger at his message. Did Callum think she was playing some kind of sexy game with him? He'd done this before when he'd persuaded her to go for dinner with him: made a show of "begging" her over text until she'd agreed. Was this all a game to him?

No. I choose me, and I'm not playing.

You should not ever sleep with a woman and then ignore her. I'm only bothering to tell you this for my own peace of mind and not because I have any interest in talking to you after this. You should know that what you're doing right now is really bad behaviour.

Lottie was surprised to find that she didn't feel particularly upset writing these messages, knowing that this meant there was no going back to Callum. She was disappointed and vaguely resigned to the fact that she apparently had to point out to a grown man how his behaviour was utterly childish, but she realised that she wasn't losing anything.

Lottie had had one wonderful night with Callum, but she probably wouldn't ever get more than that from him. She could never lose what she'd never had. Callum wasn't able to give her what she wanted or needed. He was proving that in every message now, and every moment he hadn't talked to her before.

If you sleep with a woman and you don't want to see her again afterwards for some reason, then at the very least communicate that, politely and kindly. Please know that although our night might not have meant anything to you, it did to me. I don't give

*myself to just anyone and what we did was very personal and
intimate. You abandoning me afterwards hurt me.*

*You either lied to get me into bed, or you did genuinely like
me, and you really can't manage a grown-up relationship with
a woman. Either way, I'm not interested.*

*I'm over it, and I'll be blocking your number now. Be
better. All the best.*

Lottie watched the screen for a moment as the messages
sent, and watched as Callum read them.

He started to reply, but Lottie had no interest in reading
what he wanted to say. He'd had weeks to communicate with
her. She would have read the messages then.

Well done, dear, Gretchen's voice sounded in her mind.

Lottie tapped on Callum's name at the top of the screen and
selected "block number". Then, she deleted all of her and
Callum's messages.

For a moment, she sat and looked at her phone, then went to
the "Archived" part of the messaging platform, where she still
kept Tristan's messages.

She looked at his photo for a moment, and thought about all
the lovely messages that were still there; she could scroll back
and find them if she wanted to. She'd done that so many times.
Photos, memories, sweet words. They were all meaningless
now.

Taking a deep breath, Lottie blocked Tristan's number as
well, and, after a moment more, deleted all those messages, too.

She sat for a moment in the silence, waiting for regret to
overwhelm her, but nothing came. She only felt a kind of quiet
relief. *I chose myself,* she thought.

She'd been feeling awful for the past few days, but being
decisive with Callum had unexpectedly made her feel better.
She was still sad about Gretchen, and she was still sad that she
didn't have the love in her life that she wanted.

But, at least, she'd signalled to herself and the universe – if it was listening – what she didn't want. And what she was uninterested in entertaining in her life. And, that felt good.

Lottie closed her eyes and lay back on her pillow. At least now she could stop obsessing over Callum and wondering if he was going to call. And she could focus on the person who needed her most, right now: her friend, Gretchen.

44

GRETCHEN

It's dark now, most of the day. I sleep a lot, but even when I'm awake, it seems as though I see everything through a dark curtain.

They are talking to me, in the distance, but it's hard to hear them. I know people come in and out, but I am far away already, walking into the forest.

I remember the fairy tales I read as a child. I remember Father reading them to me. Hansel and Gretel, Little Red Riding Hood. Beauty and the Beast. All of them set in the dark pine forests, where the trees cluster together and block out the sun. And, yet, there is a fresh smell of earth and rain in the air, and, as I walk further and further in, the feel of soft pine needles under my feet.

I feel a sense of peace, finally. I have told my story to Lottie, and I have laid it to rest.

She knows everything, and that is my gift to her. It is also my gift to myself, I realise now; I never got to know Emma, my child. But I got to know Lottie, my granddaughter, and she is, along with Stella, the best gift I could ever ask for.

Now, I can go.

Eenty teenty tirry mirry, ram, tam, toosh
Eenty teenty tirry mirry, ram, tam, toosh

The childhood rhyme repeats in my mind as I walk. I am old now, and have forgotten the rest of it. It doesn't matter.

I am losing words now, losing the ability to speak. The cancer has taken so much already: my eyes, my lungs, my mind. But there is *Waldeinsamkeit*; the bear in the forest waits for me, and he is kind. He does not mind that I have lost all these things, because in his arms, I will be free.

45

'Hi, Kimberley.' Lottie rubbed her eyes and peered owlishly at her bedside clock. 'Is everything okay?'

'Lottie. Hi. Yes, it's okay. But I just wanted to give you a heads up that the doctor says... ummm...' there was a pause. 'Gretchen... probably doesn't have that long now. So, if you'd like to come and say goodbye... maybe today is best.'

'Oh no. Right. Okay.' Lottie's heart twisted; she'd known that this day was coming, but she still wasn't prepared for the thud of grief that hit her. 'I'll be there as soon as I can.'

She got up, ran to the bathroom and showered quickly, with a sick feeling in her stomach. She wanted to see Gretchen, but she didn't want to go, knowing that it would be the last time. It was too sad. It was too soon. She wasn't ready to say goodbye to the friend she had just found.

She was heading back into her room to get dressed, wrapped in a towel, when Fred opened his door and stuck his head out.

'Hey. What's up? It's early,' he said, blearily.

'Sorry if I woke you. I got a call from the care home. It's Gretchen.' Lottie's voice cracked. She had visited, a number of times over the past few days, but Gretchen had been unconscious on every occasion. 'They said... it's time.'

'Oh, god. Okay. Give me five minutes, I'll come with you.' Fred stepped out and gave her an impulsive hug.

'You don't have to...' she began, but he frowned and gathered her into his arms.

'Don't be daft. I want to.' He kissed the top of her head, then gave her a little push into her room. 'Go on. Get dressed and I'll be ready in five.'

When Lottie had dressed, plaited her hair and applied a little makeup – she wanted to look nice for Gretchen, somehow – she made her way downstairs and found Fred waiting by the front door, holding a flask and a couple of what looked like sandwiches in cling film.

'For the drive. As we don't have time for breakfast,' he explained.

'Fred. You didn't have to do that.' Lottie was already feeling emotional, and Fred's kindness wasn't helping. She felt her throat ache with the weight of unshed tears.

'Come on. We don't want to have our stomachs grumbling when we see her.' He opened the front door and ushered her out.

'All right, all right,' she acquiesced as she got into Fred's car. 'I could drive, you know,' she added.

'As if I'd let you drive today. I'm driving.' He frowned at her and started the ignition.

'Okay,' she said. She didn't have the energy to argue.

'How's work?' Lottie asked, once they'd driven out of the village. She unwrapped the sandwich Fred had made her. He was right: she was hungry.

'Not much to report. Books will be books.' Fred shot her a shy smile. Lottie thought again how handsome he was. Maybe that was a good sign. If she'd stopped fancying bad boys like

Tristan and Callum and started finding Fred attractive, at least that meant her taste was changing.

'And Helen?' she asked. *Remember he has a girlfriend, Lottie,* she chastised herself.

'Oh. Fine, I guess,' Fred said, evasively.

Lottie frowned at him. 'You don't sound sure.'

'Umm... well, we're not seeing each other anymore.' Fred looked embarrassed. 'So, no, I guess.' He stared ahead at the road.

'What happened? You seemed so happy!' Lottie looked across at him. After seeing them the other day in the woods, this seemed like an abrupt change. She didn't say that, though; she didn't want Fred to know that she'd been spying on him and Helen. She hadn't been spying, anyway. It had just been an accident: she was there, they were there.

'Didn't work out.' Fred shrugged.

'Oh, no! Why not?' she asked, appalled that she could have got it so wrong. She'd been convinced that Fred and Helen were the perfect couple. She'd gone to bed that night feeling so sad that they seemed to have what she craved.

'Just didn't. We're really similar people, but it just never really clicked, somehow,' he said, slowly. 'We're good friends. I guess she didn't really think about me like a boyfriend and vice versa.'

'Oh. Are you all right? Do you want to talk about it?' Lottie reached over to the steering wheel and put her hand on his briefly.

'I'm okay. Honestly, we weren't that involved. We only ever went on a few dates. She's so busy with work.' He looked uncomfortable. 'Please, don't worry about me. Though it's very sweet of you.' Fred stared at her hand on his until she took it away.

'Okay. Well, if you do want to talk about it.' Lottie guessed that he felt uncomfortable with the physical contact, but when they pulled up to some traffic lights, Fred reached across for her hand, and held it for a moment in return.

'Listen, Lottie. I just want you to know that I'm here for you today. Okay?' he said, seriously. 'Me and Helen aren't important. You are. Gretchen is.'

'You and Helen *are* important,' Lottie argued.

'Fine. But it's not about that today,' he repeated. 'We can talk about it another time.'

'Okay,' she said, quietly. 'As long as you know, I'm here for you. Okay?'

'I know you are,' he said, quietly. A warmth enveloped her heart, but he just nodded and stared at the road ahead.

When they got to Apple Orchard, Kimberley ushered them into Gretchen's room; the curtains were half open and the lamp by her bed was on.

'No point taking her into hospital at this stage. She's comfortable,' she said in a low voice. 'I'll make you some tea, if you'd like.'

'We had coffee on the way. But thanks,' Lottie said, grateful for Kimberley's kindness. 'Can we... I mean... is she awake, can she hear us?' Gretchen had her eyes closed, and her breathing was weak. She looked small, like a doll. Lottie felt her chest tighten.

'She's not very with it, but she has moments of clarity. She saw her grandson earlier and he said they exchanged some words, though not much. He went home to get some sleep, but he was here half the night. Lovely lad,' Kimberley said, softly. 'Take as much time as you like. I'll pop back in a while, but if you need anything, give me a buzz.'

'All right. Thanks,' Lottie said, softly, and took Gretchen's hand. 'She looks so frail,' she said to Fred, who put his arm around her shoulders. 'I came a few times this week, but she looks smaller again. Like she's shrinking.'

'I know. I remember my nan when she was like this,' Fred

said, quietly. 'Nan was a really outgoing, funny person. Then, at the end, she was... it was just like, she'd gone already.'

'Gretchen's just like that. A big personality. She's always dressed nicely. She loved clothes. We had a lot of conversations about outfits she used to wear. She was really nice to me about the way I look. Made me feel a bit more confident about it,' Lottie said.

'I'm glad. You always came back from your visits here really animated. I could tell you loved Gretchen. Love her still.' Fred nodded. 'And, I'm glad she made you feel more confident about your appearance. Though, you always look lovely. I can't believe there was ever a time you didn't believe it.'

'Most of my life.' Lottie shrugged.

'That's a long time to be wrong.' Fred shook his head.

'I do love her,' Lottie whispered. 'We had this very close bond, right from the start.'

Gretchen opened her eyes and blinked a few times.

'Who's that?' she asked, her voice querulous. 'I can't... see... you very well.'

'It's Lottie, Gretchen. And Fred, my friend.' Lottie's heart leapt. She hadn't expected to be able to talk to Gretchen today.

'Oh, Lottie. I can't record today,' Gretchen said, slowly. Her mouth looked dry and her voice cracked. Lottie saw that there was a glass of water next to the bed.

'I'm not here to record,' Lottie said, trying to keep her voice friendly and level, like she and Gretchen were chatting in their usual way. 'Gretchen, would you like some water?'

'Yes.' Gretchen nodded, so Lottie tipped the glass very gently towards Gretchen's lips. She was mindful not to give her too much. Gretchen took a couple of small sips, then coughed, so Lottie took the glass away.

'What have you been up to, then?' Lottie continued, in the same conversational tone. 'It looks like you've been partying way too hard, Gretchen.'

'No... rest for the... wicked,' Gretchen whispered. Lottie could see how hard it was for her friend to speak, and it brought a lump to her throat that Gretchen was still trying to make jokes, in her last hours.

'You are wicked. But in a wonderful way,' Lottie replied. 'I wanted to say thank you, Gretchen. For everything you've told me about your life. You've shared so much, and I'm so grateful. My project is going to be amazing because of you. But, you've been so much more than that to me. You're my friend.' Her voice strangled at the end of her sentence.

'Is... this... your... young man?' Gretchen asked, and Lottie chuckled, despite the sadness of the moment. Even close to death, Gretchen was a keen observer.

'Umm. No, Gretchen, this is Fred. We live together in the same house.'

'Hello, Gretchen,' Fred said.

Gretchen opened one eye wide, which appeared to take some effort. 'Oh. Fred Mackenzie. Give my regards to your mother.'

'I will, thank you,' he replied, polite as ever. 'We've missed you in Pageturner's. But I've enjoyed listening to Lottie tell me all about your interviews.'

'All... entertaining... I hope,' Gretchen replied. Lottie could see that the interaction was taking a lot of energy for her friend, and that even just a few sentences were demanding.

'Very entertaining,' Fred said. 'Lottie really loves you,' he added, squeezing Lottie's hand.

'I love her,' Gretchen said, remarkably clearly. With a clear effort, she opened her eyes and met Fred's surprised stare. 'Take care of her,' she said, as firmly as she would have usually.

'I will,' Fred said, exchanging a look with Lottie.

'If... there's one thing... I'd tell you. Live life... on your own terms.' Gretchen seemed intent on saying what she wanted to say, and Lottie knew that she was far too bull-headed to be dissuaded – even in her final moments. 'But...' Gretchen coughed, fighting for breath; fighting for the strength she needed to finish her words. 'If... if there's one thing... I regret. It's. Not... opening myself up... to love. After Alex.'

Gretchen closed her eyes.

'I know. But I read the journals, Gretchen. I know that Alex hurt you,' Lottie said, gently. 'That's not your fault, Gretchen. Anyone would be wary, after that.'

'The baby...' Gretchen whispered, and Lottie put both hands on Gretchen's. Her little hand felt like a featherless bird: light bones and a thin covering of skin. 'I should have told you. The locket.'

Lottie put a hand to her locket, her breath catching in her throat. This was what she had been waiting to hear. She had almost lost hope that she would be able to talk to Gretchen. Sudden nervousness overtook her; her heart started to pound.

'Was this yours?' Lottie asked, holding the locket up to the light. 'Was this what you wanted me to know, when you gave me the journals?'

'Ross family. The eyes. I saw it... the first... day you came,' Gretchen said, opening her eyes again and fixing them on Lottie's. 'I knew. And when you said you were Emma's child...' Gretchen coughed. She closed her eyes, drifting. 'I knew.' Now, Lottie could see that she was exhausted. 'Tired,' she sighed.

Lottie took in a deep breath to steady herself. She had to know, unequivocally and for sure. 'Gretchen. Are you my grand-mother?' she asked, outright. She saw Fred's shocked expression.

There was a silence. Gretchen appeared to have dropped into unconsciousness again. Lottie bit her lip; she was so desperate to know.

'Gretchen?' Lottie asked, softly. 'Was Emma your baby? The one you gave away? All that in the journals? Was your baby my mother?'

Gretchen didn't open her eyes again, but she murmured something. Lottie leaned in so that she could hear better.

'What was that, Gretchen?' she asked, gently.

'Yes,' the old woman whispered, her voice cracked.

Lottie started to cry.

'Lottie. Sweetheart,' Fred said in a low voice, putting his arm around her. 'Shhh. It's okay.'

Lottie buried her head in Fred's shirt and sobbed. Despite the fact that she had suspected she was right, she still hadn't quite believed it until Gretchen had said *yes*. That tiny word had changed everything; now, she wasn't just sitting at the bedside of her friend, who was dying. She was sitting next to her grandmother, and that made it so much worse.

Yes, Gretchen was the same person; Lottie was still losing *her*, and that was the toughest thing. But Lottie had already lost her mum, and knowing that she might have gained an unknown member of her family had been an amazing feeling. A gift, from nowhere.

And, now, all too soon, that was being snatched away.

'It's not fair. It's not fair,' Lottie sobbed into Fred's shoulder. He rubbed circles on her back.

'I know, sweetheart,' he said, soothingly. 'I know. I can only imagine.'

'The blue album,' Gretchen murmured thickly; she slumped against her pillows. 'Take it. It's yours.'

'What did she say?' Lottie asked, sitting up and wiping her eyes.

'Something about a blue album,' Fred said, frowning. 'She wants you to take it. I think she might mean that blue photo album, on the shelf there.' He pointed.

Gretchen's eyes fluttered closed, and her breathing slowed. Lottie's heart caught – *was Gretchen going? Were these her last moments?* But then she took in a long, jagged breath, and her breathing seemed to right itself. Lottie exchanged looks with Fred.

'We'll stay as long as you need to,' he murmured. 'Okay?'

'Okay.' Lottie bowed her head, only wanting to be here for Gretchen. But her eyes strayed to the blue photo album on the bookshelf that Fred had identified. What was in it that Gretchen wanted her to see?

46

'Thanks for stopping here. I just wanted to see Gretchen's old place.' Lottie stepped out of the car in front of one of the white-washed cottages on Queen's Point. The wind whipped her hair across her face – today, she had worn it loose for a change, rather than self-consciously trying to hide it in a plait or pinned up – so she took a hairband off her wrist and tied it up quickly to avoid it getting tangled.

'Of course. How are you feeling?' Fred closed the driver's side door and stood next to her, looking at the cottage.

'Better. Still sad, though. And kind of... overwhelmed, I guess,' she said, quietly.

'That's understandable. It's been quite a day.' Fred took her hand, gently.

They had stayed at Gretchen's bed until the evening. Gretchen's breath had become laboured and irregular. Kimberley had said, kindly, that they could stay if they liked, but Lottie knew at a certain point that it was time to go. She had said her goodbyes, and she had found a kind of peace between her and Gretchen.

'So. I kind of joined up the details in my own mind from

what you said when we were there, but – you think you and Gretchen were related?' Fred asked.

'Yes. And, thanks for what you did, back there. Just being there and being supportive. I'd read the journals Gretchen gave me, and I had a pretty good guess that we were related from the details in them. My mum's birthday tallied up with the date of the baby being born that Gretchen gave away for adoption, for one thing,' Lottie explained. She hadn't said much in the car coming back from the care home; there had been a lot to process.

'And your locket? It was hers?' Fred asked. 'I kind of put that one together. Was that mentioned in the journal too?'

'Yes. When she gave the baby up – my mum, Emma – she gave her a locket that had belonged to her family, and she put a lock of her own hair inside it. It's still in there.'

'Wow. That's... yeah. Quite the thing.'

'I know. It's so strange that we should have met, after all these years, apparently by chance. She never met my mum,' Lottie continued.

'That's hard. I'm sorry,' Fred sighed. 'But I guess at least you met Gretchen, right? The odds were definitely against it ever happening.'

'Yes. You're right.' Lottie let out a long breath. 'It's just... a lot, I guess.'

'It definitely is,' Fred said, taking her hand. 'You know, I used to come up here and play when I was a kid. I think I might even remember one of the old ladies who lived in one of these cottages giving us biscuits.'

'It's certainly nice up here,' Lottie agreed. 'It's sort of... comforting, being near to her old place. My grandmother's old house. Strange to think that.' The sun was setting over the loch, and had turned the strips of cloud that seemed to blanket the sky a deep orange.

'It's beautiful. Sometimes these sunsets are straight out of a painting,' Fred agreed.

Lottie stared out at the loch. Her heart was still raw from their visit to Gretchen. Kimberley had said she'd call when *it happened*; Lottie knew that meant when Gretchen passed. When they departed, she had slipped into a deep unconsciousness and hadn't said any more to them after mentioning the blue photo album. Lottie had taken it with her when she and Fred left.

Lottie turned her gaze to the cottage, trying to imagine Gretchen there with her daughter Stella. Or, Gretchen being there as a child herself. She wondered how Emma's life would have been different if Gretchen had kept her and not given her up for adoption. Would Emma, Alex, Stella and Gretchen all have lived there together? What would that have been like? She had no idea, but from what Lottie had read about Alex, she suspected that it would not have been a happy existence.

Lottie led Fred to a bench at the edge of the Point that over-looked the loch. There was a plaque nailed to the back of it, which looked relatively new:

IN MEMORY OF SERENA MCKELLAN
DAUGHTER OF LOCH CAMERON
HER LOVE SHOULD INSPIRE US ALL

'I wonder who Serena McKellan was.' Lottie touched the plaque gently with her fingertips.

'Oh. I know that, actually. She jumped off Queen's Point, broken-hearted. Her lover left Loch Cameron and never came back. A famous ballet dancer. I forget her name. Serena couldn't get over the loss.'

'Oh. Goodness. That's tragic.'

'It is.' Fred came to sit by her on the bench. They stared at the cottage that had once been Gretchen Ross's for a while, together. 'There are a surprising number of sad stories in this village,' he added. 'I know about Serena because there was a dedication ceremony for the bench a couple of years back, and it's a bit of a local story. But there's other stuff that's gone on that I've probably never heard about. You never know, in a place like this.'

'But some happy stories, too.' Lottie felt that she needed to hang on to something good, on today of all days. 'Gretchen's story was mostly happy.'

'That's true. Let's look at the album,' Fred reminded her. 'You brought it with you, right?'

'Yes.' Lottie reached into her bag and pulled it out. 'But I don't know what she meant. I mean, I think it's probably just an old photo album. She was so confused. She probably didn't know what she was saying.'

Lottie opened the album and carefully turned over the first, tissue-thin covering page. The album was spiral bound, with a fake blue leather cover. The photo pages were the kind popular in the 1970s to the 1990s: glued pages with a covering cellophane layer that pressed down on the pages. Lottie knew that this was what people had before digital cameras and then, later, phones, had taken over as the means to take photos.

The photos were mixed, with no particular order, but Lottie recognised a younger Gretchen straightaway: she smiled and pointed her out to Fred. In the pictures, she looked in her thirties or even forty, and the fashion and the sepia tones looked as though it was the 1970s.

'Look. That maxi dress. And look at her here. Those flares.'

'Ha. She looks great.' Fred nodded. Lottie turned a few more pages. There were some pictures of people she didn't know, and then some pictures of a baby.

'That must be Stella,' Lottie said. And, it seemed that it was, as the album continued with more pictures of Stella, growing up: smelling the flowers in the cottage garden, dressed in a tutu, opening presents on Christmas Day.

But, then, wedged in at the back of the album, there was a series of pictures of a different child. Another girl, not Stella.

These pictures weren't laid out under the cellophane, but just collected and pushed into a pocket at the back of the book.

Lottie took them all out and began to look through them. A strange feeling, partly disbelief, partly grief, bubbled up within her.

'What is it?' Fred asked, watching her.

'That's my mum.' Lottie looked up from the album. 'She was telling the truth. About all of it.'

'Did you doubt that she was? Telling the truth, earlier?' Fred leaned forward.

'No. Not really. But, you know. This just makes it all the more real.' Lottie stared at the photos. She turned the page, and shook her head in amazement. 'This one! I actually remember this picture. We had the same one at home.'

'This is your mum?' Fred peered at the picture again.

'Yeah. She's ten years old there and she won the egg and spoon race at school. Look. She's holding the spoon.' Lottie pointed to it. 'It was a school picture, and she always liked it of herself. She said it was a happy time. We had the framed picture on top of the sideboard,' Lottie said, not believing what she was seeing.

'Wow. That's really weird.' Fred stared down at the picture.

'Look. Here she is again.' Lottie turned a page and tapped her fingernail on another photograph. In this one, her mother was younger – perhaps five or six. 'Younger, but that's her.

'This is wild. We looked almost the same as children. And I recognise that house that she's standing outside. It's my grand-parents' house. That's their garden. Their summer house.'

'So strange, isn't it?' Fred peered at the pictures. 'Gretchen's written something there, look. The date. Would your mum have been alive then?'

Lottie did some quick maths in her mind.

'Yeah. I think she would. That's the right year for her to be that age. As if we needed more proof. But how would Gretchen have these pictures? She gave my mum up when she was a baby.'

'Oh. Look! A letter!' an envelope fell out of the back of the album and onto Lottie's foot. She bent to pick it up and saw that it was addressed to Gretchen Ross at the cottage on Queen's Point: the same cottage that they were sitting opposite.

She showed Fred the address, and his eyes widened.

'Read it,' he said. Lottie reached into the envelope and took out a folded-up piece of paper which looked as if it had been creased, read and re-folded many times.

Dear Gretchen,

I hope that you are well, and things are going well at work and with Stella.

As per our agreement to send pictures once a year, please find enclosed some pictures of Emma. She is growing well as you can see, and is a happy child. She loves to draw and colour, and she has a good circle of friends at school.

You were concerned that Alex might have found her, but we haven't heard from him. Rest assured that I would inform you if we did. I have your phone number.

We are still open to the idea of sharing Emma's true parentage with her, if you decide that is something that you'd like to do. I know that the adoption agency advocates openness with adopted children when they are ready, and Graham and I are secure in our parenting of her. If you would like her to know about you – and if you would like to send us a picture of

*yourself to show her, or perhaps of you and Stella – then we
would happily oblige.*

*She is a sweet, wonderful girl, Gretchen. You would be very
proud of her.*

All my best wishes,

Sharon

'Oh, my goodness.' Lottie blinked repeatedly. 'They knew.' She looked at Fred. 'Sharon... that's my grandmother. I mean, the one I grew up with. They knew Gretchen. All these years and they never told me.' She stared at the letter in disbelief. 'They could have told me. I could have known her for longer. Much longer. Mum could have.'

'But, it seems from reading this that Gretchen didn't want them to tell you, Lottie. I guess they were just doing what she asked.' Fred exhaled. 'That's rough. Maybe she kept in touch with your grandparents long enough to know that Emma had a daughter called Lottie. And when you turned up at the care home to do your project, maybe she put two and two together.'

'But if she did, why didn't she say anything to me?' Lottie looked back at the photos. 'Why wouldn't she tell me?'

'I don't know. Maybe she meant to, but she didn't know how. And, maybe, the longer she knew you, the deeper your relationship got, then she couldn't find a good time.' Fred shrugged. 'I don't know.'

'I can't believe it. I was talking to a member of my family this whole time, and I never knew.' Lottie felt a wave of deep sadness wash over her. 'My biological grandmother. And, now... Now... I'm losing her. I won't talk to her again.' She started to cry helplessly, and Fred pulled her into his chest. She wrapped her arms around him and started to sob again.

Fred held her, steadfast, letting her cry. Finally, she looked up at him, aware that her makeup must be half way down her face, and that she needed to blow her nose. She sniffed and wiped it with her sleeve. He handed her a tissue from his pocket.

'Keep it,' he said, after she blew her nose and attempted to hand it back to him. 'Really. It's fine.'

'Thanks.' Lottie's eyes met his; she blinked, suddenly aware of a shift in the energy between them. 'What? What is it? Do I have something on my face?' She rubbed her nose, and then under her eyes. 'I must look like—'

But, she wasn't able to finish her sentence.

Fred kissed her. His lips met hers softly, and lingered there, barely touching, but enough to send an unexpected electricity through her body. She made an *oh* noise, but it was subsumed in a deeper, longer kiss that made her breathless.

She felt all of her grief, all of her sadness resonate in the kiss, as if Fred was willingly letting it all break over him; as if he was a rock and she was a wave of tears. He held her against him firmly, not letting her go, holding her, being there, being so fully and manfully *present* that she had to take a deep breath to steady herself.

'I...' she began, not even knowing what she was going to say.

'It's all right, Lottie. I've got you,' he murmured, and kissed her again. She felt herself melt against him, and a deep sweetness in the centre of her open. Suddenly, she felt an overpowering combination of comfort in Fred's arms – a grounded sense of being protected, safe and cared for – as well as being deeply aroused.

Her whole body was alive, tingling, warm and alive. She felt like a *woman*, in a way she never had before. Strong, and centred, knowing – all of a sudden – that she had so much love to give. That there was so much sexy, loving sweetness in her that was just waiting to feel like this. Over the past months, she had become more confident in herself and her appearance; she had made herself take more pride in how she looked and, slowly, had started to feel more confident.

But, it had taken this moment, deep in her grief, to release something in her and let it shatter the walls of her heart. The walls she had put up to protect herself, so many years ago, and been so afraid to lower. Those walls had protected her, to some extent, but they'd also been responsible for keeping her from... whatever this was. And, it had taken a sudden moment of grief to make her vulnerable enough for her to lower them, just for a moment.

'I want you to know that I'm here for you. And that I always have been,' Fred said, quietly, putting his finger under her chin and gently tilting her head up. 'From the first time you walked into our house, I knew that you were special. And then, when I got to know you, I realised just how special you really are. You're caring. Sweet. Thoughtful. Smart. You make me laugh. And we've always been able to talk. Like, really talk. I've never really had that with anyone else.'

'I... I don't know what to say, Fred. I like you a lot too. I just... never knew you felt that way.' Lottie wiped her eyes. 'I'm sorry I cried on you.'

'Never be sorry for that.' He kissed the tip of her nose. 'I'm sorry. It's such an inappropriate moment, what with Gretchen, and everything. I just... I had to.'

'It's fine. I just wish... I dunno. I must look a state.' She felt self-conscious. 'It's not very romantic, kissing a tear-stained girl.'

'You are the most beautiful woman I have ever met in real life,' Fred said, completely seriously. 'You could be wearing a dress made of dead fish and I'd still want to kiss you.'

'Oh, Fred,' Lottie half-laughed. 'That's very sweet.'

'I wouldn't have been with you all day, on this day in particular, holding you, being there, unless I cared about you. And I do. Care about you. Very much.' He met her eyes, seriously.

'This has been quite a day, huh. But you *were* there for me all day. Thank you,' Lottie said, quietly. 'I thought... that day at the castle... but you were with Helen. I didn't want to get in the way. I guess I just thought, you seemed happy with her. And I felt bad for suddenly finding you attractive.'

'I told you. Helen and I didn't actually date that much. And she's a really nice girl, but I never really had *the feelings* for her.'

'Do you have the feelings for me?' Lottie asked, cautiously.

'Damn. YES. From that first time I met you, I couldn't think about anyone else. I've never met anyone like you,' he confessed, blushing a little.

'I'm not sure that I deserve you,' Lottie said, her self-doubt rising up. But, she looked at Fred's expression, and saw in his eyes that he was completely genuine.

'You do,' he said, taking her in his arms again. 'As much as I deserve you.' He kissed her again, and Lottie felt warmth glow between them as if she was standing in the sun. 'You need to believe in this, Lottie. I do.'

'I do believe it,' she breathed, thinking of the little mantra Gretchen had made her say every day in the mirror. *I am more than enough for anyone. I am lovely, I am beautiful, I am talented.* Gretchen had told her that she was a goddess among women, and that she deserved love.

I choose me, Lottie thought. *And one way I can choose myself is to be open to good men who treat me right. I don't need Fred; I don't have to depend on his affection to be happy. I can be happy in myself. But I can want him, and be secure in knowing that he wants me.*

'I guess if I've got Gretchen's blood in my veins I guess I should start living up to it,' she added, a smile playing on her lips.

'Attagirl.' Fred grinned. 'I've always seen that spark in you. It's sexy as hell.'

'If you say so,' Lottie murmured, as Fred kissed her again. This time, it was passionate, purposeful; she gasped a little as his hand found her back and pressed her to him.

'I do,' he said, and Lottie dissolved into his arms.

47

GRETCHEN

I am finally in the arms of the bear, and all is peaceful here.

I bury my face in his deep, warm fur, and I am a child again.

Finally, I know the love I have been searching for, all my life. Finally, I know what it is to be held and known and accepted for all that I am.

We will all come to the bear's arms eventually, but for many, they still have a life to complete. They have trials to endure, people to love and work to do.

I hope that Lottie's young man treats her well. I think that he will.

I hope that Lottie one day knows the joy of being a mother. If that is her will, if that is her path, then I wish that she will have a peaceful and happy home life. She deserves it.

I murmur into the bear's fur that I wish for happiness for my granddaughter, and he makes a low, reassuring growl in his chest.

Then, I look up, still in his arms, and I see Stella, waiting for me in a sunny clearing in the forest. She holds out her hand to me, and the bear releases his grip.

48

Six months later

'Gosh. It looks lovely, Lottie. What a wonderful job.' Kimberley picked up the copy of the book from her chair and looked at it in wonder. 'This is the most wonderful testament to Gretchen's life I could think of.'

'Thank you. But I really couldn't have done it without Hal and Zelda's help,' Lottie said, watching as the Laird of Loch Cameron and his beautiful fiancée walked into the Great Hall of Loch Cameron Castle. 'When I told Hal my idea for the book, he funded the printing of it. Fred's shop is going to stock it, and I've sent a copy to some of Gretchen's old contacts at Hatch Publishing. You never know,' she said with a shrug.

'Goodness. Wouldn't that be wonderful, if they published it? They should. Gretchen was a tour de force, and, from what I understand, still a bit of a legend where she used to work.' Kimberley flicked through the pages. 'I can't wait to read this. And this is her whole story? Everything she told you?'

'Pretty much. And, she gave me a couple of her diaries before she died. I've added those in, and some photos from her

albums. Zelda helped me go through them and contact
Gretchen's grandson. He was able to supply some more, and
some other memories of her.'

Lottie was nervous about today, but there was also a sense of
poignancy about the day for her. She had forged a friendship
with Gretchen Ross for what had turned out to be the last few
months of her life, and, in Gretchen's final days, had found out
that Gretchen was her biological grandmother. Somehow, she
had been called to Loch Cameron before Gretchen had passed
away, as if life was bringing them together at the last minute to
connect.

Maybe it was her mother's spirit, in the afterlife, that had
guided Lottie to Gretchen. She didn't know. But she was so
grateful that it had happened.

'All right, then.' Hal Cameron stood at the front of the
Great Hall, its stone walls festooned with the Cameron coat of
arms, tapestries featuring ancient battles, and swords and
muskets in protective glass cases. On another wall, a display of
Cameron clan swords – bloodied in wars hundreds of years ago
– were arranged in an elaborate criss-cross pattern.

'Can I have everyone's attention, please?' He clapped his
hands a few times. 'Bit o' hush! All right.' He smiled, as the
hubbub calmed. 'If everyone can take a seat. Fantastic.' He
waited a moment for everyone in the Great Hall to make themselves comfortable. Lottie, Fred and Zelda had put the seats out
in rows earlier, and most of the village had come out for
Gretchen.

She had had a small funeral at the chapel on top of the hill,
which had been a lovely service. When her coffin had been laid
in the small graveyard, Lottie had found herself looking over at
the corner of the graveyard, remembering what Gretchen had
said about the women that were buried apart from everyone
else, at one time. After the service, Lottie had asked the vicar
what had happened to those women's graves.

The vicar, a friendly woman who had been in post a few years, had told Lottie that the graves hadn't been moved, but that the boundary had. And that the graveyard itself had been landscaped to be an inclusive space for all the community, now. Lottie could see that: there were no partitions, no separate areas, and the space felt welcoming and calm. The view overlooked the loch, and, on the day of Gretchen's funeral, it had been warm with a soft breeze. *A beautiful day for a beautiful soul*, the vicar had said.

'No more stigmatising women. Or anyone,' the vicar had said, sternly. 'There was a time when the village felt a certain obligation to uphold what they saw as moral behaviour. But I'm glad to say that we've moved on since then.'

Lottie was glad, too.

'Now, then. I'm chuffed that we're all here tae celebrate the life of one o' Loch Cameron's most loved residents, Gretchen Ross,' Hal began. 'We all knew Gretchen. We knew that she was a powerhouse of a woman, aye. Bold, inquisitive and bright. She and I shared a love o' books, an' I know that many of you here will have had some fantastic book recommendations from Gretchen over the years.' He smiled as people nodded and smiled in remembrance. 'But, books wasn't all there was to Gretchen. Many of ye are here because Gretchen helped ye out; she was a great listener, a great judge o' character. She'd lived quite the life. Now. I'd like tae welcome Lottie Fox tae the stage, who's put this fabulous book together, and can take it from here. Lottie?' He held out a hand towards Lottie who stood up, nervously, and joined Hal in front of everyone.

'Hi, everyone,' she began, a copy of the book in her hand. 'For those of you who don't know me, my name's Lottie, and I came to Loch Cameron about a year ago to do some oral history research for my Master's degree.'

Fred, who was sitting in the front row with Celine, Zelda

and Gretchen's grandson Eric caught her eye and nodded encouragingly. *You got this,* he mouthed.

'I met Gretchen Ross at Apple Orchard Care Home, where she lived for the final years of her life.' Lottie smiled at Fred, starting to warm to her story. Zelda was nodding along, a look of love on her face. 'I know that many of you loved Gretchen, and as soon as I met her, I knew that I was in the presence of someone who was one of a kind. She instantly engaged me, and started telling me the story of her life. And it was quite a story.' Lottie paused for a moment, unsure of how to phrase what she was about to say.

'My trips to see Gretchen soon became a pleasure rather than just a research project. We became good friends, and, as I think she'd done in many of her friendships, Gretchen helped me regain my confidence in myself and start to see life in a more positive way.' Lottie knew that there were several women in the audience who had stayed at Gretchen's old cottage up on Queen's Point over the years, and benefitted from Gretchen's wisdom; Zelda had introduced her to a few of those women as she'd arrived for the event.

'Sadly, what I didn't know, in the course of our conversations, was that Gretchen had got a brain tumour, and that the cancer had spread to many of her organs.' Lottie's voice wavered. 'She hid it, but her eyesight was failing her, probably when we met. She didn't want to make a fuss, which was Gretchen all over. But I think she knew she was dying, and so I think she was happy to have an opportunity to tell her story before she went.' Lottie took a breath.

'The other thing that I didn't know was that Gretchen Ross was my biological grandmother,' Lottie continued, blinking back tears. 'I think that she realised that quite early in our relationship, but I only found out just before she passed.' She stopped for a minute to gather herself, feeling her strength waver. 'I...' her voice broke.

Fred got up and came to stand next to her, taking her hand. Lottie felt reassurance and warmth flow from him to her.

'It's okay,' he murmured. 'Take your time.'

'Gretchen had my mother and gave her up for adoption as a baby, and she gave my mum this locket.' Lottie touched the necklace she still wore every day. 'Gretchen specifically asked my grandparents not to disclose her identity to me or my mum while she was alive, and, in accordance with her wishes, they didn't.' Lottie took a deep breath. 'I didn't understand why Gretchen didn't want me to know I was her biological grand-daughter, until I read something in her journal. I'd like to read that to you now.' She cleared her throat and opened the book to the page she'd marked.

5 July 1980

I received Graham and Sharon's annual update abut Emma today. She is looking really well and Sharon says that she is doing really well at school, and is happy. She looks very like Alex. It's painful for me to look at her face, in a way, as the spectre of him seems to look back out at me: the ghost of a man I tried very hard to forget. Yet, at the same time, hers is a beloved face because I can see my mother in her; she has a strong look of the Ross women too.

I will never forget that day up at the chapel graveyard, when Mother told me about the women buried at the edge.

"Those women are something you never want to be. Women that had babies out of wedlock. Babies are supposed to come inside marriage. Not out of it. God frowns on women that commit the sins of the flesh outside holy union." That's what she said. And I never forgot it. Even when I became a woman and I knew that she was wrong, I still never forgot.

I flouted the rules. I always did. I adopted Stella as a single parent and I ignored the comments at work, the questions about whether she looked like her father because they couldn't see a resemblance with me. The looks at playgrounds. I was a single mother and I was proud.

And, yet, when I became pregnant with Emma, that day in the graveyard played on my mind.

My decision wasn't made in shame. My decision came from a place of protecting my girl. I gave Emma up because of Alex. If he had been a better man – a man that I knew we would be safe with – then I would have married him and allowed him to be a father to her – and, possibly, Stella, if I had still adopted her later on. But, Alex couldn't do that. Alex showed me the violent truth of himself under the patina of a gentleman, and, as much as he might tell me that he wanted to protect and love me and the baby, he showed me who he was when he slapped me across the face and screamed abuse at me.

When people show you who they are, believe them.

I could not let Alex near Emma. Her perfection must never be marred by violence. So, as much as I would love to see her one day, I will protect her by insisting that Graham and Sharon never tell her who I am. For as long as I am alive, and he is, I will protect that girl.

Lottie stopped reading. She looked up and saw her grand-parents, Sharon and Graham, in the second row of seats. Sharon's eyes were closed, and her head was on Graham's shoulder. Lottie's grandfather caught her eye, and gave her a reassuring nod.

'It's okay, hen,' he said. 'Carry on.'

'Alexander O'Connell – my biological grandfather – died in 2010, and my mother, Emma, died three years ago,' Lottie continued. 'Gretchen knew that Alex had passed, but she lost touch with Graham and Sharon – the grandparents I grew up with – some years ago. When we met at the care home and I told her that I had lost my mother quite recently, that her name was Emma and that I wore her locket, Gretchen must have known that the daughter she gave up for adoption had also died.' Fred squeezed her hand, and she squeezed his back. She was so grateful to have him with her.

'I don't know how that must have felt to her. Or, why she didn't tell me who she was to me. Perhaps it was habit that kept her from saying anything, or she just didn't know how.' Lottie smiled at the audience. 'But, whatever it was, I'm glad that I had the chance to know her, and even gladder that I got the chance to share Gretchen Ross's remarkable story with you all. This is the manuscript of my Master's project, with some additions. Hal has very kindly paid for a run of 2,000 copies of the book, and there's a copy for everyone to take home. Oh. The title. I called it *Freedom is the real abundance: The Gretchen Ross Story* because of a quote that she mentioned to me once, from one of her favourite writers, Marge Piercy. The quote is included at the front of the book. It's from a poem called 'The Sabbath of Mutual Respect'.

Lottie read the poem aloud, pausing at the end with the line *freedom is our real abundance.* How true that was of Gretchen's life, she thought.

'That's it, I guess. Here's to Gretchen. She was a great lady.'

There was a moment of silence as Lottie stopped talking, followed by a loud round of applause.

49

———

'To Gretchen!' Zelda stood up, clapping furiously. She had tears in her eyes; Hal enveloped her in a hug and held her for a few moments.

'Gretchen. Gretchen Ross!' the crowd called out, as the clapping abated. A hum of chatter replaced the applause, and a rustling as everyone picked up the books and started to look at them.

'Well done, little bird.' Lottie's grandfather came forward and tapped Lottie on the shoulder. 'You did so well.'

'Was it okay?' she asked her grandparents.

'It was wonderful,' Sharon said, hugging Lottie. 'You did Gretchen proud. And yourself. Lottie... I hope you understand, about Gretchen. Why we couldn't tell you about her. It would have gone against her wishes.'

'I know. I understand,' Lottie said. 'I just wish we'd had more time to talk about it all, before she died.'

'We wanted to tell you, little bird. When we found out that you were coming to Loch Cameron, we wondered if you'd unravel something of the story. We hadn't been in touch with

Gretchen for some years. We didn't know she'd moved from the cottage; I tried to call the line there a few times and even wrote her a few letters, but either they didn't get to her, or she didn't want to reply.' Her grandfather continued, 'The last thing we heard from her was that she still didn't want us to tell you and Emma anything about her. I wrote to tell her when Emma passed, but I don't think she got that letter, either.'

'I don't think so. Because when I mentioned that mum had passed, she seemed shocked,' Lottie remembered. 'At the time, of course, I didn't know about everything she suspected. She knew who I was as soon as she saw the locket. Before that, maybe. I think the first day we met, she looked at me as if she recognised me. Maybe she did.'

'It's very possible,' Sharon said. 'But, anyway, you did such a wonderful thing in collating her story in this book. It's such a testament to an amazing woman. I'm so proud of you, pumpkin. And your mum would be, too.'

'We really came close to tellin' ye a few times. We should have,' Graham said. 'I'm sorry, my sweetheart. If we got it wrong. We were just tryin' tae do the right thing.'

'I know, Grandpa. It's okay.' Lottie gave him a tight hug. 'I love you.'

'I love ye too, ma little crow maiden. Always.' Graham wiped a tear from his eye.

Sharon shook her head and reached out her hand to Fred, who was standing patiently next to Lottie.

'Please excuse us, Fred. It's good to see you again,' she said, smiling warmly.

'Good to see you too, Mrs Fox,' Fred said, politely. 'And you, Mr Fox.'

Lottie had introduced Fred to her grandparents a couple of months ago.

'Sharon and Graham, please,' Lottie's grandfather said,

clearing his throat. 'Makes us feel a bit less ancient. How are the two of you getting on? Treating my little bird like a princess?'

'Of course.' Fred nodded, seriously. 'As she deserves.'

'Right answer,' Graham chuckled.

'Grandpa.' Lottie nudged him. 'Stop it! You're embarrassing me.'

'I will speak as I find,' Graham said, archly.

'Lottie! Your speech was so super!' Celine approached the group and waved her copy of the book in Lottie's face. 'And, look at this excellent thing you have made! It is wonderful.'

'Thanks, Celine. Grandpa and grandma, this is my house-mate, Celine,' Lottie introduced them. 'And this is Gretchen's grandson, Eric.' She beckoned over a tall, lovely looking young man who had been standing shyly on his own. 'Which I think means we're related, somehow. But I'm not sure what that makes us.'

Eric was in his early twenties and was tall, rangy and with a bouncy gait. He was dark haired and wore jeans and a shirt with a black suit jacket over the top.

'Oh. Pleased to meet you, Eric.' Celine batted her eyelids at him. Lottie gave her friend a discreet eyeroll. When Eric turned away slightly to talk to her grandparents, she lowered her voice.

'I thought you were seeing Tom?' Lottie asked.

'Oh. No. That didn't work out.' Celine shrugged. 'We got into an argument about Callum, in fact. Tom defended him over what he did to you and I was not having it,' she said, firmly. 'As they say, sisters over misters, no?'

'Celine. I didn't need you to do that,' Lottie said, but she was touched at Celine's being in her corner. 'I thought you really liked him.'

'He was okay. But when he tried to talk about you and tell me what Callum had said... it was a big turn off. You are my friend, and a wonderful person. If he wants to take the wrong side, that is that, eh?' Celine eyed Eric appreciatively. 'We should take Eric out for a drink though, what do you think? Now you're related, no?'

'Celine. Really,' Lottie laughed.

'But I'm not related to him,' her housemate protested.

'That's true, I suppose,' Lottie chuckled.

'Lottie. Thank you for doing this.' Zelda caught her arm as people started to gather at the back of the room; Hal and his housekeeper Anna were serving drinks and snacks. 'When I first came to Loch Cameron, Gretch and I became real good friends. She was always such a sweetheart to me and Hal and I can't imagine the world without her. So, thank you for this. I know I've already said thank you. But, again. It really does mean so much to all of us.'

'I was glad to do it,' Lottie said. 'I'm waiting for my results for the MA but it almost doesn't matter now. I gained so much from doing this.'

'Well, sure. You got to meet your real grandmother who just happened to be Gretchen Ross, one of the coolest women who ever lived. You know she had an affair with Norman Mailer? She was friends with some of the biggest writers in the world. They sent flowers and cards to her funeral, do you remember?'

'I do. I managed to collect some comments from some of them for the book. I've sent copies to some of her good friends.'

'That's great, Lottie. Listen, I was thinking, as well – maybe we could feature your book in the magazine I work for? Do a whole piece on Gretchen. We could put an extract from the book on the website as well. Kind of a long form thing. What do you think?' Zelda looked at Lottie expectantly.

'Wow. Zelda, I'd love that, if you think they'd be interested.' Lottie knew that the magazine Zelda worked for was one of the glossy ones you saw in the shops. It was international, and Zelda had a super jetset life because of her job there.

'They would. And I'd like to do it. As my own personal tribute to Gretch.' Zelda nodded. 'Okay. I hoped you'd say yes. I'll be in touch to organise it.' She gave Lottie a kiss on the cheek. 'You and Fred should come to New York, too. The four of us could go out. On the magazine, obviously. Or Hal.' She twinkled.

Fred and Lottie exchanged incredulous looks.

'Are you serious?' Lottie asked. 'New York?'

'Sure. Why not?' Zelda clapped her hands. 'Gretch would love it. I know she'd be so happy for me to take you. Say yes!'

'Err... yes!' Lottie laughed. 'That would be fantastic! What do you think, Fred?'

'Well, I guess Pageturner's could manage without me for a week,' he said, mock-seriously. 'Though the cut and thrust of Loch Cameron is a tough market for a village bookseller to look the other way from, even for a minute.'

'I think he's joking. Is he joking? I still don't always get the sense of humour here.' Zelda looked carefully at Fred. 'You're joking, right?'

'I'm joking. I'd love to come,' Fred told her with a grin.

'Okay. See you guys later then. I'm going to help Hal. Do the Lady of the Manor shtick.' Zelda grinned back and did a mock-curtsey, leaving Fred and Lottie alone.

'This was quite a day,' Fred said, taking her hand. 'Thanks for having me here with you.'

'You're welcome,' Lottie said, shyly. 'I think I'd like to kiss you now,' she said.

'I think I'd like to kiss you too.' He smiled.

Lottie wrapped her arms around his neck and kissed him. She was so happy in that moment; happier than she thought she had ever been. And, as if she was nearby, Lottie heard Gretchen's voice in her ear:

You deserve a real man, Lottie Fox. And as soon as you start believing in yourself as a beautiful, powerful woman, believe me, one will appear. They will hear your siren call.

That was what Gretchen had said to her, once. And she had been right. He was here. And, Lottie's new life had begun, with Fred as a wonderful part of it, and none of it would have happened without Gretchen Ross. For that she would be grateful, forever.

A LETTER FROM KENNEDY

Dear reader,

I want to say a huge thank you for choosing to read *Lost Memories of the Cottage by the Loch*. If you did enjoy it, and want to keep up to date with all my latest releases, just sign up at the following link. Your email address will never be shared and you can unsubscribe at any time.

www.bookouture.com/kennedy-kerr

I hope you loved *Lost Memories of the Cottage by the Loch* and if you did I would be very grateful if you could write a review. I'd love to hear what you think, and it makes such a difference helping new readers to discover one of my books for the first time.

I love hearing from my readers – you can get in touch through social media.

Thanks,

Kennedy

KEEP IN TOUCH WITH KENNEDY

facebook.com/kennedykerrauthor
x.com/kennedykerr5
instagram.com/kennedykerrauthor

AUTHOR'S NOTE

I quoted from Marge Piercy's poem 'The Sabbath of Mutual Respect' from her book *The Moon is Always Female* (Knopf, 1977).

The phrase "well-behaved women seldom make history" appeared in an academic paper in the journal *American Quarterly* in 1976 by Laurel Thatcher Ulrich.

In 1976 Ulrich was a student at the University of New Hampshire, and she earned her Ph.D. in History in 1980. She is now an eminent Pulitzer-Prize-winning Professor of early American history at Harvard University.

The article containing the phrase was titled "Vertuous Women Found: New England Ministerial Literature, 1668–1735". The goal of the paper and much of Ulrich's work was the recovery of the history of women who were not featured in history books of the past. She was interested in investigating the lives of ordinary women who were considered "well-behaved" or "vertuous" (an alternate spelling of virtuous).

The 1990 book *A Midwife's Tale: The Life of Martha Ballard, Based on Her Diary, 1785–1812* by Ulrich reprinted and extensively commented on the diary entries of an ordinary midwife in Maine who also acted as a healer. The book illuminated the medical practices and sexual attitudes of the era and was awarded a Pulitzer Prize and Bancroft Prize.

I have a similar goal to Dr Ulrich when writing, which is to highlight women's histories that are too often forgotten. In this book, I also greatly enjoyed giving Gretchen's story full rein. As the Loch Cameron series developed, I fell in love with Gretchen, who is modelled on my own Scottish grannie, who was tons of fun, a writer herself and loved books. Gretchen Ross is an homage to my Grannie, with a dash of Fran Lebowitz and Joan Collins thrown in for good measure.

Gretchen mentions the sexist advertising used by airlines in the 1960s and 1970s that objectified air stewardesses. I found an excellent article by Nell McShane Wulfhart on the National Geographic website that was a great summary of what was going on at the time. Wulfhart reminds us that in the 1970s, airlines in the United States sold tickets predominantly based on the perceived sexual availability of their stewardesses rather than the airline's safety record or flight times.

The time when flight attendants said: 'Go fly yourself!' www.nationalgeographic.com/travel/article/the-time-when-flight-attendants-said-go-fly-yourself

I am indebted to Dr Jenny Keating's presentation on adoption legalities in the UK in the twentieth century, which can be found here: dfe-jenny-keating.pdf (historyandpolicy.org). I based Gretchen's story of the private adoption of her daughter Stella on the real and lived experience of a close friend who was privately adopted in the 1970s as a baby from a poor family where it was felt his life chances would not amount to much if left there. His birth mother was a teen runaway, and he was not her first pregnancy. He was legally adopted by his adopted mother and father, his mother knowing the family but not being related to them. Nowadays, in the UK, private adoptions are limited to existing relatives.

Lottie's mother Emma passed away due to Sudden Arrhythmic Death Syndrome which I learned about from the work of the charity The Alex Wardle Foundation Fund. This charity raises awareness of the syndrome and raises money to provide defibrillators into communities in Hampshire in the UK. Alex – a young man studying medicine at university – died at the age of twenty-three from Sudden Arrhythmic Death Syndrome, which is when a disturbance in the heart's rhythm causes death in a person who has not been diagnosed with physical heart disease. Alex's life might have been saved if a defibrillator was nearby and able to be used, which is why the charity has worked with public bodies such as rail networks to fund defibrillators at train stations. Find out more at https://www.thealexwardlefoundation.org

UK Member of Parliament Jess Phillips reads out the names of women killed by men because of domestic violence every year in the House of Commons. In her most recent speech, she said that whilst it was an honour for her to commemorate each woman, she grew weary of having to do so. Phillips remains an advocate for women and was previously the shadow minister for domestic violence and safeguarding.

PUBLISHING TEAM

Turning a manuscript into a book requires the efforts of many people. The publishing team at Bookouture would like to acknowledge everyone who contributed to this publication.

Commercial
Lauren Morrissette
Hannah Richmond
Imogen Allport

Cover design
Emma Graves

Data and analysis
Mark Alder
Mohamed Bussuri

Editorial
Kelsie Marsden
Sinead O'Connor

Copyeditor
Claire Rushbrook

Proofreader
Tom Feltham

Marketing
Alex Crow
Melanie Price
Occy Carr
Cíara Rosney
Martyna Młynarska

Operations and distribution
Marina Valles
Stephanie Straub
Joe Morris

Production
Hannah Snetsinger
Mandy Kullar
Ria Clare
Nadia Michael

Publicity
Kim Nash
Noelle Holten
Jess Readett
Sarah Hardy

Rights and contracts
Peta Nightingale
Richard King
Saidah Graham